The Snow Leopard of Moscow & Other Stories

THE SNOW LEOPARD
OF MOSCOW
& OTHER STORIES

by

MATTHEW G. REES

A WORK OF FICTION

RED STEPPE PRESS

Шаттнеш Я. Яеех

Matthew G. Rees grew up in the border country between England and Wales known as the Marches. He trained as a journalist and served on the staffs of newspapers in the UK for ten years. He later entered teaching. In Moscow he taught English at a school near the Kremlin. He lived in flats dating from the Soviet era in neighbourhoods beyond the central tourist zone, using the same shops, markets, post offices, pharmacies, barbers, cafés, parks and transport as his Russian neighbours. On days off he either wandered the city or caught trains to outlying districts. He visited the one-time homes of Chekhov, Gogol, Tolstoy, Bulgakov, Pasternak and Lenin, among others. He also visited monasteries, cathedrals, cemeteries and cinemas. He swam regularly in open-air swimming pools (during snowfalls on occasion), including the one used for the 1980 Olympics. He saw parades commemorating Russia's role in the Second World War. He also witnessed protests against the government.

As boy and man, Rees has visited some twenty countries and a number of the smaller and more remote islands of the British Isles and Channel Islands. His life has included a variety of activities. He has, among other things, been a night-shift taxi driver. His writing includes the story collections *Keyhole*, *Smoke House & Other Stories* and *The Feast*. He has also written plays. He has a PhD from the University of Swansea, Wales.

More about Matthew G. Rees can be found at
www.matthewgrees.com

Author's Note

Once upon a time I lived in Moscow. This book draws its inspiration from then. It is not a memoir, nor is it journalism. It is a collection of stories of the kind that I'm inclined to write.

The roots of the fiction that follows lie not in the Russian capital of brochures and tourist trails. These tales – extraordinary as some may seem – are from what I think of as the hidden Moscow – the *real* city – which, for a short while, was my home.

Although perhaps known as a writer who explores the strange and the uncanny rather than mere matters of gore, I warn that violence and blood will at times be encountered in these pages. I make no apology for this, given that the backdrop is a city where, come winter, for example, pavements are often taped-off to protect pedestrians from falling icicles, and where murder – albeit official figures suggest a gradual reduction – has reportedly been running for most of this century at a rate of several hundred homicides a year. This offence, though, is far from the only topic of these tales.

In one (very loose) sense it might be said that my subjects are not entirely unlike those of Dostoyevsky, who, though more often associated with Saint Petersburg, was Moscow-born and raised. Other authors who perhaps come to mind – for the arenas into which their fiction sometimes stepped – are Bulgakov and Gogol (and possibly Chekhov), whose homes and graves I visited in my time as a resident of the Russian capital. The story writer and satirist Mikhail

Zoshchenko, who was censored in the post-War Soviet era, has, I think, been an influence. Likewise, the émigré Vladimir Nabokov.

Ultimately, though, these are my stories. They have been written how I wanted to write them. Readers must make of my tales what they will.

Matthew G. Rees

Acknowledgements

In terms of overall words the greater part of what follows is published here for the first time. Early versions of some of the stories appeared in anthologies and reviews. Revisions have been made. At times the changes have been significant and substantial: we may talk of 'short fiction' but it can be argued that the writing of a story never truly ends. Acknowledgements are due to *Belle Ombre, Bewildering Stories, The Lonely Crowd, The Gull, Horla, nation.cymru* and *Waterfront* for publishing initial versions of certain stories that appear here. The photographs were taken by me. Except where a link is self-evident, as, for example, in the case of Lenin's Rolls-Royce, the images are published simply because I feel they may be of interest; no connection should be inferred with the content of any of the stories, which, as I have said, are fiction, from beginning to end.

MGR

To Moscow, to Moscow, to Moscow!

Anton Chekhov, *Three Sisters*

I haven't understood a bar of music in my life,
but I have felt it.

Igor Stravinsky

Stories

Firebird

At that time, Alexander Antonovich must have been about seventy-five years old, and it was unusual in my part of Moscow to see a man of that age still around.

Tall (in spite of a stoop), pale and lean, he seemed to me like a bird – a crane of the kind my mother would point at in storybooks.

He wore an astrakhan hat of the type some older men still had, which he bumped every time he got into Dad's car.

A port wine stain the shape of Italy ran down his right cheek and was to me a source of intense fascination. When I once questioned my father about this, he told me it was a war wound that I was never again to mention (this reference to wars and wounds only serving to increase my curiosity, of course).

His hands were enormous and, compared with my father's own knotty, stunted versions, seemed like wings. If ever he removed his sheepskin mittens in winter, he revealed fingers and thumbs that had the startling purple-pinkness of new-born babies – so different from the cadaverous rest of him that I'd wonder if they weren't actually someone else's: a fare-dodger's, buttoned-up, secretly, under his long, dark coat.

His teeth were horse-like and mustardy. Sometimes, his big, grey tongue lolled over them, like an eel on ice on a stall at our market. Enormous ears drooped from his head like the sails of a boat becalmed on Baikal, while his watery, pale-blue eyes wandered in distant worlds of their own. For its part, the back of his neck, which I had opportunity to study at length from my seat in the rear of Dad's car, was home to a thicket of white hairs which sprouted from cracked, hide-like skin of the kind I thought dinosaurs must have had.

Considering Antonovich now, I can see how the thought of him might have slackened the bladder of many a small child alone in their cot at night. But he was only one part of the story. The cause of my night terrors was more complicated than that.

My boyhood nightmares... how well I remember them.

I'd wake up screaming (when their events became no longer bearable): blankets and bedsheets bunched over my bottom half... lukewarm and wet.

Suddenly, the whole world would go yellow, as my mother – my saviour – threw the light switch and hurried into my bedroom: her arms locking around me, my nose sinking with snot into the shoulder of her nightdress.

She'd set about cleaning me up.

My pyjamas she'd throw at Dad, who by now would be in the doorway. He'd disappear, in search of a clean pair.

When he got back, Mom would fling him my sheets.

Next – tiny as she was – she'd flip my mattress, so it was dry-side up. After which, she'd squish my pillows and tell me to 'jump back in'.

Apart from a few hushes and shushes to me, Mom would do all this in silence, finishing her tasks in what seemed like seconds (though it was longer than that, of course).

In time, I came to see that this wordless, beetling precision of hers was, in fact, a statement – as unmistakable as anything bawled in the street – of her fury... her *absolute* fury... with my father, who she'd shoo from my room as if he were some intruding dog.

Finally, she'd light a lamp by my bedside and pull my door not quite shut as she and Dad retreated into the dark of the hall.

And then I'd lie there... and wait for their row to begin.

My mother's voice would be first through the thin walls of our flat: asking my father (in a way that wasn't really 'asking') why he took me to see Antonovich...

demanding that the visits he took me on be brought to a stop.

My father would respond sharply, saying that he took me to see Antonovich because he had to and if she had ever listened to him in her life she would know that he had no choice.

My mother would then speak over him, asking the same questions again. My father – louder – would then speak over her, giving the same replies.

After some moments of this, they'd fall quiet. Then my mother would start up once more, and my father would do so also – like two clockwork toys that had been rewound and set go again on the floor.

Sometimes, a neighbour would bang on the wall, and my father would shout or bang back. My mother would then resort to whispers (that weren't really 'whispers'), telling my father to hush. He'd venture some other loud comment about the neighbour before, finally, falling quiet. My mother would be on his side – for that moment – telling him to 'leave it there' and to go back to bed.

I'd then hear them shuffle from the kitchen to their room, followed by the creak of their bed as they climbed in.

Softly, my father would be saying now: 'I can't say no. I *have* to take him.' And my mother – I somehow knew – would be turning from him, setting her face to the wall. And then he would say to her, 'Marta?', before doing so again, a second time (which I knew would come) with a slightly different pitch: 'Marta?'

This, like his first enquiry, would go unanswered, as I listened and mouthed my mother's name, on my pillow, in my dry pyjamas. in the lamp-lit seclusion of my room.

❦

My father drove a taxi. He didn't have a sign that said *Taxi* and I doubt he had a licence or anything official like that. But that's how he put food on our table. For a while, he drove limousines in the smart parts of the city for a firm that serviced hotels and ran rich people to their restaurants and shops in Kitay Gorod, Okhotny Ryad and Tverskaya. But he had a tendency to do rough things that, to be fair, he didn't know were rough, such as blowing his nose loudly and listening to the radio (which he turned up if his customers started to speak). Sometimes he put down his window and spat.

The guys he worked with weren't the nicest and mocked him for, among other things, not having a jacket to go over his shirt. One day he came home with it torn and told my mother he'd been fired. He had a cut on his hand and a lump on his cheek. After that he drove local people to places around our neighbourhood in his own car, Beatrisa (as we called her), and occasionally further. Sometimes they paid.

The reason my father couldn't say no to Alexander Antonovich, in the way that my mother wanted him to, was because Alexander Antonovich was his best customer by far. Put bluntly, Antonovich paid our bills, with some help from my granny and whatever Mom could scrape from selling bits of junk, in the same way as other of our neighbours, on the cut-through to our metro station (when the cops weren't chasing them off).

The inconvenient truth was that Alexander Antonovich *liked* me to go with them on those trips he made with my father. In fact, he sort-of insisted upon it. If ever I wasn't there, because of school or sickness, Dad would promise I'd be present for the next ride out. My being there also made my father's life easier. Dad hailed from peasant stock. Antonovich on the other hand was from gentry (though by now almost all his money had gone and he lived in a flat in a run-of-the-mill neighbourhood, just like our own). His family had had land once and lots of it; one ancestor had been a general, another a magistrate. My father didn't know what to say or how to behave around a man from a background like that. Having me there, on Beatrisa's back seat, while Dad sat beside Antonovich up front, eased the awkwardness that he felt. Sometimes, if Antonovich thought I'd made a funny or smart answer to one of his many questions, Antonovich would say something like, 'But of course, professor.' My father would then laugh and nod and say the word *professor*, several times over, proud of – and grateful for – the juvenile absurdity that I'd uttered.

It was my father's practice to drive Antonovich to a farm – it wasn't even that, really – outside Moscow, which was the last fragment of an estate that had belonged to the old man's family. There'd been birch forests, hay meadows, pasture and fishing lakes once – not to mention the shooting grounds where my father claimed Tsar Alexander (in some versions of the story, Tsar Peter) had killed a giant wolf. All that was left now was a house, a huddle of tumble-down buildings and a small acreage of land grown wild. Sometimes, when we were out there, we'd see big, foreign-made cars crossing ground that was formerly the estate's, the occupants heading to new houses built in the hills or by the sides of the lakes. At the sight of them, Antonovich would frown and move his lips in a whisper.

When we got to the farm, Antonovich would disappear inside the old house, leaving Dad and me to our own devices. What he did in the house was a mystery and I'm not sure that he actually did anything very much. Once, I stood on a trough and looked in through a grimed window. Antonovich was sitting in a wooden chair in a room as big as our flat. Save for him and his chair, the place was empty. He faced a huge fireplace of blackened stone that resembled a cave, and he just sat there... and stared.

Dad and I usually ended up in an orchard of apple trees that bore sour and knobbly fruit. I seldom strayed from his side. You see, it wouldn't just be *us* on those rambles of ours. Always – and I mean *always* – Napoleon would be there, too.

I didn't have to hear the clicking of his feet on the cobbles of the yard, or see his shadow, creeping at corners and looming at ledges, to know he was on our heels. I just knew. His aura preceded him. He was, to my youthful eyes and ears, evil *personified*... if such a term can be used for a farmyard cockerel. He dripped with it: from his brittle pink comb to his scaly-skinned claws... his black, sickle tail to his hooked and spiteful spurs. Evil – above all – in his glaring, staring, blood-red eyes, which *nothing* escaped.

In my fevered dreams, Napoleon and Antonovich became one, their union yielding not a beautiful musical avian like the Alkonost and Sirin of ancient legend, but a different creature entirely. This *thing* occupied a dank, brambled shed in a shadowed gully, which only the two of us knew. It roosted there by day (the sole sound being the occasional scratching of its hands at its feathers) and came to life at night... when small boys were in their beds.

In my night horrors, it landed with a heavy *clump* at the foot of my mattress, the sullen beat of its wings on its flight from the farm having already roused me from sleep.

Sitting-up, I would see a huge dinner-plate of a crimson eye, staring at me in the dark. Then, as I sat there, too terrified to move, it would stride – one giant claw after the other – towards me, over the bedclothes.

Within moments, its broad and muscular breast would eclipse all else in my room, stifling my ability to utter a single word. Then, when right above me, it would lower its enormous beak, so that its giant and glacial mandibles skimmed my forehead and cheeks.

Next, it would lift its great neck, cast sly looks left and right, and then shoot out its tongue, on which waved a forest of feathers that erupted into flames.

Further, shocking fireballs exploded from its nostrils and its eye sockets.

And now I would begin the screaming – my hose-like pissing would already be in full flood… and, with it, the wailing that would summon my mother.

As she marched out of the dark, the Hellbird would disappear into its depths, beating its wings, and winding-back its terrible, flaming tongue…

Affecting not to know Napoleon's ghastly nocturnal purpose, I once asked Antonovich, 'What does he do?' (while gripping my father's hand, as the three of us studied the cockerel, holding court amid the old and broken cobbles of Antonovich's farmyard).

'Do?!' responded Antonovich, with mock astonishment. 'Why… what he likes! He's the boss round here. It's *his* farm… *his* land.'

Associating the business of 'bossdom' with people much older than me, I asked Antonovich how old the bird was.

'Ancient!' Antonovich replied.

When I asked him what he meant by *ancient*, he said, 'As old as the plains. As old as Russia. He'll be here when I'm ashes… when *all* of us are ashes.'

The bird stood its ground before us, as if it understood every word the old man had said… as if it were waiting to see if we had anything to voice by way of contradiction (which we did not).

When the time came for us to leave, with or without Antonovich (depending on whether he was staying at the farm for the night) I'd pull ahead of my father, anxious to get into our car.

Dad would fiddle with his keys, mutter and try to get Beatrisa to start. I, meanwhile, would be standing on the back seat, looking out for Napoleon. Eventually, Beatrisa would snort to life… and settle to the shudder that would last all our journey home.

Near the top of the track that led from the farm, I'd finally find the courage to look back.

Without fail, Napoleon would be coming after us: springing – from one claw foot to the other – in resolute pursuit.

Even after the thrum of the wooden bridge under our wheels, he'd still be there… on our tail, squawking and jumping, as Dad steered Beatrisa onto the road.

I'd watch him, watching us, till a grass bank with birch trees on it intervened.

From a hillock, I'd stare back, and see his speck: determined, defiant.

❦

My mother died first – an illness that ate through her. My father held his life together for a while, but, in time, he fell apart. Antonovich's trips to the farm – Dad's sole source of meaningful money, and companionship – grew fewer.

As I got older, I left home (in part because my university studies took me to the opposite end of Moscow; my move relieving me of long hours travelling across our great, sprawling city). Dad scratched a little cash driving the likes of Irina Budayeva, a fat, malingering and malodorous woman who wouldn't walk anywhere, and Father Leonid, who, as a priest, my father was embarrassed to charge: a situation which Father Leonid found to his liking.

An added problem was that Beatrisa, Dad's by now heavily patched-up and very elderly car, started breaking down a lot. One time, when he was taking Antonovich, a wheel flew off, so that he and Antonovich careered down a ravine. Antonovich, virtually blind by this stage, stayed in his seat as my father went for help. A farmer put a chain around Beatrisa's fender and dragged her out with his tractor, like a cow from a river.

One night, just over two years after my mother's passing, Dad phoned and said Antonovich was dead. The old man had been found by the caretaker of his block, cold as stone in his bed, dressed in his coat and his hat.

After some confused words – my father had been drinking, I could tell – he told me he loved me and put down the phone.

Next day, he drove out to the farm and gassed himself in Beatrisa.

In one hand, he held the wooden cross that used to hang over my parents' bed; in the other, a wedding photo showing the two of them, smiling.

A police officer called me out of a lecture to inform me of the circumstances of my father's death. The officer expressed his condolences in a routine fashion and advised me of certain regulations, mainly regarding the release of my father's body. He gave me some paperwork, and left.

A short while later, I went and hired a car – with one thing in mind.

In failing light, I searched for Antonovich's farm.

I felt sure I must have become lost.

I was about to give up, when the sound of my tyres on the slats of the wooden bridge told me I was there: I had found my way back.

Tall weeds and grass brushed against my doors, as I nosed my way down the track. Moths fluttered – by the dozen – in the headlamps.

As I rolled deeper, thorns scratched the car's wings; the branches of ghostly, white birch trees – uncut for years – raked at the roof.

Finally, the slope eased, and I came into the clearing occupied by the house and the huddle of barns that I remembered.

My lights fell on Beatrisa, illuminating her in a way that made her seem pale and ghostly, like something in an old negative of a photograph.

She was parked where the police had left her.

I stopped my car and got out.

The air was cooler than in the city, but heavy… still – as if all life and sweetness had been sucked from it.

Crickets chorused in the fields.

From the edge of the woods, came the sound of something muffled. An animal, I presumed: a boar… or rabbits, perhaps.

I looked at Beatrisa and thought of my father.

I wondered if he might have had some last-minute change of heart.

Her doors were always sticking. I remembered how, if ever I, or my mother, or Antonovich, wanted to get out of her, my father had to do so first (on account of how our doors were always jammed). He'd yank open the door in question, with a shrug of his shoulders, as if he couldn't understand what our problem was.

I thought of Antonovich – his long, stooped form, sitting in the way that I had once seen him – in his chair in the great room of the farmhouse, staring at the mouth of the fireplace, his talk of ashes, the time when *all* of us would be no more than that.

Then I reached into my pocket, drew out the small box that I'd put there, slid open the drawer and struck the first match.

In that dark emptiness, the rasp of the strike, the eruption of the head, were – to my ears – like cannon and bonfire.

I tilted the match downward, between my finger and thumb, coaxing the flame to caterpillar up the slender stick.

When my fingers felt its singeing heat, I let my little flambeau fall.

Spits and crackles began at my feet. The brittle weeds and parched grass that in the intervening years had overtaken the farmyard caught light.

At first, the small beads of fire seemed harmless: tiny *teardrop* flames.

But soon I had to step back. The force that I had unleashed was ravenous.

The fire went first for Beatrisa: surging over her sides, dancing on her roof.

I left her ablaze… and walked on.

I let my second match fall at the foot of the door to the farmhouse – a tongue of flame that illuminated a straggle of vines.

Fire quickly embraced the rotten wood, like a lover long denied.

I stood back and watched as flames garlanded the old dwelling, with colours that waved like beds of summer poppies and fields of ripened wheat.

The whole place seemed to sigh and moan: more alive now at its moment of immolation than it had been in perhaps a hundred years.

I thought how much better it would have been had Antonovich perished there: smiling as he sat in his ancient coat, gratefully aflame, in his vast, grey chamber.

I heard him repeat those words of our rides out in Beatrisa, in his bronchial whisper: 'But of course, professor…'

The house surrendered – no… it *rejoiced* – as the inferno consumed it.

The crickets in the fields beat their wings with thunderous intensity.

It was as if – rank upon rank – they were relishing the conflagration: spectating… salivating; the flames leaping in their black, bulbous eyes – an insect equivalent of those *tricoteuse* women threshing their needles in the blood-soaked shadows of the French guillotine.

For a moment, the house seemed to stagger, as if shuddering in the ecstasy of the glorious, shimmering destruction wrought by my tiny, awesome torches… my shock troops.

As I was leaving over the bridge, something told me to look back.

The farm glowed like a village razed.

But it was another sight that seized me.

For in the dark womb of my car, behind me… at my shoulder, a red eye glared, and a pair of wings raised themselves… triumphant… in the manner of an *aquila* carried by the legions of ancient Rome.

I followed the road to that incline beyond the trees where, as a boy, I had looked back on the farm, from Beatrisa's rear window.

After a short distance, I parked and, not unlike my father might have, I held the door for Napoleon – in all his imperial glory – to get out.

With one leviathan step, he lifted himself onto the bonnet.

With another, he planted his huge claw foot on the car's roof.

Massive… ancient… terrifying.

Standing above me, he shook from his frame a firestorm of gold and ruby feathers… and drew open his cavernous beak.

Then, as the farm burned in the blackness below us, he crowed into the night's cold darkness – with a scathing, steepling, flaying fury.

His summons demanded the ears of everyone and every creature. Not just in Moscow, but in Saint Petersburg, in Arkhangelsk, in Vladivostok, in Rostov, in Samara, in Kazan, in *all* of Russia… the alert and the asleep, the young and the old, the living *and* the dead: he would have their homage, their adoration, their hearts, souls, their… everything.

Irina Budayeva was the first whom we 'took'… I and my master.

She was, it appears, gorging cake when our fire insinuated itself under her door. It ate its way along her crumbed carpet and cornered her in her kitchen – that same place, on the ninth floor, where week after week she had had my father lumber her bags without ever giving him even the smallest of tips.

Her corpse, when recovered, resembled a charred pig.

Next came our burnings of those houses that the fat cats – with their big cars and arrogant looks – had built on Antonovich's estate. Twelve in one night: how beautifully they burned. No hope of salvation. The bonfires soared and shone, in Napoleon's approving gaze.

The destruction, a short while after, of a fleet of limousines in Tverskaya was something in which I took particular pleasure. Their burnt-out shells were strikingly apocalyptic, like a convoy of incinerated battle tanks.

Ordeal by fire seemed the only way to settle my account with Father Leonid, who had exploited my father's subservience so blithely.

I set his bell tower alight with a votive candle as he climbed its stone steps: the fire hurrying after him along a rope rail, trapping him neatly at the top (with the aid of the bell tower's highly flammable old beams).

A priest, you might have thought, would have been ready to meet his Maker.

But not greedy Leonid.

He leapt from his belfry, in a bid to save himself… and breathed his skull-smashed last on the pavement below, as if listening – for something buried – at a crack in its slabs.

I have abandoned my studies at the university: there is simply too much to be done. I travel the city setting new fires nightly, though to Napoleon my efforts are never enough. I hasten from one appointment to the next: his red eye upon me, his peals from my balcony exhorting me to do more. I have come to realise there is something sacred between us, and have long banished my childhood fears.

His flame is eternal. Mine flickers in the moment. Yet *together* – until I am ashes – we shall bring our light to the dark.

Firebird. My ancient, golden firebird....

Watch for our work.

Listen for our song.

driving
Lenin's
Ghost

'Should we be here?' she asked.

'Why not?' he said. 'We've as much right as any.'

'But they're locking up,' she said. 'I can hear them.'

'Good!' he said.

'What do you mean "Good"?' she said.

'Let them!' he said.

'But how will we get home?' she asked.

'In the car,' he said.

'But we came on the bus... and the train. What do you *mean*? We *have* no car,' she said.

'So what is this?' he said.

'Are you crazy?' she said. 'That's Lenin's car!'

'Well he's no need of it now,' he said. 'Not where *he* is. Anyway, it's not a *car*. It's his Ghost... his Rolls-Royce Silver Ghost.'

'You're being stupid,' she said. 'Let's go. I want to go,' she said.

She made to turn. He kept hold of her hand.

They heard voices, somewhere outside.

Her fingers tightened in his, then slackened, like the kneading claw of a cat... as the voices moved away.

'They'll kill you!' she said.

'Have to catch me first,' he said.

'It's ancient. It will never run,' she said.

'Then we'll – *I'll* – push it,' he said. 'It has skis, doesn't it? Look! The only Rolls-Royce in the world with skis and... tank tracks. It was made for us.'

He moved towards it. She pulled him back.

'It was made for Lenin,' she said.

He let go of her hand, stepped over the rope.

'I'm frightened,' she said.

"Don't be,' he said.

'So help me God, you're wicked!' she said.

'That's why you love me,' he said, not looking at her but at the Flying Lady on the front of the Ghost.

He moved to the door, held the handle... which was... *cold.* 'Just think whose hands have been here,' he said. 'Lenin... Stalin....' He tugged at the door.

'What are you *doing?*' she said.

The door came open, sagged on its hinges, like the cover of an old book.

'I don't *believe* you!' she said. 'I want to go home.'

'Let's!' he said, reaching to her over the rope.

'This is madness!' she said.

'If it was good for Lenin, it's good for the workers,' he said.

'You are a student!' she said.

'Of engineering. That's *nearly* working. Come,' he said.

'We mustn't!' she said, stepping to him over the rope. 'Seriously. Someone will hear. Someone will come!'

He held the door for her. 'Get in... please,' he said.

She slid across the leather, smoothed her coat under her with her hands.

'Will it start? It will never start,' she said.

'Shall I try?' he said.

'No,' she said. 'I can't believe we're doing this! To think: Lenin sat here...'

'In the back, actually,' he said. 'I've seen a photograph.'

'Give it a *little* try,' she said, not listening to him.

'Are you sure?' he said.

'Yes,' she said. 'I know it won't work. Not after all this time. But... *try*,' she said. 'Just once.'

She watched him through the windscreen. He lifted the side of the lead-coloured bonnet. It rose stiffly, like some ancient eagle's wing. She was thinking how it smelled in there: a dry, woody, dusty smell, like a cobwebbed dacha unvisited for years.

'How come you know all this?' she called to him.

'I didn't come all the way out here just to look at his curtains and bath,' he said.

He got in beside her, fiddled with levers, turned knobs, watched the steering wheel, which he held tightly.

Nothing happened.

'It won't start,' he said. He sighed. 'Perhaps you're right. Perhaps we should go.'

'Maybe you did something wrong,' she said. 'Try it again. Just once.'

He repeated his drill: flicking, twisting and pushing, as if operating some great musical organ.

He gripped the wheel.

Her fingers held the edge of her seat.

Deep inside the car, so deep it seemed to come from some dark and unreachable cavern, something... stirred.

First there came a groan, then a tremor, then a shudder.

The old car rattled, shook.

They jounced in their seats.

And then... *nothing*.

It was as if a bear had *thought* of waking, had even opened one eye, yawned... and then gone back to sleep.

'Try it again,' she said, putting her hand on his arm, whispering, wanting and yet *not* wanting to rouse the bear.

The Ghost groaned and shuddered as before, but *this* time it groaned and shuddered again... and again, till the shudders subsided and the car was running... actually *running*... at their hands and at their feet.

'I'll open the doors,' she said, getting out.

'Are you sure?' he called after her.

She was already unbolting the exit.

Suddenly, against her face: the cold shroud of the late afternoon.

He held the wheel. The car lurched to the grey light. She jumped in.

The Ghost climbed the track at the back of the mansion in the otherwise still and snow-covered park.

'Let me drive,' she said, as they went out of the gates.

'You don't know how to,' he said.

'But I can ski. This has skis,' she said.

She pressed against him, put her (now gloved) hands on the wheel. He shifted, let go.

Lenin's lemon-painted mansion disappeared in the trees behind them.

They did not take the roads home but instead drove over the plains and through the forests, the great headlamps of the Ghost – like cloches from dinner tables in the days of the Tsars – glowing through the birches and the pines.

As they crossed the quiet, snow-filled land, Yelena felt as if *she* were the Ghost's Flying Lady.

When they reached Moscow, they did not go home. Instead, they parted the crowds outside Red Square, and entered its paved vastness through Resurrection Gate. Choral singing came faintly from the small Cathedral of Our Lady of Kazan in one corner.

There, in the square, they circled the pyramid of Lenin's mausoleum – lap after lap, so it seemed to them – amid falling snowflakes, in the closing dark.

And they drove like that, the lights of the Ghost flaring... *golden*... on the walls of the Kremlin, until they and their laughter were stopped.

FLESH AND BLOOD

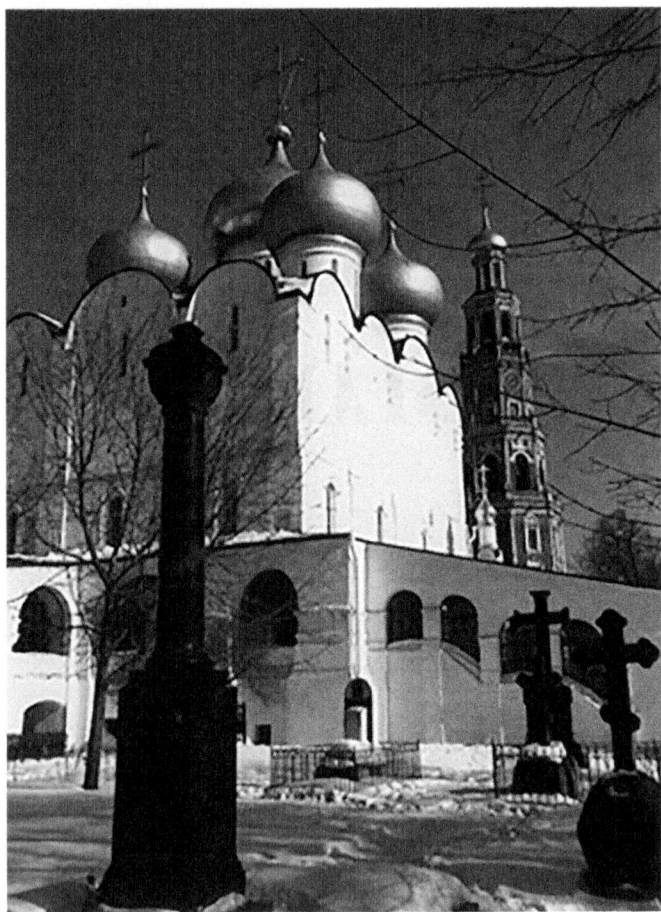

The difficulty Katerina Koptseva had with killing her husband was that, once it was in his head, the cleaver would not come out. Iosif Koptsev walked around their kitchen with the blade lodged in his skull, having the absurd look of a farmyard cock. He circled the table, holding the backs of chairs, with Katerina Koptseva in watchful, brow-furrowed pursuit. A distant onlooker might have thought them engaged in a parlour game of some kind, or even a romantic romp. Her husband being a good foot taller than her, made the cleaver's wooden handle doubly difficult for Katerina to grasp. Yet in her mind there was no doubt: Iosif Dmitrievich would *have* to receive a second – and hopefully mortal – blow, if only she could get hold of the cleaver.

She had registered the first (and, so far, the *only*) strike when, at her request, her husband had bent to look under their sink (there being, Katerina Koptseva claimed, a blockage of tea, or maybe cabbage leaves, in the neck of the pipe).

As he had pushed and pulled at the plumbing, in his clumsy, ham-fisted way, she had snatched the cleaver from its hiding place, beneath a baking tray for baklava, and drawn it down – two-handed – into his skull... thinking, as she did so, how pronounced his bald patch had become (like a brushwood-bordered forest clearing left by loggers in Siberia).

Far from falling to the floor, like the sack of swedes she had imagined, Koptsev had merely risen and straightened himself, while giving her a puzzled look (as if wondering how and on what part of the underside of the sink he had managed to bump himself). Then, he had begun his zombie-like lurch around the kitchen table, gripping, with his left hand (for balance), the tops of the chairs that were tucked beneath it.

This wasn't what Katerina Koptseva had expected at all. When, in the kitchen three days earlier, she had brought down the cleaver – double-handed – on a watermelon, its fearsome-looking blade had sliced the fat, green fruit clean apart: the twin halves rocking pleasingly on the steel draining board of the sink.

Iosif Dmitrievich had gorged first one half, and then the other, at supper: his grey teeth sinking again and again into the watermelon's wet, red flesh, in the manner of the steel forks and scooping buckets of the mechanical diggers he drove at his work… pink juice dribbling from the corners of his chomping mouth and dripping to the grubby fibres of the grimy vest he seldom bothered to remove.

Now, as he walked around the kitchen, with the cleaver lodged so ridiculously in his cranium, Katerina Koptseva wondered if Olyesa Gusova hadn't taken advantage of her at her fruit stall near the metro station, somehow craftily swapping the firm melon (that she had herself felt and selected) for another that was old, soft and liable to yield to the pedestrian fall of any random axe.

She thought also of the manager with the swept-over hair at the hardware store (on the other side of Moscow) where she had bought the cleaver: the way he had entreated her to take care as – in readiness for her journey home – she had zipped it in her bag. 'We don't want anyone getting hurt,' he had leered. Amid this pantomime with Iosif Dmitrievich, her mind at sixes and sevens, she wondered – for a moment – about returning there, to ask for her roubles back.

On what must have been their third lap of the kitchen table, Koptsev buckled at the knees – at last.

Reaching for one of the chairs, his hand missed its back and slid over the table, sending the blue check cloth and all that was on it – crockery, condiments, the cloche for their butter that was shaped like a country cottage – *crashing* to the floor.

Behind him, Katerina stretched for the cleaver – and even got her fingers around its handle of dark wood.

But then Koptsev pulled himself up… and was off – in his absurd, heavy-gaited walk of the undead – once more.

He turned to look at her, albeit still without speaking (this pursuit of theirs having been wordless from the start), wondering – so it seemed by his face – why his wife was not now pushing him aside and bending to clear the mess of smashed crockery from the linoleum floor.

A saucer snapped under one of his feet, as – momentarily – he staggered, while fixing her with his mystified stare.

After several seconds of this, Koptsev (still seemingly unconscious of the cleaver in his head) turned to carry on – his wife stalking, and stretching on tiptoe behind him, as before.

Suddenly, this *danse macabre* of theirs gained a musical score.

The drunk whose flat was above theirs dropped the needle on some old American song. Trumpets *wah-wahed* and a girl singer *boopy-dooed* and *coochy-cooed*. The sound came through the ceiling and the window of the kitchen (which Katerina realised she'd left ajar beneath its blinds). She abandoned Koptsev for a moment, to pull and fasten the pane.

The music from above became muffled. But the sounds of the drunk – bumbling and stumbling about in his flat – annoyed her. How come *he* was falling over… up there, while her husband, with a cleaver in his head, down here – So help her, God – was not?

She turned back to Koptsev (who was pale but still walking).

She looked at his head and the cleaver, which remained sunk there, as if embedded in some plum pudding, or the stump of a felled forest pine.

Koptsev's hair was matted with blood now.

A raspberry rivulet ran down his nose, settling in a teardrop on the end, betwixt the hairy caverns of his nostrils.

He pinched it and looked down at the borscht-like smears on his finger and thumb.

As he did so, Katerina's mind spun to another, who – in his way – had brought her to this bloody juncture: their neighbourhood butcher, Sergei Dedov, who she'd seen cutting mutton chops behind his counter at the mini-market... his cleaver hacking and his flabby white hands pushing and pulling red meat from grey bones. 'Saints give me strength,' she had stood there – at the glass counter, arrayed with its cuts and joints – and whispered...

The fact that Koptsev was still standing did not come as a total surprise to his wife. She had, after all, long been aware of his physical strength: the strange, disproportionate, animalistic strength that some men possessed – men who were neither particularly big nor muscular but had a wiry stubbornness that might be thought of as mulish or goat-like.

And so it was that, with a look of bafflement (but – bizarrely – not pain, or so it seemed), Koptsev now lifted his arms above his head, wrapped his palms and fingers around the handle of the cleaver, and began to rock and wriggle it, so that the blade started to see-saw in the bone and gristle of his skull.

It was a motion that might be imagined of a shrimp trawler, riding the northern swell of the Barentsevo More.

※

The first vision that Daria Koptseva had – at least, that is, the first that she could *remember* – came after her mother, Katerina, had taken her to Novodevichy Convent when she was five or six years old. Katerina Koptseva was a devout woman whose devotion had grown as her life, and particularly her married life, had soured. The more that she prayed and kissed her icons, the more she came to believe that in her son Pyotr, and her daughter Daria, there existed something pure and Godly. At weekends, she took to escorting them to monasteries, cathedrals and similar holy places. Part of her reason for doing so was that all three might, for at least some of the time, escape the rages of her husband Iosif Dmitrievich. These were at their worst when he had been drinking, as was often the case when he was not at work, making home life unpleasant, and at times unbearable, for his wife and children.

On that first trip to Novodevichy, Daria had found herself utterly captivated by the Cathedral of Our Lady of Smolensk. The snow-white building, with its gold and silver domes, was sweeter to her than anything she had ever seen – like something from a fairy tale.

By contrast, the great octagonal red-brick bell tower, on the other side of the convent's lawned precincts, had quite the opposite effect. The sky-steepling tower startled and unnerved her. Looking up, and holding on tightly to her mother's hand, it seemed to Daria as if the tower had no end.

One day, Katerina took the children part of the way up.

Pyotr, who was excited by the tower to the same degree that his sister was daunted by it, ran ahead.

From the gallery in the belfry, they saw the colossal bell.

It hung still before them, heavy and sullen.

Daria, who had never seen anything like it, stepped away and stood behind her mother who, despite the hotness of her daughter's hand, seemed not to notice the child's unease.

Afterwards, the three of them ate sandwiches on a bench by the ponds, outside the convent's walls. Then they caught the metro home.

That night, Daria had her vision – in her bedroom, in the dark.

She saw the red bell tower... soaring above her, then heard and – so it seemed to her – *felt* the fat ball of its thick clapper... striking and striking... in the mouth of the bell. Next, she saw children dancing, threading through arches which other children had made by raising their arms. After this, a train hurtled before her eyes. Finally, rockets wreathed with flames flew over a black land in which ragged people walked barefoot, with their heads bowed.

Daria shuddered and passed out on her pillow, her cheeks flushed and her forehead beaded with sweat.

Daria's visions, as she thought of them, lasted for nearly nine years. Sometimes, she saw – or thought that she did – the face of Christ, looming over her in the dark. This particular image would come to her after visits with her mother to cathedrals where drab plaster statues of His thorned and lanced likeness hung in gloomy chapels, coated with dust.

✠

When he was sixteen, Pyotr Koptsev left home and entered a seminary to train for the priesthood. This was seen as a cause for celebration by those who lived in their block. Neighbours brought gifts for him and his mother. Women asked for his blessing and stood before him, with their heads lowered.

On his day of leaving, both he and Daria were tearful, but he assured her that he would, in time, come back. And he duly returned every three months – by now wearing a beard, the wispiness of which highlighted, rather than concealed, his pale and slender youthfulness.

At such times, Koptsev, their father, would make sure that he was out, even if this meant only drinking beer with other men on the street corner.

If ever Pytor passed, the two would nod, but that would be all.

On the other hand, as he neared the block, children from the neighbourhood would run to Pyotr and shout his name – 'Pyotr! Pyotr!' – and he would humour them: kicking their footballs, ruffling their hair and handing them sweets.

҉

Iosif Koptsev was the first to notice Daria's 'bump'. Initially, he wasn't sure and for some days he studied her as she moved around the flat. When he heard her vomiting one morning, he was convinced. The girl was with child, he said to his wife Katerina. She would have to get rid of it. *They* – mother and daughter – would have to get rid of it. He would not have her bringing shame on him with her bastard, he said. Make her have a hot bath, push her over, use a coat hanger, do whatever it was that women did, Koptsev said.

But Katerina, who had also noticed the swelling in her daughter, said she would do no such thing, and if she caught him laying a finger on her—

He would do what he liked! he interrupted her. He would not have her shame him, the little whore!

So much as one finger! said Katerina. And she would kill him, so help her God!

Koptsev raised his hand to his wife, but something in her eyes, a defiance that he had not seen before, made him stop. He made sure, though, that he had the last word. If *she* did not kill the bastard… *he* would, he shouted, as he stormed from the flat. What was more, he yelled (aware as he was of his wife's devoutness, which he disliked), both she and her God could go to Hell!

In her husband's absence – he would be drinking, she knew, and spitting, with certain other men of their neighbourhood – on one of the street corners – Katerina Koptseva sat down at the kitchen table and wondered what to do.

She knew how impulsive and dangerous Koptsev could be, especially when full of drink. (Once, in a typical rage, he had threatened to break the nose of the manager of a shop that sold cell phones; on another occasion, he had pushed down the stairs of their block a debt-collector who had dared to come to their door.)

She decided to placate him with a good meal... and play for time. So it was that she hurried to the mini-market and its meat counter (where she saw Dedov, working his saw and his cleaver), from whose till she returned with two mutton chops... and one deadly idea.

And now her husband Koptsev, after much pushing and pulling, with that inherent, animal strength of his, was threatening to draw the bloodied blade clean out.

Katerina Koptseva watched in horror, as he tugged and he lifted, so that more and more of its smeared steel came free from the matted scalp of his skull.

Two more rocks of that handle, Katerina Koptseva calculated, and – Pop! – that blade would be out.

She prayed that none of this was real: that she had never bought the cleaver; that she had never married Koptsev; that she was still a girl with grips in her hair who loved her school and her colouring books.

She prayed for help... from the Virgin; the Saints; from anyone – the Devil Himself.

Fearing the worst, she shut her eyes and prepared.

By now, the drunk's music in the flat above had long ceased, and all that Katerina Koptseva seemed to hear was the sound of an awful *squelch*, as her husband wrestled with the blade in his head.

At this point, she and Koptsev no longer found themselves alone, being joined in the kitchen by their cat Mushka. Or, rather, Katerina Koptseva's cat (for Koptsev hated the animal – its every claw and hair – and had more than once tried to kill it by hurling it

against walls or out of the windows of their block…
only for the creature to somehow always land on its feet
and come back).

Now, as the cleaver was but one, last heave clear
of his head, Mushka wrapped herself around Koptsev's
ankles (in a way that she surely knew he would detest).
Her long, tortoiseshell tail twined itself below Koptsev's
knees so that – already unsteady – he wobbled even
more.

The next thing that Koptsev knew – in so far as he
knew anything – was that – in the manner of someone
whose laces had been tied together (as if in some
clownish race) – he was falling to the floor, with his eye
socket in close proximity (*very* close proximity) to the
doorstop that his wife kept in the kitchen… of an iron
ballerina – an object that Koptsev loathed with almost
the same hatred he felt for Mushka the cat.

The figure's graceful, yet ferociously rigid, upraised
arm was Iosif Dmitrievich's last sight on this earth, as –
his body falling, like some old pillar that he had brought
down with a wrecking ball at work – it rammed through
his eye and into the depths of his skull… exterminating,
once and for all, whatever was left of his bovine, bullying
brain, numb as it had been for so long – regardless of
plunging cleavers – to the needs of any in this world but
his own.

For all of his strength, Koptsev was, as has been said,
not a particularly big or heavy man. In fact, he was
sufficiently manoeuvrable for Katerina Koptseva to drag
him from the kitchen and then along the hallway and
into the bathroom of their flat. There (her whole body
empowered by her husband's long-awaited expiry), she
removed – finally – the cleaver from his skull – it came
out with a pronounced *suck* – and, in the absence of her
daughter, who was away on a trip with her school, she
proceeded to strip Koptsev of his shoes and his clothes.

Next, she heaved him into the bath and, with calm efficiency, began butchering him with the cleaver – chopping and separating, in the manner she had seen done by Sergei Dedov at his meat stall at the mini-market.

As if out of consideration for her deeds, the drunk upstairs now played some jazz. The sound of a saxophone sashayed down the copper pipes into the bathroom.

When the music – she hummed with it, here and there – gave way to arpeggios and scales, she realised it was he – the drunk – who was playing the instrument.

The mellow notes made her think of him quite differently, and she stopped for a moment and mopped her brow.

Then she resumed her hacking and her tearing, bagging her husband's butchered parts in black plastic sacks that she'd bought for the task.

After nearly two hours, a final swirl – and gurgle – of reddened bathwater took away the last dregs of her late husband's plentiful blood.

Katerina Koptseva scattered Iosif Dmitrievich's remains far and wide. This she did partly to reduce the risk of his identification and, therefore, her detection. However, she also feared that – irrational though she knew the thought to be – his body parts might somehow intuitively gravitate towards each other and coalesce, horribly, in something of the manner of Frankenstein's monster (the thought haunting her that one day the buzzer to her flat would sound and he would be there, grunting and cursing into the intercom of the block's front door).

She wrapped his head in tinfoil (as if it were a cheese) and took it with her in a holdall on the night train to Saint Petersburg. When asked by the clerk at Leningradsky station how many tickets she required, she very nearly said 'Two' – correcting herself at the last moment.

She wandered the northern city's thoroughfares for several hours, before finding a bin in a back street where she squeezed Koptsev's severed head under several layers of trash.

On the way home, she had the strange feeling that she had left him there on holiday, and that – in his semi-literate way – he might even send her a card (as sometimes had been the case when they were young).

Over several following nights, she crossed Moscow, disposing of the rest of Koptsev in sorties by train and by trolleybus. She threw pieces of his legs into the waters of the Volga and the Yauza. His right arm (minus its hand), meanwhile, entered the Vodootvodny Canal, and his left the Tushino Sluice.

His 'manhood' – that part of him which she had detached with the deepest disgust in the abattoir of the bath – she now reserved for a special rite.

Needing to satisfy herself of its irreversible destruction, she took it to the block of flats where she and Iosif Dmitrievich had first lived, remembering the coal-fired boiler in the basement, and hoping its antiquated iron furnace would still be there.

Entering the block by night, by means of an old key, she found – to her relief – that, yes, it was there and, what was more, it was burning. 'Thanks Be to the Virgin – Mother of God,' she said, crossing herself.

Tossing Koptsev's member to the bright coals within, she watched as – like a cheap, squashed sausage – it hissed and it spat (as if resentful of its fate), before melting to nothing in the consuming flames and heat.

'To Hell with it – and *you*,' she whispered, as – with a blackened poker – she pushed the heavy furnace door shut.

It was only on the very last of these 'dispersals' that a 'problem' arose.

Katerina Koptseva had taken a train to the pine woods at Peredelkino. to bury Koptsev's right hand.

The burial itself – in a dark piece of needle-strewn soil – proceeded uneventfully.

However, as the locomotive departed from the local halt for her return to Moscow, a dog – quite from nowhere – came bounding beside the track.

The animal ran till it was level with Katerina's window.

It had something in its jaws which, because of the movement of the train and the dog's shaking of its head, she could not properly discern.

It seemed to her as if the object was Koptsev's hand.

Like a bizarre item of lost property, or a duck shot by a hunter, the dog, it seemed, was dutifully bringing it back.

She expected – at any moment – the other passengers to pipe up with incredulity and alarm; that the small boy on the knee of the babushka opposite her would point a finger and shout, 'Smotryu!' *(Look!)*

But no one else in the carriage seemed to notice or care about the running dog. It was as if they were all somehow wearily engaged in a waxen tableau (one of the 'surrendered' kind she had noticed before among travellers on trolleybuses and trains).

As the train pulled away and left the dog in its wake, Katerina Koptseva composed herself.

Eventually, she wondered if the bounding hound had even been there.

Back at home, and having always liked a clean and tidy flat, she scrubbed and swilled the bath over and again, till no trace of Koptsev – not so much as a tooth or an eyelash – remained.

'Bun,' *('Good')* she said to herself, finally.

After a while, Katerina Koptseva told certain of her neighbours that her husband had died at work –

suddenly, of a heart attack. The funeral had been in his home village: a quiet affair.

Disliked as he was for his surly boorishness, no one really cared about, or mourned, Koptsev in that block. Good riddance to the rascal, its occupants thought.

❦

The child – it has not been seen for some time: one presumes it still lives – must now be what… five… six? Closer, perhaps, to six. *What* it is, even to this day, no one is quite sure. A boy, say some. A girl, according to others.

When the baby came, Daria must have been fifteen, at most. No one could credit that it was hers. There'd been no real signs to the casual onlooker of her getting 'big', and, indeed, no sign of her at all in the several weeks before the birth. She didn't enter hospital and, on what – through a process of elimination – was calculated to have been the most likely night of the infant's arrival, no ambulance came, and no doctor, or midwife, were called.

The delivery, so it was later said, was carried out by Daria's mother, the widow Koptseva, who, it was also said (in the way of idle talk) had fried and eaten the afterbirth (though some claimed it had been found in bloodied bags clawed open by cats in the bins of a neighbouring block).

People spoke, subsequently, of having heard Daria's screams through their walls and their ceilings – howls that died only when Daria bit on a rolled towel given her by her mother (though how they came by such details, God only knows).

Likewise, some said they heard the child scream till it eventually relented and lay still with Daria, who, after her ordeal, was pale and as weak as a new-born calf.

The baby was not properly seen until it was much older, when perhaps two years had passed: on a spring day, in the park, with its grandmother (long after the death of her brute of a husband who, said her neighbours, once again, the world was better without).

People saw the child and were intrigued by the child. But they kept their distance: pretending they were busy… saying nothing, looking elsewhere.

What they didn't understand was how it could have happened. Daria Koptseva they all knew to be a good and Godly girl, a shy and quiet thing who studied hard; a girl who, moreover, was 'visited' at times, and given to 'seeing' things in a spiritual way.

She could only have been taken advantage of, it was said.

Suspicion fell on certain men in the block.

And yet… she was really such a *waif*. Some people could not imagine her bearing a child, suckling a child, and reasoned that it wasn't even hers.

The real mother, they said, was *her* mother, Katerina Koptseva, who, despite her solemnity was (in the eyes of some) quite the merry one. Wasn't it she who was always with the child? The daughter studied and was hardly ever home, let alone *with* the infant. Yes, Katerina on *her* back, in *her* bed, staring at the ceiling, biting on the towel, an icon of the Virgin on the table beside her… *that* was how it had been; poor Daria… doing as she was told… her small hands holding the baby's slippery head as her mother shouted and gasped and bit on the towel.

As for the lengths that they went to – that they still go to – to hide the child: always taking the stairs, never the lift… walking out of the way, to avoid people in the park… keeping the child out of the nursery school… not even telling anyone its name.

It is as if they (mother *and* daughter) want to pretend that the child does not exist.

And, over time, people have come to wonder, in a strange way, if the child really does exist. Because, if a child has not been registered (as this one almost certainly has not) and is not *known* about, then – officially – it does *not* exist: there has been no birth, there *is* no child. There has only been… a vision.

Meanwhile, people give thanks for the interest shown in the infant by Daria's brother, Father Pyotr. He visits his mother and sister almost every other month and – Thanks Be to God – treats the child as if it were his own… or so people say.

The Honey Jar

When I stopped drinking, I needed to find objects other than bottles to occupy my hands. So I took to shovelling snow from the paths outside our block. I did this all winter, only finishing a shift when my spade scraped the tar and the slabs.

Most of my neighbours passed without speaking, which wasn't unreasonable given how they'd seen me do some crazy stuff over the years. Only the woman in 24 showed any interest, looking at me briefly when she opened and closed her curtains and blinds.

One morning, she came up to me as I was shovelling, and she gave me a jar of honey.

I thanked her and, having done so, I tried to think of something else to say.

My lack of words didn't matter because she said she had no time to stop.

She then walked on quickly, in the direction of the metro, without saying anything more. I sensed she was a little embarrassed by her deed.

I set the jar on the ledge of a window and went on with my shovelling, till I was done for that shift.

Then I went inside and took the jar up to my flat.

I spooned some of the honey onto a slice of black bread.

It was a delight… truly the best honey I had ever had.

A week later, I went to the market, carrying the empty jar.

In the hall, there must have been nearly a dozen stalls at which women were selling honey.

Only when I was about to pass her table, and hand my jar to someone else, did the white-coated arm of the woman – the lady from 24 (as I had come to think of her) – reach out.

She smiled, turned and drew a fresh jarful from the churn on the bench behind her.

The honey was almost the same bronze as her hair, which she wore 'up' with pins and a band.

I offered her money, but she refused.

I wanted to ask her how she came to be doing this... selling honey at the market, but I felt nervous and I sensed that she was nervous also. So I said nothing, and I let the opportunity slip.

At the exit, beside a stall where featherless chickens hung coldly from hooks, I stopped for a second and glanced back.

I thought I saw her looking my way.

My shovelling went on all winter.

Once a week, I went with my jar to the market.

As well as the honey, I enjoyed the ritual of these visits: the woman's pale hands drawing the honey from its churn, then screwing the jar's lid tight shut on her table.

I tended to go on a Wednesday. And I noticed that – on these days at least – the woman wore her hair 'down'.

I thought how lovely it looked, flowing to her shoulders. It was a sight that warmed me, on those white-skied mornings, when my hands were numb.

When spring came and the snow stopped, so did my shovelling.

I no longer carried the jar to the market.

Although I did not intend it, other glassware – the necks and shoulders of bottles – took the jar's place in my hands.

Summer was something I scarcely noticed. For the most part, it passed me by in a haze.

The autumn rains washed by me in a similar way.

Come winter, I reclaimed my shovel from the landing cupboard and re-started my routine of clearing the paths.

Several times, I went inside to throw up: my body's reaction, I think, to the shock of sobriety.

The honey jar, empty on the shelf above my kitchen sink, would catch my eye as I rinsed my face… as if to rebuke me.

Eventually, I took it to the market, wondering if the woman and her stall would still be there.

I'd seen almost nothing of her at her window, or on the paths around our block (for weeks… maybe months).

Her stall was there, amid the hubbub of the market.

As I neared it, she looked away (as if preoccupied with something).

Yet I sensed she knew that I had come.

She received the jar without a word, turned from me and drew the honey.

It oozed from the tap, like lava – just as before.

Winter sunlight streamed through the hall's high windows and fell on her hair.

I saw now that it had strands that were no longer the bronze of the honey but grey, like the churn.

I dug in my pocket for money, which – after she had tightened the jar's lid – she took.

A Capital Carousel

'Aren't you getting a little old for this?' said Elizaveta Entina as she walked past Tatyana Smekhova into Tatyana Smekhova's flat.

Smekhova looked out onto the landing for a moment. No one else was there and, despite her haughty demeanour, inside herself Smekhova was relieved.

She closed the flat's outer door and pushed the inner door *to* behind it, turning the key in the lock.

'I seek no more than that which is sought by most women,' she responded, turning to Entina in the hall, '… the love of a good—'

'So it is nothing to do with their roubles then?' Entina interrupted.

'I have no wish to end up an old maid,' replied Smekhova, '… like some.'

'Where is he?' Entina asked, disregarding the last remark.

'The bedroom,' said Smekhova.

She gestured at the door with her chin while drawing back her hair with her hands.

'What happened?' Entina asked, taking hold of the door handle.

'He collapsed,' Smekhova said, hoping her tone was sufficiently dismissive. She fiddled with her dressing gown, affecting unconcern.

They entered the bedroom.

It was light in there now, Tatyana Smekhova having opened its drapes so that only the net curtains shrouded the view of the block that stood opposite and the strip of shabby ground in-between.

Elizaveta Entina, in a grey overall of nylon, walked towards the bed.

She winced at the room's reek of cigarettes, perfume and body odour.

Tatyana Smekhova followed, barefoot in her robe, which was pink, floor-length and possibly silk.

'He is – *was* – an older man,' said Smekhova, as Entina neared the bed. 'He… gave up on me.'

She lit a cigarette.

Entina had been called to incidents at the flat involving Smekhova and men before: losses by Smekhova of her keys, complaints about the failure of the lift, accusations from neighbours that music in her rooms was too loud, or, on those occasions when she was using her bed for the purpose of sleep, her own indignant protests – not for nothing was she known by the other residents as the (self-crowned) 'czarina' of the block – about the volume of a TV or radio in someone else's flat.

But there had never been anything in the nine years of her tenancy that was the equal of this.

Entina felt the need to say something. 'This block is not a brothel, you know.'

Smekhova responded in the way Entina knew that she would. 'I will thank you *not* to lecture me about what may or may not occur in my flat,' she snapped. 'Am I behind with my rent? No! Have I given any of my neighbours just cause for complaint? No! Am I the lawful resident here? Yes! *You* are the caretaker! *That* is why I summoned you! Now… take care of it!'

Entina was unmoved by this tirade, and when Smekhova had finished the two women simply stood there in silence, staring at the man who was lying on the bed.

He lay there naked (save for a pair of black ankle socks), face down, on his belly, like a slaughtered pig; this notion being reinforced by the meadows of grey and silver hairs that traversed his shoulders and back like those that bristled on the rinds of the thicker bacon and chops sold by butchers on stalls known to the women at their local market.

'Is he really dead?' asked Entina eventually, her voice quiet (as if she were hoping the man might merely be asleep).

'Well, yes… *isn't* he?' Tatyana Smekohva asked back, her own words also spoken in not much more than a whisper now.

She did not wish to look at the man.

Her eyes, moving from him, fell on some rouble bills on the bedside table, which she reached for and pocketed in her gown.

'We'd better check,' said Elizaveta Entina. 'Come, help me turn him.'

'Must I?' asked Smekhova.

'Well you weren't so choosy ten minutes ago – or whenever it was,' Elizaveta Entina said.

'My mind was elsewhere,' Smekhova countered.

'Are you going to help me or not?' Entina asked.

Smekhova flounced forward to the bed. 'Innocently comforting some sad man,' she muttered, 'and *look* what my sympathy has brought me.'

The man's right arm hung over one side of the bed. Elizaveta Entina gripped it. The limb was still warm and, in spite of the circumstances, Entina found herself thinking of bread.

Bending beside her, Tatyana Smekhova placed her own hands over the man's hip and thigh. Aware of her diminishing ability to pick up men (in the 'social' sense), she wondered how long it might be before she found the next one.

Together the women began to turn the body, which was heavy yet also loose and awkward (like a sack of watermelons, two-thirds full), over, on the bed.

Who was he?' asked Elizaveta Entina.

'Just a man I met,' said Tatyana Smekhova. 'You know how they get.'

They let out small gasps and grunts, as they heaved the body onto its back.

In this act of rolling him, the man's right hand pawed Smekhova's gown, opening it at her waist, in a way that she found repulsive. It was as if – although to all intents and purposes the man was dead – his corpse was not yet done with what he had paid her for.

The springs of the bed squeaked, as the man's body slumped back on it.

The sound was like a chuckle in the still and airless room.

He was belly up now.

The man's eyes stared skull-wards in their sockets, as if looking for some beetle that might have been crossing his brow. His mouth hung open, the lower jaw being skewed to one side, showing teeth that were crooked and stained. On the whole, he was not so much piggish as horse-like now.

Tatyana Smekhova drew back with a shriek of disgust.

What Elizaveta Entina saw and felt, however, was something quite different.

In that moment, she remembered something that she had been trying *not* to remember… for years (decades in fact): something she had wanted any number of priests to give the last rites to and bury, preferably without any headstone, in an outlying cemetery where it could remain till it became irretrievable on account of the vastness and uniformity of the unvisited, flowerless place, or the way in which it had become so hopelessly overgrown.

And what she remembered was this: a gloved hand… on *her* gloved hand… and the tingle of breath on her neck, descending in small, warm draughts down the raised collar of her coat, as the horse, the beautiful horse – her unicorn, no less – rose and fell in a whirl of light and laughter on the wheeling and wonderfully glittering carousel. And then, afterwards, their walk, the first of many that they would have that winter, through all of the people in Park Kultury and the falling snow, over Krymsky Bridge, to the metro station and then home, to her modest flat, or, sometimes, his.

'Is he dead?' asked Tatyana Smekhova, looking away from the bed.

'For some time,' said Entina, staring.

The Bewitched Bathtub of Boris Babikov

The Deserted Bathtub of Boris Babikov

Babikov's bathtub was no longer his own. That's how he'd felt ever since Elizaveta Entina had hammered on his door to say Marusya Klimova had water coming through her ceiling in the flat below. He heard this from Entina, caretaker of the block, as he stood dripping with a towel around his waist in his hall, with Klimova scowling over the shoulder of the former.

What was going on with his bath? they demanded to know. What had he been *doing* in there?

He'd been taking a bath, he said, just like anybody else. What did they *think* he'd been doing?

The women brushed past him to see the offending tub for themselves. A big cloud of steam billowed out as they entered the bathroom. Babikov took his glasses from a sideboard and stuck them on – his lenses misting as the steam cloud consumed his angry intruders.

From the doorway, he discerned the vague shapes of Elizaveta Entina and Marusya Klimova, leaning over his bath. Beneath them, on the brimming bathwater, his yellow toy duck Demyan floated and glowed, like a lightship in fog.

The sounds of various tuts and clucks, of a female intonation, carried forth through the vaporous mist.

As these reproofs reached him, Babikov felt his towel slacken on his hips.

He thought he had tightened this loincloth (of a kind), though he wasn't quite sure, distracted as he had been by the events in his bathroom… disorientated, too, by the steamy state of his specs.

Elizaveta Entina emerged from the bathroom, like a not very lovely figurehead on the prow of some old wooden ship.

From behind her, came the sound of bathwater… whirling away.

'Your bath has been far too full,' she said, severely. 'I have unplugged it. Do *not* let it happen again.'

From amid the clouds, Marusya Klimova – or at least her head – appeared at Elizaveta Entina's shoulder, as if – thought Babikov – Entina had become some multi-headed Hydra.

'And the state of your tilework and grout!' Marusya Klimova snapped.

'My grout?' queried Babikov.

'Quite the disgrace! No wonder this flat is so full of leaks,' Klimova continued. 'Fix them! And quick!'

Only when his front door slammed behind the departing women did Babikov realise he was naked… courtesy of the sudden draft.

His bathtub, meanwhile, let out a satisfied burp, signalling the removal of the last of his water into the hidden innards of the block.

Regardless of the allegations of irresponsibility levelled against him, not to mention his exposure of himself, which – thankfully – neither woman seemed to have seen, it was he, Babikov, who now felt violated: *sinned* against by this home invasion, in fact. For if a man who had worked hard all his life – well, for *some* of his life… on certain days… here and there – if such a man was not entitled to security and comfort in his own bathtub, what *was* he entitled to? Indeed, what was life's point?

And yet he knew that Elizaveta Entina and Marusya Klimova were forces not to be crossed in the block. And that, in *their* eyes at least, there was already the problem of his 'record'.

As far as Babikov was concerned, his past misdemeanours, if some really insisted on calling them that, amounted to no more than innocent slips, errors of the kind anyone could make in what he liked to call in philosophical moments The Great Watermelon of Life.

The baring of his arse while talking to his tomato plants on his balcony the previous summer? Wholly inadvertent and, in any case, the real question was this:

why had some arse even been looking at his arse in the first place?

His misappropriation – when not wearing his glasses – of certain parcels of mail meant for his neighbours that had happened to have in them pickled herrings and chocolate cake? Blunders, yes, but hardly crimes worthy of the firing squad.

And as for the rest of his infractions... falling asleep on the slide in the children's playground... urinating through his window on the tenth floor... once or twice... when tipsy. Well! Citizens! Please! Minor offences, the lot.

Yet Babikov sensed that Elizaveta Entina and Marusya Klimova were talking about him in ways that were not 'good': the twin gorgons, as he saw them, doing so over cups of black tea and moist squares of baklava, behind his back, totting-up his so-called 'offences' in some heavy ledger or book: a grim thing of the kind written by a misery like Dostoyevksy: *The Dark Deeds of Boris Babikov*, in which his 'crimes' were enumerated, his fate decreed. He saw each woman taking turns with a goose feather pen, spearing its nib in a well whose ink was darker than any forest in Siberia, more poisonous than the venom of any slithering snake.

All this worried Babikov deeply. He remembered only too well how he'd been required to leave his previous block. He recalled with a wince the rough sleeping that had followed... on railway stations and in derelict buildings and parks.

Something else also played on Babikov's mind, and that was this: the goblin-like figure he'd seen in his flat. On shaking himself one night, he realised the unwholesome stranger was him, caught in the cracked mirrors of his bedroom and lounge.

Babikov was growing old. His time and his chances were running out.

Keen to keep a roof over his head, Babikov resisted all thoughts of a bath for more than a week.

But in the days and nights that followed, the allure of his tub grew (never mind that it was a grimed and ancient thing, with crusted 'tide' marks and a plug whose chain was red with rust).

In bed, he twitched and jabbered while dreaming of the tub's – in his eyes – comely curves and teasing taps. His toy duck Demyan winked and smiled, so it seemed, as it sailed the sparkling waters.

Temptation swelled in Babikov, like snowmelt inundating a mountain stream.

One afternoon, as the falling sun lit up his shabby flat, a bizarre and glorious vision appeared to him. He saw himself seated – naked – in his bath, in a chamber of mirrors and chandeliers. The President of Russia leaned over him and clipped the chain of Babikov's bathplug around Babikov's neck. There, the grey rubber plug hung, as if it were the medal of some respected order dating back to the days of the Revolution, if not before. The two men shook hands. Applause rippled through the many assembled (and smartly dressed) guests.

For several minutes, Babikov sat in a state of wonder in his threadbare armchair. Finally, he rose, as if from a throne, and declaimed to no one in particular that *he* was Boris Babikov, holder of a noble honour, and no one would stop him from reclaiming his rightful bath, least of all those evil witches Elizaveta Entina and Marusya Klimova, who he would see in Hell first, so help him God!

So it was that, for the first time in an entire ten days, Babikov filled his tub almost to the top, armed himself with his loofah (as if it were a sabre), set adrift his duck Demyan, and lowered to the water's surface one gnarled and yellow-nailed toe.

Yet, as he did this, Babikov was seized by the strangest sensation: the feeling that, there, in his bathroom, he was not alone. More to the point, that he was being watched... in particular, by the sharp eyes of Elizaveta Entina and Marusya Klimova. And not just by those harridans, as he considered them to be, but by the eyes of what seemed like all of the other occupants of the block: the widow Koptseva for one, her daughter Daria for another, even her son Pyotr who had long since left to become a priest – that he, too, was there, in his robes and his kamilavka hat, swinging a thurible of incense this way and that so that thick and almost choking clouds of smoke filled the small and crowded bathroom. Others were outside, Babikov believed, pressing their ears to his door, spying through its keyhole: ready to storm in at the sound of the slightest splash.

The truth was that Babikov could now barely bring himself to enter the bathwater he had so hungered for. And when, finally, he did slide his bony self into the tub's hot depths, he immediately hurried back out.

That evening, Babikov took a small sip of vodka – for his nerves – which was followed by two or three other small sips, after which his mood improved markedly. (That was *his* judgment, anyway.) In his armchair, he fell into a reverie in which, despite his earlier aborted attempt, he saw himself luxuriating in a beautiful, bubbling bath.

Suddenly, however, the steam clouds parted in this trance of his... to reveal the furious faces of Elizaveta Entina and Marusya Klimova, who were *in* the bath with him, seated at the other end... each naked as the day she'd been born. Next, Babikov saw that his loofah had come to rest, like some drifting log, between the bristly chin and crinkled bosom of Marusya Klimova. Meanwhile, his duck Demyan was advancing into the harbour that lay between Entina's large and buoyant breasts.

Babikov came-to from this hallucination with a shriek – *Nyet!* – just as Demyan was about to dock.

Babikov shook himself.

Something, he ruminated – if only he knew what – would have to be done. Move flat... put it all behind him — *that* was the thing. But who would have him? And who would author his letters of introduction: the testimonies that he, Boris Babikov, could be relied upon not to lower the dignity of a block? No, it was all too late for any of that.

This, he finally decided, was the time for action, the time for all hands to the pump. He would redecorate his bathroom and, what's more, do so in such a way that it would inarguably be both his own realm *and* water-tight. Yes, that was it, Babikov nodded to himself. 'And quick!' he added, mimicking Marusya Klimova, in the way she would surely have snapped.

Two weeks later, after several small doses of vodka (for the sake of his nerves), Babikov set to work. He would, he said to himself, create the finest and most leak-proof bathroom in the block, if not the whole of Russia.

First, he hacked away at the tatty tiles that surrounded his bath with scenes of blue windmills, clogs and, for some reason, cattle and sheep.

Beneath these, lay more tiles that had on them flowers and smiling fish of the kind seen in illustrations of folk tales.

In some areas, where the tiles came away easily, Babikov chipped right down to the brick. In doing so, he had the curious feeling that he was flaying the hide from some big and untameable beast: heaving aside its blubber, flensing it, to its bones.

With this, consistent with the philosophising turn that his mind sometimes took, he had the peculiar sense that he might be doing something even more: excavating its secrets, exhuming what some might even call its 'sins'.

After about an hour's labour, Babikov felt himself hot and dirty and in need of a bath.

He downed his tools (and a small glass of vodka) then jumped into the tub while its dusty taps thundered.

How wonderful! How democratic! he thought as he lay there, were the pleasures of a simple bath. Babikov shut his eyes and let himself soak as the steam rose around him.

After some long while of idling, Babikov felt there was something different about the bathwater in which he lazed. He also had the eerie sense of not being alone.

Scooping with his hands, he separated the steam that hung over the bath. At the tap end, was a young woman: grey-faced, her forehead beaded with sweat. She was, so it seemed, delivering a child. Blood, like so many red rose petals, clouded the water.

Babikov looked about him in horror.

On the old tiles that he'd exposed, the fish gushed crimson waterfalls from their eyes and their mouths.

He looked back to the young woman, only to find that she was gone. Her place had been taken by an unshaven man dressed in the clothes of a labourer, whose notable feature was the cleaver that was buried in the top of his skull.

Babikov again turned away in terror. As he swung his head, he saw that this time it was the old brickwork that ran red, spouting scarlet streams into the foaming tub. He looked back to the man, whose slumped figure retreated – slowly – into the steam clouds, like some mysterious riverboat in a misted creek.

Babikov wanted to move. Oh, *how* he wanted to *leap* to dry land! He leaned forward in the bath and scrabbled in the air with his hands. Yet his buttocks seemed soldered to the base. It was as if he were trapped in the tub... *by* the tub – as if he and it had somehow become one.

Suddenly, great crashing sounds filled the room. Through the clouds of steam, Babikov saw water sheeting over the tub's sides – in thick and powerful falls.

He sat there not knowing what to do.

Within seconds, any choice he might have had in the matter was snatched from him as – with an ugly groan and a shuddering crack – the bathtub sheared from its plumbing, shook off its anchorages and, like some Arctic berg on the move, sailed towards the bathroom door.

Jets of water from the torn pipes pummelled the sides of the tub. Others arched over the hunched figure of Babikov, in the style of towering sprays sent up by tugboats at times of special salute. The bathroom door now flew open and the mounting tide propelled Babikov out into the hall. There – as he clutched the sides of the tub – various bookcases, his sideboard, and a wormed hat stand left him by his mother, were already afloat, like flotsam from a sea liner that had sunk with all souls.

Elizaveta Entina – her faithful lieutenant Marusya Klimova at her shoulder – was, caretaker keys in hand, at that very moment in the act of unlocking Babikov's front door.

As the women threw it open – their raw fury overcoming the great weight of water at the door's back – Babikov steamed between them on a wave that first bowled the women over and then swept him and his vessel across the landing and on towards the stairs.

Babikov gripped the tub's sides as it bounced down the stairs, the floodwaters from his flat surging all the while beneath and behind it.

In the downstairs hall, the tub barrelled against the walls like some berserk bobsleigh, before finally shooting out through the front door of the block and into the gutter of the street.

That very week, Spring had shown herself in Moscow, and the melt of the winter snows was proceeding apace. Far from coming to a halt, Babikov and his tub now raced onward, even faster. Dogs and grannies leapt out of his way as the water sloshed and slapped both inside and outside his charging, barging bathtub.

The runaway tub roared on through the city – over trolleybus tracks, through red lights and beneath the very noses of stunned officers of police. Soon Babikov had left the suburbs completely and was sailing past Pushkin Square. Before long, he and his tub were surging down Tverskaya Ulitsa in the capital's very heart. Red Square and the Kremlin were in his sights, above the taps. The bright domes of St Basil's Cathedral beckoned. Stallholders and ice cream vendors dived for cover as Babikov stormed irresistibly on.

It was somewhere (very roughly) near the back end of the Bolshoi that Babikov underwent a change of temper – the fact dawning on him that he was no longer scared but actually rather enjoying himself on the crest of this wave of his. He noticed that people were watching, and, what's more, that some were even clapping and calling out 'Bravo!'

Babikov waved to them, as if he were a racing driver taking the chequered flag. He was even about to stand and salute – in the manner of some victorious yachtsman – when he remembered, at the very last moment, the nudity of his lower half.

Suddenly, amid this heroic progress of smiles and nods, Babikov had the ghastly sensation that his stomach had abandoned him and that his heart had jumped into his mouth.

Paying attention to his direction not before time, he realised that he was plunging... and fast... from a terrace above the Moscow River to the broad, brown waters lapping its banks below.

Babikov lunged forward and grabbed the tub's taps – like a pilot fighting to save a plummeting plane.

As luck would have it, the tub landed quite safely, and it proceeded to sail rather regally among the river's various busy tugs and ferryboats filled with trippers.

Our hero lay back now, in the sunshine, and enjoyed the view.

After all that he had been through – the invasions of his privacy by the living and the ghostly dead, the awful blood, the terrible flood – Babikov felt a tremendous… satisfaction.

So it was that, in the shadow of a high-sided steamer and watched by all those on board, he pulled the plug from his tub – doing so with a great, theatrical flourish, like some adored matador or magnificent magician.

And that was the last that – on that day, at least – was seen of Boris Babikov.

His corpse was found three weeks later, near a beach downstream popular with bathers: his waxy white face fixed with a ghastly grin… a rusty chain – seemingly from a bath plug – coiled tight around his neck.

Since that time, a peculiar eddy and bubbles on the surface have been reported by crews that ply the reach of river where Babikov's bathtub went down.

Some have said the tub remains there – restless on the riverbed, like an enigmatic squid or an unrecorded whale – dreaming, in the depths, of fresh adventures with a new admiral at the helm… explorations elsewhere: the Don, the Rhine, the Rhône.

Our story has one final footnote, which concerns Babikov's crewmate on that runaway day: Demyan, his toy duck.

The custard-coloured plaything has never been found.

It has been speculated that the orange-billed bird bobs – in splendid isolation – on a swell of the Caspian Sea.

There, some like to think, it smiles and even winks a black-lashed eye, as it rides the foaming waves… under skies that have no end.

The Snow Leopard of Moscow

An appropriate place for me to begin might be the Christmas of two years ago. Not an unhappy occasion. I was dining at the home of my prospective in-laws – my fiancée's father was in fact in the very act of carving the goose – when, feigning receipt of an urgent message on my cell phone, I announced that my attendance was required at my hospital. The reason, I – discreetly – indicated, was the performance of an emergency procedure on one of our most senior political leaders (whose identity my ethics, naturally, forbade me to reveal). I rose from the table. Apologising to my hosts (who showed only reverence for my professional devotion), I insisted they continue with their meal. I then collected my gloves, hat and coat, and saw myself out of their apartment.

There was, of course, no senior political leader and no medical emergency for me to attend. The truth was that my mind was consumed with my private fixation, which, in the way that our minds like to taunt and play tricks, had all day – even amid the liturgy of the Mass – been setting me one particular challenge.

So it was that I departed to find 'my' father and daughter. Not my own flesh and blood, of course, but two fixtures, if you will, in my collection… my extraordinary collection… of the beggars of the great city of Moscow.

The aspect of this man – the father's – conduct that – in my many years of fascinated observations of our city's beggars – had impressed me most, was his doggedness. Although profoundly unimaginative, he was a mendicant unmatched in terms of his sheer persistence.

That element apart, I counted this parent and child as 'beseechers' of the most prosaic kind in my 'cabinet', so to speak, of the beggars of our metropolis. It never seemed to occur to the father that everyone had seen their 'act' thousands and thousands of times. Even robed priests passed them by. As a 'collector's item', they were of almost no merit. At times I despaired of the man's lack of creativity.

But, peculiar as it will doubtless seem, the fact was that, on that evening of blizzards in the outside world and warm festivities within, I simply *had* to know if he and his daughter would be there... at their customary pitch.

A shiver (of anticipation) ran through me as I walked the pavements through a swirling shower of snow.

Checking my wristwatch, I saw that time was short but that, yes, the lines of the metro would still – just – be open.

If I hurried, I would make it to the trains.

Having reached the nearest station, I bought my ticket from a machine and skipped down the escalators to the platforms.

My own platform was almost deserted (as perhaps was only to be expected for the time of year).

A drunken couple groped in the gloom, the woman's heels clacking and scraping as she staggered under the man's pawing weight.

They looked at me and sniggered, having doubtless detected my disgust.

A train arrived, with the customary rush of warm, dry air.

When I boarded it, I found that it was nearly empty.

I chose not to sit, and instead stood looking at my reflection in the glass of the carriage door.

My face was pale, even ghostly, as the train jerked out of the station and hummed through the darkness.

I cannot explain why but a picture (that I remember vividly) came to me... of a strange seaside scene: a mother with three children perched on a blue-grey rock from which she was refusing to permit any of them to descend owing to the presence at the foot of the rock of a dog – a lugubrious English basset hound – which was toing and froing, with its belly sagging almost on the sand, as the mother protested, loudly, in French, about the *chien estrange*.

The family faded into darkness as quickly as they had appeared. It was as if a wave had swept over them. I wondered if the mother's over-protectiveness had brought about their doom.

Alighting at my intended station, I climbed one escalator and descended another. I entered the pink-marbled archway with which I was highly familiar, forked leftward and quickened my step along that cream-tiled passage that I had come to know so intimately from my visits over the years.

Normally thronged with travellers, the thoroughfare was deserted. The fall of my shoes was strangely loud.

The tinny sound of a burlesque instrumental version of *Santa Claus Is Coming To Town,* that metro officials liked to play on holidays, regardless of the time of the year, waxed and waned through speakers as I advanced. Gigantic images of crass so-called celebrities, alongside models of almost indecent beauty, loomed above me on billboards. In the absence of the ant-like armies who normally passed below them, their faces appeared anxious, even desperate, for my attention – the countenances, it seemed to me, of furious spoilt children.

In any event, I had my own pre-occupations.

Christmas… of all nights, I wondered. Could they… *would* they… be there?

I reached the passageway's critical curve, after which I knew I would see them *if* they were there: halfway down the straight that led to the footbridge: the tiny acreage of inviolable soil that they had made their own – their equivalent of the sacrosanct territory of a diplomatic embassy.

Another shiver passed through me.

Almost unconsciously, I crossed my gloved fingers behind my back.

I rounded the curve.

Doing so, a fresh wave of the ridiculous music assailed me, much louder than before.

I found myself involuntarily mumbling the missing lyrics: about my need to be good.

And then....

No, it couldn't be, I said to myself. Not on Christmas Night.

Because, yes... *yes*... they were there!

They stood motionless in the yellowy light: the father – as I had seen him so many times before – holding his home-made board with its beseeching words and blessings in the names of the saints, so childishly written in green crayon; the daughter, next to him, with her rolling eyes and twitching head. Hollow-cheeked and pale as consumptives, the pair of them, from their hours – *lives* – underground: his eyes far more dead than hers, not even acknowledging me as I approached.

I stole a glance at the coins on the grey blanket at their feet.

My eye (experienced in these matters) told me the 'scattering' of change had – of course – been arranged.

I wondered if this Christmas vigil of theirs had earned them a single fresh kopek.

I passed them and walked to the footbridge. They barely made a sound in my wake.

Truly they were the most faithful (yet utterly burnt-out) of Moscow's beggars.

Their devotion was unquestionable... admirable, in its way, I thought to myself, as I made for a train that would take me home to my apartment.

So... are you judging me yet? Are you already repulsed? Were I to ask you to join me for tea, here, in my railway carriage, while I go in search of the standard, Russian-issue, old lady who must be aboard somewhere (with her samovar), will you wait for me to come back? Or will you (disgusted) hurry off as soon as I have gone, insistent upon alighting at the very next halt? Is it your (already fixed) view that, in what I am telling you, *I* am the freak? Someone with whom no decent person would have anything to do? And yet… I sense that you *may* indulge me… for a while… and that you may even take a cup of tea with me *if* I can find one.

I understand, of course, that – beyond our window – the weather worsens, and I accept that the snow may be your only reason for staying with me. It's not a matter of anything ghoulish (or perverse) on your part, I know – heaven forbid! Still – seriously – I thank you.

Anyway, permit me now to take you back to my past, so that I may better explain myself and my… 'collection'.

How and why my behaviour began – and continued – isn't the simplest thing to unriddle. But my strong sense is that it was forged in the mesmeric stare I received as a child one night from a down-and-out near the Bolshoi.

I and my mama had been to the ballet and were leaving in our chauffeured limousine when the man's eyes met mine on a corner. He was not, in case you are wondering, a wretched or tragic creature. Far from it, in fact.

Staring at me, and I at him, through the side window of our automobile, he ejected a mouthful of spit that landed on and slid down the glass. Having done so, the bum gave a black-toothed grin as my mother – angry and disgusted, but in a quiet, dignified way – urged our driver to speed on.

I was shocked… but fascinated.

Some while later, accompanying her on a visit to a bank in Tverskaya, I caught sight, down a side street, of a large cluster of vagrants who had gathered at the rear of a small cathedral (in apparent anticipation of the opening of a soup kitchen). A steam cloud rose from their huddle (that must have stunk to high heaven). With their wild beards and manes of hair, and the blankets and sacking that they draped about them, they looked – to my childish eyes – like nothing so much as a corralled herd of bison.

Again, as with the tramp spitting from his street corner, I was intrigued. Nervous, yes: doubtless I tightened my clasp of my mama's gloved hand. But I wanted… *needed*… to know more about these people, who both appalled and attracted me… who were figures to me of both fear and fascination.

Gradually, in the way that perhaps more orthodox souls collect porcelain, coins or postage stamps, I began my acquisition of beggars: entering sightings in diaries, drawing sketches… giving them names, at times with childish poor taste (something to which I shall return).

Could these experiences have led to my later calling in life? My entry into medical school and progress along the professional ladder? A connection, I believe, is not impossible. After all, what draws a medical man to *want* to treat sufferers of a particular disease or disorder? Is it not some kind of fascination with the disease or disorder itself? A desire to become close to it… *intimate*, somehow?

Sufficient to say here that, alongside my more conventional studies, I began to compile a 'taxonomy', I suppose it might be called, of the mendicants of Moscow, whose chief categories I shall briefly outline.

First, there were the 'beseechers', such as the duo of the father and daughter. Another from their genre, by way of illustration, would be the young girl who knelt – and possibly still kneels – on a street corner close to the principal tourist hotels of the Garden Ring: an almost permanent presence – come rain or shine – at her pitch. However, unlike the doleful double-act of the parent and child, this young female did enough to cause me to place her in a slightly different class: the way that she *knelt* for one thing, her puppy dog eyes for another, the alternation of icons (Christ, Mary and sometimes George) that she laid on the pavement before her. People staying at the hotels threw coins and even notes, and she would lean forward and cross herself while uttering her bless yous (*'bud'te zdorovy*) and thank yous (*'spasibo*) in a display of devout piety.

(I was pleased to once see her perform in similar fashion outside the smoked glass of the more expensive shops at Kievskaya and even, on another occasion, on a pavement near a private medical facility that engaged me from time to time in the north of the city. I gave her a nod and entered this migration of hers in my notebook.)

Markedly different in my eyes, were those I called the 'browbeaters'. These I cared little for. In fact, what interested me was the intense dislike that seemed to exist between us.

Like the beseechers, I found this stratum of beggardom to be very largely female (though I concede that, in the city's darker shadows, it may well have been a case of – as with the child I've described – male puppet *meisters* pulling their strings). These (in my eyes, at least) fierce women operated on the metro trains, their method being to stand in the centre of a carriage and hold up cards bearing typed and photographic accounts of sick children they said were their own. Doubtless in some cases this was true. But the suspicion existed that in others it was not.

Often I would find myself virtually the only person in the carriage looking at them, as almost everyone else – even the old ladies – turned away. Invariably, they passed either empty-handed or with – at best – a few kopeks, from one carriage to the next – the sense of division, it seemed to me, between *us* and *them*, deepening with their every metro ride.

The least interesting branch of beggar – on grounds of their abundance – was, of course, that male-dominated category: the bum. By which I mean those filthy alcoholics to be found in derelict buildings and patches of scrub in so many neighbourhoods of our city, particularly beyond its inner ring.

For me, only those who had survived to an exceptional age (by which I mean, in their case, past fifty years) or who, from their language or some other small trace of refinement, seemed to have suffered a noteworthy fall from grace, were of any interest.

Once, on the outskirts of an old fire-ruined bakery known for its colony of dossers, I heard one fellow, with a great grey mane of hair, proclaim himself a lawyer. On seeing me, he asked for money (with a bow). I made my excuses and left. Behind me, his fellow drunks mocked him with raucous catcalls and laughter: 'Lzhets!' *(Liar!)*.

At one time, I heard a story about a former professor of mathematics who it was said could be found in a large cardboard box on the stairs of a fire escape in a shopping mall in the south-west of our city. I made several visits to the scene (even attracting the attention of the police as I sat outside the locked premises in the early hours in my idling car). To my disappointment, I never located him and eventually dismissed him as a figure of folklore, perhaps invented in some allusion to our country's internal economics.

In time, I formed the opinion that the only collector's piece in this world of the bum worth having was, to use the English, the Formerly Good Woman. And, if you were particularly lucky, a 'specimen' who had not only been good but who had also been well-heeled.

In this underground world of mine, there persisted talk of a nun who had lost her faith and who now, in the ragged robes of her past order, and amid all weathers, pushed a shopping trolley of junk among the remoter neighbourhoods of the northern reaches of the Grey Line.

At the height of my fascination – my fiancée having, by now, broken off our engagement over what she called my *dark side* – I trawled those neighbourhoods religiously (if you'll pardon the pun): stopping at late-night beer stalls, enquiring at kiosks, asking questions at cathedrals, while buying votive candles and small books of prayer.

Once, and once only, I seemed to catch a glimpse of her: a hunched, grey figure, disappearing between tenements on the far side of a busy carriageway.

By the time I had surfaced from the underpass beneath the road, she was gone – lost, with her trolley, amid the endless flats. Not, to my eyes (perverse as it may seem), a wretched old woman with a cargo of trash, but something rare and wonderful, like a Siberian tigress… disappearing into the great, white wilderness. Or perhaps a saiga antelope, shyly lapping water at a lake's edge on the Steppes.

By contrast, I once found myself assailed in the backstreets of one district by a crone who claimed to be the daughter or grand-daughter – she couldn't decide which – of Princess Anastasia, the 'missing' child, as some would have it, of our last tsar and tsarina.

Her face horrifically rouged, she rasped that she would tell me her story and allow herself to be photographed – naked, if I wanted it – for money, of course.

She spat absurd sums in American dollars through horrible, rotten teeth. Five hundred for her breasts. One thousand for *all* of her.

She had heard of me, she said: I was a surgeon, and she knew where I worked.

At this, people began to stop and listen.

I walked on.

She staggered after me, jabbing the air with a bony, turkey-claw hand, calling out 'Vrach! Vrach!' *('Doctor! Doctor!')*.

I brushed her off and made for a taxi (which I was lucky to hail).

As the driver pulled away, I glanced back. I saw her squatting in the gutter… urinating.

I confess that sometimes I did wonder about the strangeness of what I was doing.

When, finally, I told my fiancée the truth about my night wanderings (after several terrible rows in which she had accused me of seeing other women… and even men), she responded that I could have her or my beggars, but not both.

Such was my state of mind at the time, that I chose… my beggars.

For a while, her parents threatened me with scandal, but in time they relented (perhaps realising that my idiosyncrasies might drag their own good name through the mire).

So, are you still with me? Yes? Well, that's good and I'm grateful. What a night it's becoming! You know, it's so cold in the carriage of this train that my eyes are streaming. And a minute ago, when we jolted over some points, I was practically thrown from my seat. We seem to be forking somewhere, but it has grown so dark outside that it's difficult to tell. Moscow lies behind us. That much I know: her lights aren't even embers now.

Aloof from all those I have described, stood – in his own way – one who was neither a beseecher, nor a browbeater, nor a bum… nor even really a beggar at all. A *barker* is perhaps the word for him – and one of the five-star kind.

He was not so much a seeker of alms, it seemed to me, as a collector of (what many might think of as justified) tithes. By that I don't mean to say that he engaged in the seedy vaudeville that so many of my beggars took up. Among them an old and toothless fellow who tap danced (very badly) in shoes splayed open at the toes on the promenade to Sokolniki Park. Elsewhere, a defrocked priest who picked pockets for show (very neatly) beside Vodootvodny Canal. Still more, who need not detain us here, doing things with cards, small dogs, filthy handkerchiefs and tuneless guitars.

'Sawn-Off' (as I came to call him) was, emphatically *not* of that set. You see, when I say he *barked*, I mean that he demanded your money, called out for it, *insisted* upon it, quite shamelessly, in fact. With him it was not beggary, it was… *beration*. And done with a ferocious pride.

His fearless belligerence, together with the fact that the metro was his milieu, caused me to think of him – not that he was the least bit criminal – as being faintly with the glamorous highwaymen and pirates about whom my mother read to me from English storybooks as a child.

But the most remarkable thing about this fellow (the most notable of all my 'discoveries'), particularly to a surgeon such as myself, was not his voice (no matter how compelling its boom), nor even the nobility of what might be called his 'Stand-and-deliver!' (which any hero of the highway or high seas would have envied). What enthralled me about him, and set him above *all* of his inferiors, was his partial nature. The fact that he was a fragment of a man. *Half* a man, to be exact.

I shall never forget our first encounter. The train was pulling out of Park Kultury (I had been visiting a private patient – a wealthy woman, of fading looks, prone to call me with complaints of a hypochondriac nature – who lived in the Ostozhenka district). As usual, I was pretending to read my newspaper while scanning the travellers who were seated and standing around me for any small matters of interest.

Suddenly, a furious voice filled the carriage… and I can remember every word.

'Look at me! *Don't* turn your backs. "Look at me!" I said. All of you. You owe me your eyes, at least. A man like me is worth the attention of your eyes, isn't he? Put down your papers! Look at me, I tell you!'

Well, I was electrified, of course. I looked both ways for the source of this bellowing, reasoning that it could only have emanated from some huge bear of a man.

'That's better,' the voice said. 'I deserve your respect, don't I? After what I have done…'

I craned my neck this way and that. Yet still, on account of the crowded nature of the carriage, I could not make out the fount of this oration.

'… after what *I* have given!' barked the voice.

Beneath my coat, my heart raced. My newspaper trembled in my hands.

The commuters standing near the doors at the northern end of the carriage parted, and, from their midst – like a fist-pumping charioteer entering the Circus Maximus in Rome – came the figure… the half-figure… of Sawn-Off (as, disrespectfully, I know – in those early days – I christened him).

As a surgeon, I was not unaccustomed to arresting sights, but there was, about this man, something remarkable.

I found myself rising to my feet (only just resisting the urge in my hands to applaud).

When I speak of him as a half-figure… a half-man… that is because *physically* that is what he was: a double amputee (cut through, in both legs, high in the upper thigh, so it appeared).

He propelled himself on a square platform, rather like a tray, that had beneath it castors or wheels of the kind used on roller skates.

With his muscular arms, he held heavy blocks that he placed on the ground in front of him, simultaneously, to project himself in a rhythmic, machine-like motion of clumping forward, shouting and clumping forward again.

His head passed those in the carriage at the height of waists and laps: a powder keg, is how I thought of it, topped with greying black hair in a neo-Roman cut.

His burly torso was buttoned-up in a battledress jacket across which, in the style of a bandolier, was strung a belt with a pouch.

'Both legs!' he barked as he advanced down the carriage. *Clump*. 'Taken by terrorists!' *Clump*. 'For you!' *Clump*. 'What are they worth?' *Clump*. 'YOUR legs?'

He stopped before me... head at my waist, jerked his chin to the pouch on his chest.

Although as a rule I *never*, for all sorts of reasons, gave to the beggars whose activities I observed, I found myself emptying my trouser pocket of all of its change and placing my coins in his pouch.

He nodded.

I re-took my seat as he continued down the carriage. 'Twenty years' service!' *Clump*.

A young woman opened her purse.

'Both of my legs!' *Clump*. 'What is that worth?'

Others reached into their pockets and wallets.

The train now pulled into Okhotny Ryad. My new man – as I (arrogantly) already considered him – was about to alight.

I moved to the window, keen to study his technique.

He departed with impressive efficiency: first reaching out of the open doors with those blocks of his, then swinging the rest of his tray-borne self onto the platform.

He then scooted off – part clumping, part freewheeling – till he veered into an arch and was gone.

I re-took my seat (conscious of how the carriage's other passengers were looking at me owing to my conspicuous interest in our erstwhile companion).

I wondered if I would see him – this marvel – again.

We have pulled in somewhere – you and I – at last. Somewhere in the middle of nowhere, I suspect. The platform has only the weakest lights, and there is complete silence now that the train has stopped. And yet there should be noise here, shouldn't there? Carriage doors opening and shutting, passengers boarding, others getting off; not to mention whistles, shouts, our engine hissing... And yet – in the mechanical and human sense – I hear... nothing. I wipe at the window with the sleeve of my coat. And I see... *nothing* – except snow swirling in the dim yellow arcs of the platform lights. It cannot be *my* stop. The guard, who I've yet to meet, would have come to tell me, I feel sure. Should I get out? What do you think? Maybe there's a stall. Warm borscht and bread are what I need. And yet it is *so* quiet. I swear I can *hear* those flakes of snow. What if I step out and the train should leave?

I wipe at the window anew and – suddenly – the strangest thing: every door on every carriage as far as I can see (from my vantage point beside the glass), both up and down our train, is opening and slamming... yet *no one* is boarding and *no one* is alighting. Not a single soul. It is as if the train is engaged in some surreal round of applause till, with the same suddenness that it all began, the doors cease their clattering... and fall still, and silent.

With a violent lunge, the train pulls off, throwing me back in my corner.

I wrap myself in my coat against the cold... and think again of Mr Sawn-Off and my 'collection'.

Some while after my encounter with him, I received information about a 'curiosity' which I was told would be to my liking: a husband and wife of non-Slavic ethnicity, so I was informed, both affected by dwarfism, who could be found on certain evenings at a quiet station in the southern reaches of the metro. There, it was indicated, they performed various tableaux, including scenes from William Shakespeare, followed by a collection.

The pathetic nature of this theatre appealed to me. My tip came via an informant I had used and rewarded with small sums in the past (albeit a source I'd not heard from in some time). The station was a remote one. When – on account of its distance – I havered somewhat on the telephone, my caller added that the husband and wife were begging in the way that they were because they had fled a circus whose manager had wanted them to act only as clowns – which they (not unreasonably) considered beneath their dignity. What was more, they had provoked his fury by marrying (against his will). They would, said my spy, be on the platform of the station on the evening of the next day.

I entered the details in my diary.

The following night, I alighted at the given location at the specified hour.

The place was deserted. There had, I told myself, been some mistake. I turned to re-board the train on which I had come, but it had already begun pulling away.

I waited for some moments under a light on the platform, then climbed the steps of the footbridge that led to the other side of the tracks.

I heard steps behind me.

As I crossed the bridge, a train pulled in – and out again – while I hurried down the other side.

Those same footsteps I had heard followed me down the bridge… and then stopped.

Three pairs, I told myself. One owner who was lean and nimble, two others who were heavy-set.

I quickly decided that I would give them my money, my wristwatch, my pens, my cell phone – whatever they wanted. But I would ask them not to harm me, and, in particular, to spare my hands. I would tell them that, regardless of whatever I did in my private life, I needed my hands because my hands helped people… they did good: I was a surgeon. They would already know that, of course.

Ahead of me, tiny specks of moisture drifted in the yellow-green glow of the platform lights. I felt the night's damp on my neck and regretted having come out without a scarf.

'Doctor?' one of them said – the lean one, I supposed.

For a strange moment, I wondered if it was me who was being called. I sensed myself half-looking for someone else: the other doctor, the *real* doctor, who would step forward so that I might then turn up my collar, pass by and go home.

'Doctor!' came the voice again. Except now it wasn't asking but telling. More than that, something in the bleakness of its intonation conjured… my father's cane, which – unpleasantly – I saw and, for a second, heard falling on the palm of my six-year-old hand.

A train flashed through the empty halt, on the far track.

'Doctor!!' the voice behind me repeated. Not asking, nor telling, but *ordering* now.

Yet still I strained at those myriad beads of moisture, shifting and switching ahead of me, in the sickly light of the platform lamps.

As I stared, a slow but steady, metronomic beat made itself heard. Faint at first, it grew louder… till, out of the murk, the unmistakable form of Sawn-Off appeared. I realised he must have alighted from the tail of the train that had come and left as I was crossing the bridge. He nodded as he passed me: tree-trunk arms pounding his blocks to the ground.

Two 'strikes' behind me, he stopped.

The wheels of his board cut a half-circle on the platform.

'Is everything all right here?' he asked.

'Move along, freak. This isn't your business,' the lean one replied.

Sawn-Off, to my surprise, said nothing in response to this remark. All I heard was the dripping from a roof gutter filled with slush: each droplet detonating on the platform with a weird intensity borne of the stillness of the scene.

'I said, "Move"! Freak!!' the lean one said again. 'I won't tell you a third time.'

I turned around.

Sawn-Off (for whom this disrespect had, understandably, been too much) smacked his blocks on the platform and stared at the would-be bandits – like some dark, pawing bull.

The lean one, and his stodgy lieutenants, seemed to sneer.

Suddenly, Sawn-Off was in flight – as if catapulted – bulldozing those hoodlums, swinging and smashing with his blocks, like a combatant in some medieval battle where the fighting had degenerated to the close-quarters kind… hand-to-hand.

My three would-be robbers – youths not long out of their teens by the looks of them – held up their arms to shield themselves, before scrambling away, pitifully – whimpering and vanquished – into the vaporous dark.

Sawn-Off glanced at me while letting out deep breaths.

Then, with his fury sated, my saviour re-began his *clump*, and rolled away, wordlessly, into the night.

After that, I kept from the outlying stations and confined myself to the stops within the Garden Ring (where a police presence was assured).

If I'm honest, this new carefulness of mine – I no longer made expeditions after nightfall – caused my 'diversion' (if I may call it that) to lose its frisson. I contemplated rekindling my relationship with my fiancée but drew back from the idea as I replayed in my mind the scenes of our final row: her slaps and cries of 'Urod!' *(Freak!)* – the same epithet that the leader of those louts had used to my defender.

I was pleased when, some weeks later, my path again crossed Sawn-Off's, in more benign circumstances.

I was heading to a branch clinic of my hospital on a northern stop of the Green Line.

He came pounding along my carriage in his now familiar fashion.

I wrapped a good-sized bank note around my business card, inscribing on the latter that date of my endangerment when he'd been my knight in shining armour. I wrote under it 'Spasibo' (*'Thank you'*). These I placed in his pouch as he clumped his way down the carriage.

He recognised me, so it seemed, gave one of his curt nods, and clumped on.

Some days later (and somewhat to my surprise) he telephoned me. With a few gruff words on his part, we arranged to meet at a coffee house in a backstreet in Kropotkinskaya. He, of course, knew by then that I was a surgeon, and, as I walked to the coffee house from the metro, I thought about how I might best handle what I had anticipated would be his inevitable enquiries about surgery (which experience had taught me to expect).

In fact, as we sat at a table – he lifted himself backwards onto his chair by means of his blocks – he made no mention of medical assistance or anything of the kind. Indeed, it was a case of me seeking something from him.

'I would like to do something for you, in return for the help you gave me,' I said.

'There is no need,' he said, in that proud way of his.

'If you will permit me,' I said. 'I feel the need.'

He gave me a long, hard stare and then said, 'What I would like, doctor, is not yours to give.' He drank some of his coffee then brought down his cup with a finality which said that, as far as he was concerned, our conversation was over.

Albeit somewhat puzzled, I decided to respect his position. Once again, I stated my gratitude for the assistance he'd given me.

He lowered himself from his seat to his board.

'Be careful, doctor,' he said, 'about the places you frequent. Your interests are known. Next time, it may be different. My legs were of consequence to me but – arguably – not to the world. Your hands *are* of consequence. People *need* your hands. Watch what you do with them.'

'I am sorry for my… "intrusions",' I said.

'God made us all, doctor – *damn* Him (as sometimes we're all perhaps, in our darker moods, given to think).'

And with that he clumped through the coffee house and hauled himself into the street.

You haven't forsaken me, have you? No? Well, Thanks Be to God for that! I was beginning to wonder if I was the only person on this blasted train. Apart, I mean, from the girl who's been here. You've just missed her. A beautiful girl, in fact. She was of few words, but she gave me what I needed: cigarettes. Yes, yes, I'm a medical man and therefore I shouldn't partake, I know. But don't be shocked. You *can't* be shocked. Not now, anyway. Not after what you've come to know. They are company – these small, seductive tubes – and, more important, they will help me get through what I must share with you next.

When the atrocity happened, I was dining alone: a quiet Chinese restaurant in Kitay Gorod, after work. For several days, I had been congratulating myself on what I supposed others would call my 'rehabilitation'. My various notebooks, journals and photographs I had shut away in a closet in my apartment, having lost all appetite to search the streets in the manner that had been mine. I had also vowed to cease my use of tasteless puns – such as 'Mr Sawn-Off' – in my superior and foppish English and French. Something else: I had begun to pay more attention to the opposite sex: smiling at women in coffee houses, leaving tips for waitresses, and suchlike. I was even toying with the idea of issuing an invitation to a female colleague to join me at a viewing at an art gallery off Pushkin Square.

But then, as I say, the *atrocity* – and I abandoned all thoughts of anything else.

As a surgeon, I was among the first that my hospital summoned.

If you were to ask me now, on this train, for my thoughts on what Hell might be like I would say to you that it might very well be like the 48 hours in which I *amputated* the blood-soaked hand of a small girl that was hanging from the rest of her by the merest of arterial threads; *cut* loose the crushed and barely recognisable foot of a sportsman that hung from the rest of him like some dog's gnawed bone; *separated* from her skull the pulverised ear of an elderly lady whose eyes had been so filled with flying shards of metal and glass as to render her almost certainly blind; *detached* from the rest of him the horrifically mangled and unpreservable right leg and genitalia of a young man due to be married that very next weekend.

I would tell you also of the pregnant mother whose twin foetuses were lost, and the fair-haired boy of ten (who reminded me of the child I once had been) who died on the operating table in front of me.

And *still* I would not stop.

I would have you inhale the charnel-house smell of flesh… freshly burned, till you vomited as I vomited, and then have you hear – again and again and again – as I heard it, the infuriatingly banal *clack* that came with every nail, bolt and screw that I extracted from skin that would almost certainly be permanently scarred, which I placed in steel receptacles, beside my scalpels, where the projectiles piled up, one on top of the other, in horrific heaps of bloodied scrap, which, in those moments of sleep that I was able to snatch, became, in my fevered dreams, mountainous pyres that erupted into flames, on which were thrown the severed limbs and even heads of the living and the dead, in fires that raged and *never* went out.

That, if you asked me, is how I would describe Hell.

In the days that turned into the weeks that followed, I attempted to repair painful ruptures, make the best of cruel mutilations and performed or assisted in the removal and transplant of countless organs. I felt myself so steeped in blood that I wondered if I had not ceased to be a surgeon and had, in fact, become some kind of butcher. Despite calls from my colleagues to rest, I worked on till I found myself in a state of both mental and physical exhaustion. When, finally, I passed out in the operating theatre, my employers *insisted* I took leave.

And I went home and slept.

Eventually, I came-to… in the middle of the night… three maybe four days after I had been ordered to go on leave.

I groped my way, weak-legged and disorientated, to my balcony window, slid it open and stood there.

I thought how beautiful – in a strange, primitive way – my neighbourhood seemed. The few lights in the otherwise black blocks and towers made me think ours a temple city in a remote and peaceful mountain range.

Then a jackhammer started in the street below, and I pulled the window closed.

I walked into my bathroom and tugged the light cord. The flare of white light all around me was so overpowering that I almost collapsed. I shielded my eyes with one hand and reached for the cord with my other.

The flimsy line evaded me till, finally, I had hold of it and yanked it so that the darkness was restored.

I breathed deeply, calmed myself and fumbled for the small light above the washbasin.

I threw water over my face in the light's soft glow.

I abandoned an attempt to clean my teeth. Two, three, four – I lost count – slugs of toothpaste fell and glued themselves to the walls of the basin. I put down the tube and my brush. I held up my hands in the mirror... and watched them waver.

Returning to my bed, I told myself – like a doctor encouraging a patient – that I was tired and that – given time – all would be well and that my hands would recover.

But they did not.

My shake – *my* shake – how personal, how intimate and precious that sounds, as if it were a creation of mine of which I could be proud... grew more pronounced.

I returned to work, even so.

However, when my incisions for the removal of a growth from a patient's spine descended into a grotesque and meaningless zigzag, the anaesthetist quite rightly put her hand on my wrist and forced me to stop.

And so now here I am... as you find me... *riding*... *joyously* riding.

I think I have the better of it these days. My '*shake*', I mean.

You saw – and said – nothing while I was smoking. Maybe I really am steady again. Or maybe you were just being polite?

There's something I... obtain... for it. A sweet little something, it has to be said. Mine by virtue of my position as a surgeon (according to my business card, at least).

It does the trick. Mostly.

On days when I've rested, and my hands are (relatively) still, I ride the metro – and sometimes the out-of-town trains (as we are now).

I go... nowhere... in circles... for hours.

My fellow travellers don't want to know me, of course. I'm the madman in the carriage who no one wishes to come near.

That is why I've been so grateful to you, for your company, on this particular trip.

Recently, on one of my dead-eyed excursions, I saw Sawn-Off – or thought that I did. (How I must *stop* calling him that!)

He came clumping down the carriage where I had sunk myself in a corner seat.

He was berating no one, not even speaking, in fact. I'm not sure he saw me. If he did, he didn't want to know.

He clumped and rolled himself to the door of the carriage.

Then *she* came – the beautiful flame-haired girl… one of those whom – on that earlier excursion of mine… into Hell – I had done my best for (though my best had not amounted to much).

She clumped and rolled after him: halting, by his side, the two of them facing the exit.

The pair of them were like parachutists, waiting to jump.

When they did, they freewheeled away quite wonderfully… along the platform and out of my sight, as my train tunnelled on… into the dark.

And so, as I said at the start of our meeting, it's time now for you to tell me… to give me your answer. Where do *I* stand? How should *I* be judged? More dog than wolf? More sinner than saint? Somewhere in-between?

I feel that soon I may disappear entirely… in this half-light, this shadow-world, where I drift.

I've come to think of myself in the same way that I once saw the old nun with her shopping trolley. Not yet, I hope, a down-and-out of the gutter, but a vagrant 'creature' of the dawn and the dusk – an exotic beast, perhaps: paws falling softly on the Kremlin's ramparts, leaping silently from one cathedral dome to the next.

The Snow Leopard of Moscow, if you will.

A rare creature, a sight worth seeing.

One for the scrapbook. Truly, a collector's item.

Yes, if you'll indulge me, I'll settle for that.

Remove the rime from your window... and you might just see me.

Look.

Look.

The Red
Vineyard

Frost-feathered pane, porch of Tolstoy's townhouse, Khamovniki, Moscow

From the corner of his eye, Malikov caught sight of the small pools forming on the parquet floor as the melting snowflakes dripped from the hem of his coat on its hook on the stand.

Sveta Sukhanova was standing in front of him talking and, although he was aware of her, he was not listening. He was thinking instead about what had happened on his way to work: the car that had nearly run him down in the street and, more disturbing, the subsequent behaviour of its driver – which he was still trying to understand.

Malikov went over it in his head. How, not for the first time, he had left the metro by the wrong exit (he was given to such moments of absent-mindedness), and, rather than retracing his steps into the underpass, he had taken the decision to walk – and then run – across the highway.

Sveta Sukhanova's lips moved in front of him. Malikov noticed a small chip in one of her teeth.

But what he was actually thinking was how, at that busy time of the morning, the roads seemed not really to be roads at all. They were, he thought, more like trails down which thousands of steaming, snorting bison ran – as if somehow compelled – from distant and misted plains, halting at times – in their great, dark herds – before swarming on anew.

Instead of Sveta Sukhanova, it was the driver of the car – a big, (and to Malikov) militaristic vehicle with smoked glass – that Malikov again now heard, shouting after him as he, Malikov, hurried… amid horns, skids and swerves… onto what Malikov had presumed would be the safety of the pavement. 'What world are you in, you stupid bastard?' the driver had bawled through a wound-down window. Malikov had glanced back… to see that the man was separating from the herd and pulling-up in his vehicle. He was big, jowly and, even though he was in the car, he wore a dark fur hat (of the kind that Malikov associated with hunting). 'Are you a fucking retard? I'm talking to *you*, shithead!' the man had yelled. Malikov had hurried on, worried that the man – clearly antagonised by his dash across the roadway – might have a gun... and intentions of using it. Next, behind Malikov, a car door had thunked shut. By this time, Malikov had quickened his step. While beetling through the snow, he had pictured what the man was now up to, behind his back: flinging open the car's trunk, shoving shells in a rifle, aiming it. How on earth was it, Malikov had wondered, that an act as trivial as him crossing the road had led to all this? In next to no time, there had then come the sound of the man's boots – crunching the frozen pavement in furious pursuit. 'Hey! Shithead! I want to talk to you!' His life had flashed before Malikov – not Malikov's life, but the *man's*: school bully, small-town thug, some sort of boss who'd made his way to Moscow after greasing fleshy palms belonging to other bosses even more brutish than him. For an instant, Malikov, who was becoming short of breath, had seen in his mind the owners of these palms – big men, with boils on their backs... birching their walrus bulks in bathhouses, drinking frothy beer from glasses brought to them on trays by flunkeys.

Although safe now, Malikov – with Sveta Sukhanova speaking in front of him – listened to the sound of his heart. Yes, it was *still* racing. And *No wonder!* – he told himself – because, only a few minutes earlier, he'd been running... well, *practically* running... his briefcase flapping and hitting his side and his knee. The other man, the maniac from the car, had been closing-in on him, like he was some sort of enraged bear (and he, Malikov, a kind of skittering, fleeing goat or small deer). 'For Christ's sake!' Malikov had thought. 'This is insane! What on earth is this all about?' Maybe the man's wife had left him... or his dog had died... or maybe a doctor had told him *he* was dying. Maybe *that* was it:

madness of the kind that could be expected when men were told their days were done. Malikov remembered reaching the gallery's steps... a police car speeding past. He remembered looking back and seeing the man... who was staring at him, and then the man's figure... turning and running, clumsily, back to where he'd left his car. The patrol car had pulled up behind it. As its lights flashed, two officers had stepped out... other cars in the street weaving around them. The officers had then begun to speak to the man, who seemed to produce some papers, which one of the officers looked at while the other prowled the man's vehicle. The next thing Malikov had known was that he was in the office at the gallery, 'listening' to Sveta Sukhanova, while looking at the pools of snowmelt beneath his hung-up coat, on the herringbone patterned birchwood of the heavily varnished floor.

Malikov now looked over Sukhanova's shoulder at a wall calendar. With a deal of concentration, as if he were reading an optician's chart, he was able to make out the date and the day. It was a Thursday, and there was one place that he went to – come what may – on Thursdays. When it seemed to him that Sveta Suhkanova had finished, he nodded and said 'Of course' (though he had not listened to a word she had said). He then left the room, closed the door and went upstairs.

Everything else was behind him now, as – thawing, thinking – he stared at *The Red Vineyard*. Mentally, Malikov wandered among the vines. Around him, the women of the canvas worked. My goodness, how they worked! How they picked and filled and bundled their baskets, barely speaking, seldom stopping, so that a by-passer unacquainted with such harvesting might suppose that their intense inclinations to the earth were nothing less than entirely natural: strong, muscular, sweating women, who themselves, so it seemed, had been grown, sickle-shaped, as tools of the shadowless land.

Malikov knew the painting well. Better, he sometimes thought, than Vincent. After all, how long did *he* have with the painting... van Gogh (the only one in his life he had managed to sell, or so it was said)? It had been 'nationalised' – that's what they called it – by the Bolsheviks (with the rest of Sergei Shchukin's collection): its destiny perhaps signalled by its colour, thought Malikov... its future foretold in its name.

Not for the first time, he considered the markedly contrasting figure of the white-shawled woman who, amid this scene of toil, walked – processed, it might even be said – in the shade of a parasol.

Around Malikov, the day ticked away.

Beyond the windows of the gallery, Moscow was losing its light. Malikov readied himself to leave. He had no desire to go home. There was nothing for him there. He envied the gallery. It was, he felt sure, a place of illumination – even theatre – after dark. He frequently pictured the darlings of Edgar Degas – his ballerinas – coming to life, spinning and leaping along and over the landings, their *pointe* shoes falling softly in the gloom. Meanwhile, in the background, the whinnies of Edgar's racehorses would – he felt sure – be audible, as their riders settled them in the newly dimmed lights.

Malikov turned his keys in the staff door and wished them all goodnight.

Outside, in the cold air, on the pavement, Malikov heard steps... coming from behind him: boots cracking its surface of ice.

Instinctively, he began to hurry.

Rounding a corner, he slipped and nearly fell. Steadying himself, he saw the reassuring glow of the café where he often stopped.

Suddenly, though, the boots were at his back.

Something smashed at his head, and – as one – all of the lights in the street went out.

A kick to his stomach and a second to his ribs brought Malikov to his senses.

He saw the window of the café.

It was at a weird angle.

He realised then that he was on the ground.

A boot drove into his head and he no longer saw the café but the bricks of the wall on the other side of him.

Malikov now became aware of a woman's screams, and a struggle above him.

Turning his head, he made out the figure of the waitress from the café. Alongside her was her colleague, the cashier. They grappled a figure much bigger than them, who stared down at Malikov.

It was the driver of the car who'd pulled over, in the street, hours earlier.

'That'll teach you, you bastard!' he yelled.

'Stop it! Stop it!' screamed the waitress. 'My God, what is wrong with you?'

The man shrugged off the two women and lurched away.

The waitress knelt beside Malikov, holding his head in her lap. Blood from his nose and mouth smeared her apron.

Although she knew nothing of Malikov and had, at the very most, only ever nodded to him while noting his orders, she was shaking now and sobbing. 'My God!' she repeated to the cashier, who stood looking half at her (supporting Malikov), and half at the retreating figure of the man.

At a table in the café, Malikov dabbed at his bleeding nose with paper napkins, and let the waitress go through his tufts of hair in search of any wounds to his skull.

He dismissed all suggestions of summoning the police.

After some time, he rose, insisted that he was quite well, and left the café for the metro station at Borovitskaya.

On the concourse outside the station, a man, with a satchel on his shoulder, gave Malikov a small magazine, which Malikov, taking no particular notice, placed in an outer pocket of his overcoat.

Having returned home, Malikov lay down in his coat on a sofa in the lounge of his flat and slept. Some while later, unaware of the hour, he woke and fingered his face and his head. Although tender, any bleeding – it seemed – had stopped.

He rose to make some tea.

The strip light in the kitchen made a pinging sound then settled to a hum as he filled a kettle and placed it on the gas stove.

He emptied the pockets of his overcoat, hung it in the hall and then went back to the kitchen. As he went to open the cupboard where he kept his tea, Malikov saw – along with his keys, some coins and other detritus – the magazine that the man with the satchel had handed him.

He opened the publication and began to leaf through it.

It was a compendium of advertisements for prostitutes, who, to Malikov's surprise, were alleged to be 'available' all over Moscow.

Behind him the kettle began to blow.

He was about to close the magazine when his eyes fell on a small box-type advertisement that had no photograph.

Services
Mature Woman - Youthful Looks
By Appointment

Malikov made a pot of mint tea. As it brewed, he looked again at the advertisement.

He walked into the lounge, picked up his phone and dialled the number given on the advertisement.

To his astonishment, the phone began to ring in the flat next door.

He looked at the wall for a moment, then threw the phone back onto its cradle.

The ringing next door stopped.

Malikov moved away from the phone, as if it were something dangerous: an ill-tempered dog he'd disturbed by mistake. Leave it be and it might not bite, he thought to himself.

He went into the kitchen and sipped a half-glass of tea.

He carried it to the doorway of the lounge and stood there, sipping and looking at the phone.

Finally, he moved towards the phone once more, picked it up and re-dialled.

Again, the ringing began in the flat next door.

Then it stopped.

'Yes?' said a woman.

Malikov froze.

He stared at the paper on his lounge wall: flowers – *irises*, he thought. He realised then that it was the first time that he had noticed them – on a background that surely had once been white, and now was beige. The paper must have been there for thirty years.

'Who's calling? the woman said. 'Speak quickly or I shall hang up.'

Malikov heard her voice not only on the phone but also, so it seemed to him, through the wall.

'Are you… available?' he asked quietly, hoping that the woman would not hear him through the wall (in the way that he could hear her… fearing, also, that he was making a terrible mistake and more than half hoping, therefore, that she would *not* be 'available').

'For what?' she said.

'For what it is that you… do. *Services*,' he said, remembering the word in the advertisement.

'When were you thinking of?' she asked.

'Now,' he said, his heart beating strongly.

She hesitated.

He pictured her looking at a clock. He wondered if it was the same as his clock, above the door in the kitchen: golden beams fanning from a chocolate-brown face. He wondered if everyone in the block had them… if any still worked. His own needed a battery for the one that had failed fifteen years earlier. He wondered for a moment if *all* of their clocks had stopped at the same time.

'In an hour. That's the best I can do,' the woman said. She described a bus stop in a neighbourhood two metro stations away. She told him to go there and wait. He knew the location… that there was a coffee house on the other side of the street. He supposed she would study him from its window… decide if he was worth the risk.

When she finished all of this, Malikov said, 'I actually meant here… now… if that would be all right.'

The woman went quiet. 'Where *are* you?' she asked.

'Next door,' Malikov said.

With this, the whole block seemed to go quiet – so quiet, in fact, that he felt he could hear her clock, the one in her kitchen… ticking.

Suddenly, she went for him, like that dog in the yard that he'd thought about: snarling, barking and baring its teeth, straining on the last link of its chain.

'I could have you thrown out of here for this! You hear me? What are you? A pervert? Is that it? You phoned earlier, didn't you? How *dare* you!'

'I have your advertis—'

'Telephoning me! Like this! In my flat! Harassing me! I've a mind to report you! You hear that? To the management of this place! And get you thrown out!'

She sounded to Malikov as if she had moved, so that she was now right next to the wall.

'I expect you are some kind of Peeping Tom. You have a hole somewhere, I don't doubt. Well, let me tell you, I shall put an end to that. I have a good name in this building. You pervert! You fiend!'

With his ear that was not fixed to the phone, Malikov now heard scuffles and thuds, as if the woman were moving objects on her side of the wall: pictures, books, vases.

'A man gave me a magazine… with your advertisement… at Borovitskaya,' he said. The scuffling sounds continued. 'I wondered if I might engage you… for a fee.'

Suddenly, the line went quiet.

'What did you say?' said the woman, after a moment.

'How much would you want… please?' said Malikov.

He heard her breathing.

'Are you… *serious?*' she asked.

'Yes,' he replied.

'Describe yourself,' she instructed.

'In what way?' he asked.

'Your appearance.'

He gave an account of his stature and looks.

'I do not remember having seen you in this building,' she said.

'It is possible that I am not the most noticeable of individuals,' he answered.

'Well… come to my door in ten minutes,' she told him. 'And bring your wallet.'

Malikov rang the bell. With the exception of those with whom he worked at the gallery, he was unaccustomed to… interacting… with women. As he waited for the door to be answered, he again considered his looks (in light of the attack on him). He had examined himself in his bathroom mirror a few minutes earlier. And, though there was some swelling and reddening to his right cheekbone, there were – thankfully – no black eyes or anything 'glaring' like that. He deemed himself 'respectable'.

The woman led him into the flat. She wore a pink silk robe and had a white towel around her head. An odour of shampoo filled the air.

'This is most irregular. I was washing my hair,' she told Malikov.

She lit a cigarette.

'I do not want sexual intercourse,' he said.

She took the cigarette from her lips. '*That* is very presumptuous of you. Well,' she continued, after a moment, 'why *are* you here?'

'There is something I would like you to… perform,' said Malikov.

'I will *not* be doing any filthy or strange. You may think what you like, but I am a respectable woman. If you want anything of *that* nature, you had better leave now.'

'It's nothing like that,' said Malikov. 'Really. I would simply like to see you wear something and then do some… things,' he said.

'Do *what* things?' she responded.

'I shall direct you,' he said. 'Think of it as being like… an artist's model.'

'What is your occupation?' she asked. 'In spite of what you may think, I am not the sort of woman who accepts the demands of… *any* man.'

'Of course, not,' said Malikov. 'I am… in the Arts.'

'The Arts?'

'I have a custodial position,' Malikov said.

His answers seemed to impress her.

She unwrapped the towel on her head and drew back her hair, making a knot. 'I shall need a fee… for whatever it is that you wish me to… perform,' she said.

'Quite so,' said Malikov. 'That is only to be expected.' He placed some notes on the table in front of her. 'Will that be enough?' he asked.

'For now,' she said, taking the money quickly and putting it into a pocket of her gown. 'Take off your jacket. Sit.'

She went into what Malikov took to be a bedroom. Hangers scraped on a rack. She re-entered the lounge.

'Which do you prefer? This,' she said, holding up a flimsy satin top that was a shiny green. 'Or this?' She raised in her other hand something that was short, black and see-through.

'Oh, no. No thank you,' said Malikov. 'I was rather hoping that you might have something… plain.'

'Plain?' she said, lowering the garments.

'Yes,' he said. 'A blouse with sleeves, if you have one, and also a long skirt. Those are what I'm looking for.'

'This is most unusual,' she said, returning to the bedroom.

'Forgive me,' he said.

After several minutes, and more scraping of the rack, she reappeared. She wore a white blouse buttoned to the collar and a long, dark skirt undone at her waist.

'I haven't worn this skirt in ages. Quite the maiden and the golden slipper, aren't I? You'll have to zip me in.'

'Of course,' he said, rising from where he was sitting.

Somewhat nervously, he did up the zip at the back.

As he slid it, the teeth tightened noticeably.

The woman seemed to breathe in.

The zip – to his relief – held fast.

He let go.

A finger's width of the woman's fat spilled over the waistband of the skirt.

'A *little* tight,' she said, 'but not so bad, after all these years. It was the style back then, of course. Garments these days are tailored differently.'

Turning, she seemed to study Malkiov for a moment, taking in his drab jacket and trousers.

She was unimpressed, he sensed.

'Now, what is it that you want?' she asked.

'Do you have a basket of some kind?' he said.

'A basket?'

'Yes, a shopping basket, an ironing basket… a basket, you know.'

'I have a flower basket. Well, that's what I call it. It's for when I leave here… this place… Moscow, and go to live somewhere…'

Her voice trailed off as she went into the kitchen.

Malikov heard her open and close various cupboards.

She reappeared with a long, rectangular basket under her arm. 'I shall pick flowers and take them into my house and arrange them… in a vase,' she continued. She looked at him. 'So… are we there yet? Is that it?'

'Almost. I wonder… do you have any grapes… *red* grapes?'

'Grapes? Why no. I have no grapes. Are you hungry? You should have eaten before you came here.'

These last words seemed to Malikov like an attempt at a joke.

'No, it isn't that. I would just like to have seen you with some grapes… that's all.'

'I have cherries… in my fridge… a bowl of them. A cust— *I* bought them… in Kitay Gorod. How they manage to get them at this time of year, I really don't know. It's all against Nature.'

'Thank you, they will help. Please… put them in your basket and just… bring them. And if you could take off your shoes,' added Malikov.

'My heels? Normally men like—'

'No, they are not right… in this instance.'

She went back into the kitchen.

She returned to the lounge, with the flower basket under her arm. The yellow ceiling light fell on the glossy cherrics, which were in a plastic carton in the basket's brown wicker.

Malikov noticed that she was shorter… sturdier, without her shoes, more… *rustic* – and this pleased him.

She stood before him with the basket as he sat on a sofa that had a faux leather cover. It issued a squeaking sound as he moved on it.

'Good, *very* good,' he said. 'Now, if you would kindly incline yourself… as if you were picking grapes from a vine… a *low* vine,' he said.

'But these are cherries,' she said.

'I know, but you would be doing me the greatest kindness if you could just imagine you were picking *grapes.*'

'Where is the vine?' she asked.

'Here,' he said, leaning forward and pointing to a tall, rubber-leafed plant near the end of the sofa. 'The vine is right here.'

'Shall I loosen my blouse? Undo my buttons?'

'No. Please no,' said Malikov. 'You look…' his voice petered. 'Just as you are, please.'

She bent forward as if harvesting the grapes.

'How am I doing?' she asked, not looking at him but reaching towards the tall plant in its pot. She made sideways motions to her basket, which was on the carpet.

'Good… very good,' he said.

'*Now* what?' she asked, after some moments.

'I would like you to walk from there,' he said, pointing to a footstool on a rug in front of her TV set, '… to there,' he said, indicating the radiator below the curtained window of the lounge. '… carrying the basket,' he added.

She began walking in her normal fashion.

Malikov cut-in, anxiously. 'You *must* imagine the basket to be very heavy,' he said, '… almost *groaning* with grapes.'

She now curved herself as if straining under the great weight of the basket. 'Is this right?' she asked.

'Not quite,' he said. 'You are a strong woman, a countrywoman, remember. It is a matter of proportion,' he said.

She eased the grimace on her face. 'Better?' she asked.

'Better,' he said. 'Much better!'

'To where am I going?' she asked.

'The radiator. You are going to the radiator,' he said.

'And what do I do when I have got to the radiator?' she asked.

'Imagine that you are passing this heavy basket to someone else,' he said. 'But don't actually pass it because we need you to bring the cherries back.'

'You mean the grapes,' she said.

'Quite so,' he said, turning on the sofa to watch her, as she moved across the room.

At the moment of her imaginary transfer of the grapes, Malikov called out, 'Please! Stay there!! Like that! *Just* like that… if you would.' She had bent forward and was holding the basket of cherries in front of her in her outstretched arms. Her bare feet were planted on the rushes and flowers that patterned – in green and ginger – the room's floor carpet. A lamp on a sideboard picked out the lines of her breasts, waist and arms, beneath her thin and simple blouse.

'You are, I think, not from Moscow,' he said.

'No. I'm a country girl… originally,' she replied.

'Whereabouts?' he asked.

'You wouldn't know it. But not Moscow,' she said. 'How long do you want me to stay like this?' she asked, keeping her pose. 'It is a little…'

'Oh, I'm sorry,' he said. 'Please… return and harvest a fresh vine.'

This tableau of theirs continued for some three-quarters of an hour. Eventually, the woman told Malnikov: 'Normally, my clients have finished well before this.'

He apologised and quickly rose to leave. "Thank you for your... service. I am grateful,' he said.

'You really require nothing else?' she asked.

'No, I am quite satisfied,' he said.

He walked into the hall and stood by the door, waiting for her to open it.

'What's your name?' she asked. 'We live next to each other and we don't even know each other's names. I am Tatyana,' she said.

'Matvei,' he said.

'Well, Matvei, will I see you again? Apart from our meetings in the lift and on the metro, I mean.' Not waiting for him to answer, she continued: 'Tell me, do I ever... in here... *disturb* you? Our walls are thin.'

'Most of the time I'm somewhere else,' he said.

'Good,' she said. 'I would not want to disturb you with my... music, or anything.'

She went to open the door... paused.

'What has it been *about*... tonight?' she asked. 'In my experience, these things are normally about something.'

He looked away and then back at her.

'Being somewhere else... I think,' he said. 'Like you and your flowers... your country house.'

'Oh... one of my little foolish secret. You'll keep them, won't you, Matvei? My secrets?'

'Of course,' he said.

'Your cheekbone,' she said to him. 'It is swollen, and somewhat red. Did something happen to you?'

'I... slipped on some ice. You know how it can be: the pavements... that is all.'

'Does it hurt?'

'My cheek? Oh... no, not really.'

'You must watch your step.'

She opened the door, and he walked out, onto the landing.

Returning to his flat, Malikov made straight for the bathroom. He needed to pee. A pale red thread fell from him to the toilet bowl. His member stung. It was nothing to do with the assault that he had suffered earlier, or the events of the previous hour. His problem with his 'undercarriage' had been with him for some time. On the days when the gallery was closed to the public, it was Malikov's habit to admit himself quietly for a consultation with Dr Felix Rey. He appreciated having the doctor to himself even though all that the fellow seemed to offer was polite prevarication and sympathy. 'It depends on what you mean by... We'll see what comes of it... Have faith: discoveries are being made all of the time.' That was about the sum of things from Dr Rey whenever Malikov raised the subject of his 'rosewater'. On the whole, Malikov found him a fey, prissy little man: the small, rosebud mouth, the fussy little beard, the scarlet buttons and piping of his navy-coloured suit. Malikov loathed the portrait and, more than once, had felt like destroying it... slashing a furious X in Felix's white and weaselly face. He could not, of course, because it was one of Vincent's. It bore Vincent's name more boldly than almost anything else. Yet Malikov sometimes wondered how he – VvG – could have done it at all. It was nothing like Rey, really. Nothing at all. Malikov had seen the real Rey in a photograph: a big, bluff almost olive-skinned man. No resemblance to the little whey-faced piglet that Vincent had painted. Felix took Vincent in when Vincent mutilated himself. He was kind, concerned. And Vincent gave him the painting, possibly as a gesture of thanks. Rey had used it to fill a hole in his hen house. And now Rey had nothing to say to Malikov... nothing at all.

Malikov shook himself and lowered the lavatory lid.

In the morning of the next day, Malikov's mood lightened, at least to begin with. As he waited on the platform of the metro, he thought of 'Vincent's Express' as he called it – the locomotive that steamed through *Landscape with Carriage and Train in the Background.* Malikov liked to board the train whenever the painting entered his head. He imagined the locomotive arriving now to collect him: clouds of white smoke filling the platform as he stepped inside one of the lovely black carriages. On leaving, they would enter the tunnel at the end of the platform, but only to pass into a land of clay-tiled houses and small, whitewashed farms. Fields abundant with potatoes, peas, lucerne and wheat would roll to the railway line, all of them coming so close to Malikov that he might reach from his carriage window and trail his fingers through their flowers and leaves, spotted with droplets from the morning rain. At halts in the line, he would hear the songs of buntings and larks.

The *real* metro train now announced itself, with its customary blast of warm, dead air from the blackness of the tunnel. The grind of its brakes and the concomitant surge to its carriages of those who were on the platform around him buried all remnants of Malikov's idyll. He was almost swept off his feet as he boarded.

Inside, he was sandwiched between the belly of a bull-necked man and the backpack of a long-haired student-type. Meanwhile, a dirty-looking character of the kind that talked to themselves while riding the trains all day held the rancid underarm of his greasy jacket virtually in Malikov's face. On Malikov's other side, a woman with sour cigarette-breath pressed against him, making him aware of the bruising to his ribs caused by the battery from the maniac of the day before. More than once, the woman trod on Malikov's toes.

As well as being stinking, the carriage boiled with heat.

As the train drew closer to the central district, it was, to all intents and purposes, overwhelmed. Passengers, determined to board, ran up to the open doors and hurled themselves in, against those who were already crushed. The grotesque confusion of limbs made the train seem in Malikov's mind like some sort of ghastly mobile charnel house: one that opened its jaw-like doors to corpses while snaking through the city's awful black underbelly.

Upon his eventual arrival at the gallery, Malikov spent almost the entire day staring at Vincent's painting *Prisoners Exercising*. Malikov shut out all sense of the rest of the gallery, ignoring the visitors milling around him, disregarding enquiries from members of staff. He stared fixedly at the canvas and sensed himself falling into step with its coughing, shuffling, desperate inmates.

That evening, in his flat, he looked at the phone on the other side of the room. He wondered if he might ask her… Tatyana… to play another part. While Vincent was his favourite artist, other of the gallery's works came to mind… in which she might 'perform'. Portraits of aristocrats and even icons of the Virgin (if there were no objections from her on grounds of faith).

Malikov crossed the lounge to his telephone, and dialled.

He heard the phone ringing, both in the handset pressed to his ear and in her flat.

The ringing stopped.

He waited for her voice: the sharp 'Yes' that he felt would mellow to something softer when she realised it was him.

No words came – just the sound of a knock… as if the handset had been dropped… onto a table… off the hook.

Malikov pressed his phone to his ear, straining for sounds.

He heard laughter – *her* laughter – and then a man's voice, in a sort-of singsong, as if the man were addressing a child. 'This wolf is going to eat you… he's going to eat you all up.' And then, again, after it, her laughter… growing thin.

Malikov imagined her running out of the room where the phone was situated… skittering, in her pink gown… the man with the singsong voice chasing her… in ankle-socked pursuit.

Malikov put down the phone and moved to the wall. He leant with his right ear to the paper, and listened.

He heard… nothing.

Suddenly, he moved along the wall, sweeping books from shelves, dragging dust-covered pictures and photographs from hooks, listening with every sinew… every cell, as if for a child buried by an earthquake that had swallowed a town. He pulled over a sideboard that smashed apart. He crabbed further and further along the wall till, near his front windows, he stopped. He realised from the layout of his own flat that he now had to be next to her bedroom.

Malikov again pressed his ear to the wall.

Her cries were muffled… barely able to be caught – but they were *there*.

Malikov closed his eyes and listened.

A horrible grunting began to stifle her shrieks. The ugly and (to Malikov) primeval noise rolled over her utterances, drowning them, becoming louder, angrier and more violent.

A knocking began against the wall.

Malikov stepped away from it.

He noticed that, in the rectangle where the sideboard had been, the paper was clean… white. It was as if the patterned flowers that showed there were from stems that had freshly bloomed.

The knocking against the wall had become a slamming now.

Malikov thought of the 'bison' on the street outside the gallery… and on all of the streets of Moscow. Piercing horns, thick humps and thundering, cloven hooves.

He thought also of the crazed man from the car; how – even after the attack – the man had still shouted, still threatened, even as he retreated. 'Bastard! Bastard!!'

Malikov backed away from the wall now. He stumbled across the room until he was at the lounge door.

The slamming at his wall grew louder, heavier. It was, it seemed, no longer confined to the clean, white patch of wallpaper with its flowers, but had spread against the whole of the wall. It was as if the divide was being pummelled by not just one pawing, snorting beast, but a whole steaming herd of them.

Malikov wondered at their fury.

And then the sense of it dawned on him. This, he reasoned, was what happened when Man drove animals to extinction. They came back. They found… 'a way'. In their wisdom, in their ancientness, in their understanding of all things spiritual and temporal (which Man could never hope to equal), they somehow divined the path to their own survival. If he, Malikov, could hear and feel the beating heart of Vincent's horse that stood with its carriage in *The Red Vineyard*, then why should any animal *ever* die?

And now Malikov felt himself weakening.

He clutched the frame of the door to the hallway, sensed himself slipping.

A vision passed before him of an endless chain of bison… leaping through his lounge wall.

He collapsed under the onslaught of their stampede.

It was daylight when Malikov came-to. The curtains in his lounge were edged with bright – and rare – midwinter sun. He lifted himself, with difficulty, from the carpet. The chaos of the room – the strewn books and pictures, the smashed sideboard – confused him. He wanted to piss, and he shuffled to the bathroom.

When it finally came, his urine was borscht-black – the darkest it had ever been.

It clouded the bowl with an oily bloom.

He flushed the handle.

Then he put on his coat, hat and gloves, and he left his flat.

Rather than getting off the metro at one of his usual stops, Malikov continued on the Red Line to the loop in the river at Vorobyovy Gory.

All journey long, Vincent's painting, *Seascape at Saint Maries*, played on Malikov's mind.

On a fine day, a blue-sky day, such as that one, his fondness for the picture exceeded even his feelings for *The Red Vineyard*.

The painting's fishing boats and breaking waves filled him with vigour. The embrace of the rich, blue sea, topped by only the smallest strip of sky, was irresistible to Malikov.

He had known the painting – fifth and last of the masterpieces by Vincent in his custody – for more than three decades.

Paintings.

How inadequate that word had always seemed to Malikov.

They were his world… his life.

Malikov alighted and walked the long, echoing platform that spanned the bridge of the Moscow River.

After wandering for some while, he came to a door that forbade entry, passed through it and climbed the metal staircase to the roof.

On top of the bridge, out in the sharp air, Malikov had only the faintest sense of the tree-covered Sparrow Hills that rose to his left. Likewise, the Olympic Stadium, that squatted, in the manner of some enormous mollusc, to his right.

The water of the immense river below him was heavy and grey. It laboured its lugubrious way through the sprawl of the endless city.

All Malikov saw, however, were the billowing sails of Vincent's fishing boats at Saintes-Maries… sea foam rising at their prows, as they made for the safety of the shore – nets laden – in the last of the day's sun.

Below the high steel girder on which Malikov – precariously – stood, a train stopped, then pulled away.

Its rumble startled him.

A draught blew off his hat, which flew – helter-skelter – to the river.

As he felt it dislodge, he snatched after it and was even about to jump in pursuit, when, suddenly, he remembered where he was and awoke from his reverie.

Working his way slowly, wind whipping his face, he finally reached a door to a staircase that led down to the platforms.

Once there, he waited for a train.

When one arrived, the peripheral nature of the station meant that Malikov was able to sit and not have to stand whilst hanging from a strap.

Looking at his reflection in a window, he smoothed his tousled hair as the carriage pulled away.

That evening, observing the arc of his urine in the toilet bowl, Malikov noticed that it had lost its borscht-blackness and seemed now to have acquired a lighter, strawberry hue. He wondered if this constituted an improvement, possibly even a sign of remission.

In the days and nights that followed, Malikov, who, over the course of almost thirty-five years had never really known the fellow occupants of his block (beyond perhaps the odd pleasantry or nod), found himself looking out for Tatyana in a way that – because of its novelty – puzzled and even unsettled him.

In the evenings, he would stand on the slide in the children's playground and peer upwards, trying to pinpoint the windows of her flat for the presence, or otherwise, of a light, or lights, inside them.

On the landing outside her door, he moved slowly, with – he realised – the hope that he might hear her, or even encounter her opening it and emerging.

Inside his own flat, he took to listening with a glass at the wall, moving and re-attaching the tumbler – as quietly as he could – as he progressed along its length, holding his breath as he did so.

However, through the concrete and the wallpaper, he heard nothing.

After several days of this, two explanations presented themselves in Malikov's head. The first was that Tatyana had left her flat in order to go and stay, or even live, somewhere else, possibly the rural village from which she was an émigré.

The alternative explanation – which unnerved Malikov greatly – was that something had befallen her, perhaps not unrelated to the conduct of one of her callers, and that she might now be in a state of unconsciousness – or worse – in the darkness of her flat.

One evening, well past midnight, when the sky was dark and the neighbourhood quiet (at least by the standards of sleepless Moscow), Malikov tapped with his hand on the lounge wall.

Hearing nothing, he tapped again.

He repeated his discreet tap a third time – to be met only with continued silence.

At that juncture, Malikov began to consider his telephone, reposing in its hideous shade of nicotine yellow, on a sideboard.

Perhaps by reason of the rarity with which he used it, and the even greater rarity with which it rang, he had forgotten how it had been the means of their 'introduction'.

To his great startlement, the phone now began to ring.

Malikov, who could not remember when such a thing had last happened, stepped away from it... to the doorway into the hall – this seeming to him a safe distance.

It was as if he had come upon an intruder in his rooms – which, in more than thirty years, no one had entered but him.

He looked, listened – his heart beating fast, as the phone rang... and rang.

Eventually, he walked towards it and – without speaking – picked up the receiver.

'I remember skating... at Park Kultury... on the ice, when I was a young woman, when I first came to Moscow,' said the voice of Tatyana. 'Oh, you should have seen me then, you should have seen my figure. I was... a picture. Graceful... slender... beautiful, if I say so myself. I glided on that ice... *glided*, let me tell you. I was like the most glorious female swan: golden hair... perfect poise. Women envied me. Men adored me. Some spoke of me as their angel. I had wings back then, you know. Wings.'

Her words stopped.

Holding his breath, Malikov thought he heard hers... in what seemed to him a sigh.

Beyond the act of listening, he did nothing, standing completely still in his lounge, the phone to his ear, like some statue in a park.

She began again: 'I have not heard from you. I had expected to. I thought that we – you and I – might have had... an engagement.'

Malikov swallowed, thought, but still said nothing.

'You know, as a child, I was so innocent, so... pure. When I was a teenager, all I ever heard about, all I ever thought about, was Moscow. "Go to Moscow! That's the place for a girl like you!" – that's what people said. My mother agreed. My father was dead. She had a man. A new man. One she wanted to keep. And I...

I was a good-looking girl. "Go to Moscow, Tatyana. In the morning. Here is the money. Make something of yourself" – that's what my mother said. But… oh, you don't want to hear all of that, do you? You have found someone else. For your tableaux. Someone younger, someone prettier. I understand. It is to be expected. It is natural enough. Tell me, Matvei… what is she like?'

'No!' Malikov replied. 'You are wrong! I have not. I… *would* not. I am not that… sort of man. Besides, I have been waiting. I have been… listening.'

'Listening! Oh! Well! Hah!! *There* we are! So, I was right the first time!'

'No, not like that. What I mean to say is that you have been… quiet. That is all. I did not know if you were… there.'

'Oh, I have been here. Where else would I have been? Saint Petersburg? Sochi? With the pretty people? No. I have been here. A little bruised, yes. But I have been here. I remain… here.'

'Bruised?' asked Malikov. He looked up from the phone to the wall.

'It happens… sometimes. You must know that, Matvei.'

He swallowed again. 'Yes, I know,' he said.

'You do? But never mind that. I don't walk to talk about it. I want to talk about *other* things… about "being somewhere else", as you once put it. Do you remember saying that?'

'Yes,' said Malikov.

'Well, I would like you to take me somewhere. In your scenes… your dreams… whatever you may care to call them. Will you do that? Take me somewhere?'

'Yes,' said Malikov. 'Yes, I will.'

After a moment, he asked: 'Do you have a parasol?'

'A parasol?' she responded. 'I'm not sure about a parasol, but I have an umbrella.'

'That will do,' said Malikov. 'And a shawl? A white shawl?'

'I think I have something that might suit,' she answered. 'Perhaps not in white, but I have shawls, yes.'

'Good,' said Malikov.

'So, we have a date then?' she asked. 'That's what the young call it, isn't it?'

'Yes. I believe so.'

'And maybe, when the opportunity presents, we could go out somewhere... on a trip? It's been such a long time since I did anything like that, Matvei. And I shall pay my expenses, of course.'

'There is a railway ride that I am rather fond of,' he told her.

'A railway journey? Good, that sounds... nice... *if* you have the time.'

'Yes,' said Malikov. 'Thank you...' he began. 'Thank you for... your call.'

'Until I hear from you then?'

'Yes... yes indeed,' he said quietly.

He heard her hang up, then he placed his own handset back on the cradle.

Looking at the lounge wall, he thought how, in the morning, he would consult Doctor Rey, at the gallery.

And, with luck, there *might* be time... time for him – and Tatyana – to make Vincent's train, after all.

Snowball

Before we go any further, there's one thing I want you to know. Arkady and me were friends. In fact, we were more than that. Our mothers carried us at the same time. And when we were due, they lay in beds side-by-side in the same hospital ward. I arrived first, kicking and screaming; Arkady showed himself an hour later, quietly and without fuss.

We grew up in the same block: my flat was on top of his. At school we were in the same class. In all our early childhood I can remember only one time when we were apart: a week when his mother took him to his grandparents' village. I knew Arky (my name for him) not just by his face and his voice, but by his step and his smell. We were under one another's skins and inside one another's heads. That's the truth of how it was between Arky and me.

One other thing I want you to know concerns the snow. In Moscow we have it for about five, maybe six, months of the year. But, when it comes, it's a cause for excitement among kids, nonetheless. I, for one, couldn't wait to go out.

So what I'm saying is that throwing my snowball at Arky was the most normal thing in the world for me to do.

I'd been waiting for him outside our block. I'd said through his parents' buzzer I was going to the park. A white lie, you might call it.

In fact, I hid behind the bins and waited for him to come out.

When he got to the corner, he was still fiddling with his hat (in that thoughtful, particular way of his). And that's when I stepped out… and threw.

I wasn't *aiming* for his face when I chucked the snowball. I just threw it – and it happened to connect.

When Arky fell, I was pleased.

'Popalsya!' *('Got you!')* I shouted and laughed.

I pointed my gloved hands towards him, like pistols.

135

'Peeow! Peeow!' I called out. 'Ty mertverts!' *('You're dead!')*

When he *stayed* lying there, by the metal rail that skirted the patch of garden outside our block, I felt sure he was fooling… that any second he would jump to his feet and counter-attack.

So I bent and scooped a fresh fistful of snow.

But Arky didn't get up. He didn't move at all.

'Hey! Arky!' I shouted. 'You can get up now.'

But, even as I stood over him, he just lay there, flakes falling – like feathers – on his coat and his face.

His head was turned to the right, as if on a pillow. Only when I leaned forward and looked closely did I see the red spots. A small spray of them on the snow between his nose and his lips.

On the metal rail, to the side of him, I noticed the gap in its white crust – the spot where Arky had fallen, in my ambush, and hit his head.

'Arky,' I said, '… Arky.'

He still didn't move.

'Arky,' I said again, this time kicking his boots.

Slowly, ever so slowly, his left eye opened.

He turned his head so that he was looking up at me, like he was waking from sleep.

He squinted.

Around his right eye was a patch of pink, with specks of what looked like salt or grit, where my snowball had hit.

He got up, stumbled, steadied himself.

Then, without speaking, he left me and went back into the flats.

I didn't see him for quite a while after that. Not until he came back to school, wearing his patch.

It was black and over his right eye – held there by a band that ran round his head, tight, like a cheese wire. When the band had been in the same place too long, it gouged a red line across Arky's head. Even so, I thought the patch made him look noble, heroic – a boy-soldier who'd been wounded doing something courageous for our Motherland.

His patch preoccupied me. I wondered if he wore it in bed, with his pyjamas; if it was there, on its band, as his mother parted his hair and kissed him goodnight.

The other kids saw it differently. They called him 'Pirat' *('Pirate')*. More than once a mob of them pinned him down in the playground and pushed the patch aside to peer at the snaggle of scar tissue where his eye no longer was.

Its removal was down to me: the snowball that I had thrown. The matter of him losing his balance and knocking himself out on that rail was itself of no consequence. What *was* of consequence was the way my snowball had rattled and damaged the delicate inner world of his eye. After complications, including the onset of an infection, it shrivelled in his head and died.

I fought the other kids who abused him, often coming off worst. More than once I asked him if he was still my friend. To this he gave no answer. On our way home from school, he would hurry on ahead.

Our parents had always been friends and, as families, we had done things together, such as going to Park Kultury and Strogino Beach. After the doctors took out Arky's eye my mother went to see his mother at their flat. I watched, without them knowing, from a corner of the stairs.

When Arky's mother opened the door, she looked white and old. She called my mother all kind of things. Arky's dad appeared behind her. His tattooed arms pulled her back into their flat. He slammed the door in my mother's face. Even with it shut I could hear their shouting. Arky's mother was calling my mother a whore. She screamed that I was evil.

My mother turned. I darted down the stairs.

After a while, Arky came to school with a false eye which, in my opinion, was a whole lot worse than his patch. It fooled no one and looked nothing like his other, real eye... which was blue and wide. His surgeons had not even screwed it in right. It just hung there, always looking down. When you saw only that side of him, his eye (the ugly thing: it was like a marble) made it seem as if his whole being were dead. I was furious on his behalf.

News reached the other kids – either through their parents or from the teachers (none of whom I'd ever really liked) – that I was to blame for Arky's eye. This caused my fellow pupils to lay off Arky and to bully me instead.

My father and Arky's came to blows at work. Arky's father brought up how my little sister had, a long time earlier, fallen (and died) from the balcony of our flat. The other men at their plant had to pull them apart.

I decided something had to be done.

One afternoon, I rang Arky's buzzer from the front porch.

His parents and mine had gone out (separately, not together, of course) to some musical event going on at Sokolniki.

'Arky, it's me – Lev,' I said. 'Come up to mine. I've something for you.'

'What is it?' he said.

'I will show you. Just come... please,' I said into the buzzer.

I let him into our flat. 'In here,' I said, bundling him into the bathroom.

'What are you doing?' he said.

'I want you to cut off my ear,' I said.

'What do you mean—your *ear*? Are you crazy?' he said.

'Of course not,' I said. 'That's what they say, isn't it? An eye for an eye?'

'But you just said your ear,' said Arky.

'I know. An eye is dangerous. You might dig into my brain and kill me. I read about it on the internet,' I said. 'Especially as you now see with only one.'

'What you did was an accident,' he said.

'I know, but Arky, I *need* you to do this,' I said, 'as my friend… for me.'

'But why? Have you thought about this? I mean, it's your ear,' Arky said.

'Exactly,' I said. 'I will be like that painter in Pushkin Museum. Van Gogol.'

'Van Gogh,' said Arky.

'That's what I said,' I said.

'Your breath is… funny,' he said, sniffing me. 'What have you been drinking?'

'My father's aftershave,' I said. 'It contains alcohol. I read that on the internet also.'

'So you are drunk as well as crazy,' he said.

'No, not yet,' I said. 'It was disgusting though. To think he puts that on himself. I could manage only half the bottle. So… you will do it for me?'

'No, I won't,' Arky said. 'I am going.'

He opened the bathroom door. I pushed it shut and swung round him so my back was against it.

'Look at me,' I said.

He turned away.

'*Look* at me!!'

He turned towards me and raised his head.

His real eye stared into mine. The other just lolled there, as always.

My mother's sharp kitchen knife was in my hand. I stuck the tip under my chin.

'If you do not do this for me, I will cut my throat… here, now, in front of you,' I said.

Above us, the lavatory flushed in the bathroom of the flat on the next level. Arky and I stared at each other, as its waters gushed.

I pressed the blade tight against my throat.

'Will you promise?' I asked him.

'No, I will not,' he said.

'Then I will cut myself in front of you this minute,' I said.

I started to skewer the knife's tip into my neck, below my right ear.

'‘Stop!' Arky said. 'You are bleeding.'

'Of course,' I said. 'That is the idea.'

'But this is mad. *You* are mad. Our parents will kill us,' Arky said.

'How can they, if I am already dead?' I replied.

'Put down that knife. Stop this. You never meant to do what you did with that snowball,' Arky said.

'Yes, and I live with it,' I said. 'I don't have your glass eye, but—'

'It's not glass,' Arky broke in. 'It's plastic… or something.'

I kept the knife at my neck. 'Well, I preferred you with your patch. You were handsome. Then.'

'Will you do it? My ear? Arky? I mean it,' I said. 'My parents will be home soon.'

Arky stared and said nothing. I pushed the knife into my neck: deeper this time, while staring back into his one eye.

'Stop! Yes! Yes!!' he cried. 'Lev, for Christ's sake! YES!'

Our bathroom had a chair in it. Not an easy chair. The place – what with our washing machine and everything – was too small for that. I'm talking just a small, foldable thing on which my mother laid towels and sometimes my socks and my pants. I moved the stuff off it, dragged it to the basin and sat as if at the barber's in the market.

My head just showed in the bottom of the mirror on the wall behind the taps. I could see the wounds in my neck, like a vampire bite. Blood escaped in a trickle from one of the holes.

Arky stood over me as if he were about to tuck a sheet in my collar and ask my mother – if she'd been there – how much (of my hair) to take off.

I handed him the knife.

'Which ear?' he said.

'I don't know,' I said. 'Which do you think?'

'Christ, it's your ear. Have you not thought about it? You know I could go to prison for this. It has to be a crime,' he said.

'How can it be?' I said. 'You have my full permission. I am the owner of the ear. This is a free country, isn't it? Have you not seen the president say so on TV?'

I thought for a moment.

'The right,' I said, pointing. 'It's always full of shit anyway. Who needs an ear like that?'

'That is your left,' said Arky.

'Exactly. That's what I mean. Get on with it,' I said.

He lifted the knife. I glanced at my father's aftershave in its bright blue bottle near the cold tap. 'Wait!' I said and took another swig.

Jesus… it was foul.

I shuddered, put it back.

'Okay—do it,' I said.

Arky lowered the knife to my ear, then stopped.

'Christ! What is it now?' I said.

'Foam,' he said, looking with his one eye into the mirror. 'Do you want foam? My father uses it when he shaves his beard. And my mother, too. Under her arms. And on her legs… I think.'

'Christ, Arky!' I said. 'What has this got to do with your mother's legs? We are talking about my ear. Will you not get on with this? Please!'

And that was when he made his move, flinging the knife into the bathtub and dashing for the door.

By the time I was out of my seat he was practically on the landing and away down the stairs.

I went back into our flat.

I picked the knife out of the bathtub. I slumped in the chair in front of the mirror. Then I sat up and set about my ear.

When my parents found me, I was – apparently – lying with my head in the basin, which had in it both vomit and blood. Among it all, like a lost shrimp (so my mother was to say), was the sawn-off form of my right ear.

They drove me to hospital – my mother weeping and wailing all the way as she held a towel to my head, in the back of my father's car.

On the front seat, next to him, my ear lay on a bed of ice under the lid of a dish that we normally used for fish stew.

In all, I was in hospital for nearly two weeks as the surgeons considered then abandoned the idea of sewing the severed lobe back on. Apparently, it was in too much of a mess, owing to how I'd hacked it off.

'When you do the other one, try to make a better job,' one doctor said.

I didn't know if he was joking. He was a miserable bastard, with sour breath, so probably not.

❦

I have been in this present hospital – not that first one – for I'm not sure exactly how long. I think five, maybe six, winters. It's a dull old joint and no mistake. The walls are more grey than white – like the snow that sometime falls beyond our windows.

Recently, my mother came.

I asked her why I was still here and how much longer it would be until I was allowed home. I also asked what had become of my ear.

She said it was being 'looked after', like me.

I imagined it on a shelf in a fridge – next to Arky's eye.

I pictured our body parts looking and listening as doctors and nurses opened the door to take out their milk and chilled melon for their break-time snacks.

What they need for company, of course – the eye and the ear, I mean – is a nose.

Mine's always running. I can't keep up with it. It's *such* a curse!

It has crossed my mind to….

But, anyway, seriously, the only utensil they permit here is a spoon. Can you believe that? And what can one do with a spoon?

We each carry ours to the refectory hall, as if they were gifts from God.

I asked one of the doctors to explain this business of a single spoon. It was for the *common good*, he said – whatever the hell that meant.

But I *think* there's a way of making mine useful…

❦

I've been digging myself out.

Slowly.

Gradually.

One spoonful at a time.

And, of course, it takes years.

My escape – when it comes – is via a long, dark tunnel: the white light at its end coming at me, enlarging, like a snowball in flight.

And, eventually, I'm outside our old block… standing on the snow-covered grass… in my pyjamas and my dressing gown… a solitary figure, beneath the watching moon and stars.

There, I pack snowflakes in my fingers, my breath climbing to the night sky through the branches of the trees.

I take aim and I throw – at Arky's window.

My cannon-fire explodes on what I remember to be his pane.

I call up to it, between pitches – with those same words that I used on that day in our childhood… except that my voice is hoarse now and old.

'Arky! Can you hear me? Get up, Arky! Get up!'

The Shaft

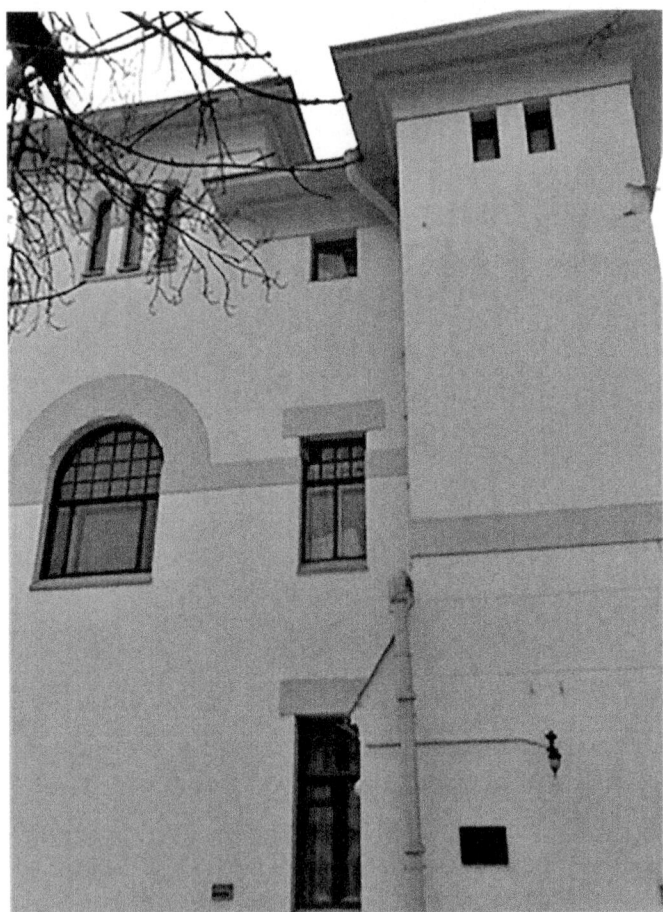

I found it – though *heard* it might be the better word – when I was hanging around on our landing.

A movement… a flap.

The sound of something *troubled*, something *trapped*… coming from the shaft of the lift in our block.

That I should have heard it before anyone else came as no great surprise to me.

You see, after what happened to my eye (with Lev), my ears sort-of… came to life. I just heard so much more. Faraway things – like a bottle, or even a book, being dropped; close-up sounds, too: how the table in our kitchen vibrated – ever so slightly – in a way no one else seemed to notice when the trains of the metro passed-by our building.

So, anyway, I called my father onto the landing and had him stand next to me, beside the shaft of the lift.

'Listen!' I said to him.

He leaned to the metal gate.

I – again – heard the flap.

There was even a rattle in the outer cage that contained the shaft.

'Do you hear it?' I asked.

'I don't hear anything,' my father replied.

'Listen!' I said again.

I put my right ear to one of the diamond-shaped gaps in the gate, bidding my father join me.

And, for several moments, we held ourselves like that.

'I still can't hear anything,' my father responded, eventually. And, to my great disappointment, he drew away.

'You are young, Arkady. You have special ears,' he said, appearing to detect my dejection at what seemed to me to be his deafness. 'Maybe one day the Army will give you a special job.'

He put his arm around my shoulders.

'Come, let's go. It's time for us to eat.'

As he said this, the lift clanked to life in the hall downstairs, and the car climbed up.

Old Golubkin, the tailor, appeared behind the brass trellis as the car rose past us.

'Dobry vecher,' *('Good evening')* Golubkin said through the trellis.

'Dobry vecher,' we said back.

My father turned to me. 'Arkady, come. Our food will be on the table. Your mother will be waiting.'

And we went back inside our flat.

It was a dropping… one dropping.

But it was enough to prove me right.

The little pellet of guano made its mark, so to speak, as Marusya Klimova was stepping from the lift, next morning, onto her landing.

It fell through the narrow gap between the shaft and the car, falling on her hand as she tugged the gate aside.

She immediately set off to the office of Elizaveta Entina, our caretaker, by way of the stairs.

Some short while later, they found Semyon Solnikov on the landing of his floor, holding a grey feather and wearing a puzzled look.

When I got home from school, half the block was on our landing.

People were peering through the cage that surrounded the shaft, noisily telling each other to hush.

'Something is *in* there. There is no doubt,' Semyon Solnikov said.

'What is it?' said Pavel Yuskov.

'A bird, of course,' said Natalya Nikonova.

'What are we talking?' said Yuskov, mockingly. 'An eagle? A stork?'

'You are being ridiculous, deliberately ridiculous,' said Natalya Nikonova, who everybody knew disliked Yuskov (in part for something he had allegedly done –

or had tried to do – in the lift, one night). 'I suggest you go back to your flat,' she said to him.

'And I would like to, but *you* are blocking my way to the lift,' Yuskov said.

He walked, moodily, to the stairs.

'How long will this nonsense be going on?' he called out as he went.

'For as long as it is necessary. There is a creature in there and it is trapped. Have you no mercy?' Tatyana Smekhova, not normally known for her generosity to others, answered him.

Yuskov let out a dismissive snort.

After hearing and seeing nothing, no matter how they strained with their eyes and their ears, the people eventually relented, and returned to their flats.

That evening, after supper, at that time of day when our block filled with the smells of meals that had been cooked and eaten, and the sounds of TV sets being turned on in lounges, I went out onto the landing.

I put my fingers in the holes of the cage around the shaft of the lift.

I looked into its abyss.

The shaft was dark, warm and had an oily smell.

Its machinery of pulleys and weights and wheels seemed strange in the middle of our block, where all of the flats were kept so very clean and tidy by house-proud women, in their soft-furnished castles in the sky.

Suddenly, the bird came and hovered right in front of me, its wings outstretched, fluttering in the air of the shaft.

It hooked its bright pink feet on the wire of the cage, just above my fingers. I could see the small talons.

It turned its head so that we were looking at each other, one eye to one eye.

We stared like that for a moment, till, as if in some lapse of its memory and thinking itself in some square or park, it tried to fly off.

It caught itself – with an ugly sound – on the sides of the cage, as it climbed, awkwardly, above me, into the dark.

As I undressed for bed that night, I told my mother what had happened.

She told me to tell Elizaveta Entina in the morning.

After my mother had turned out the light, I thought about Lev and where he was.

I didn't know what had happened to him exactly, other than he'd been taken someplace where he was being kept, whether he wanted to stay there or not.

I knew that I had to keep all thoughts of him to myself. Mention of his name upset my mother (even though it was *my* eye, not hers, that had been lost).

'Ah... a pigeon,' said Elizaveta Entina, when I went down to her flat the next morning. 'Then we must look after it, Arkady, of course.' (She had in mind the belief among some in our country that a pigeon carries the spirit of someone who is gone; that the arrival of such a bird can, in certain circumstances, be a signal of good luck.)

She placed a sign on the gates of the lift – *Closed (Till Further Notice).* The old ladies of the block cooed their agreement, even though they would now have to climb the stairs. The safety of the winged messenger would come first, they said.

That evening, I took some food to the shaft.

I held up my hand, which had sweet corn and breadcrumbs, to the wire cage around the shaft.

The bird landed just above my palm.

It pushed its small head and beak through one of the square holes in the cage and began to eat the morsels.

When it had had its fill, it flew off into the darkness, seemingly a little less clumsily than on the night before.

Next day, after school, I asked Elizaveta Entina what was being done about the bird. She gave me a weary look. Clearly, I wasn't the only one who had enquired.

She said people were already grumbling about having to use the stairs, no matter what they had told her at first.

'Arkady,' she asked me, 'are you *sure* that you saw the bird?'

'Yes!' I said. 'Definitely! What's more I have fed it… from my own hand.'

She looked at me doubtfully.

'I am not blind, Elizaveta Entina,' I said. 'How do you think I walk to school, and write in my books?'

'I know,' she said. 'I have asked the engineer to come and look. But if he doesn't come soon, I will have to re-open it. We have people here who are old, Arkady, and some who… well… you know.'

That evening, I took a small dish of water out to the landing and held it to the cage. I called to the pigeon to come. The cage rattled as the bird landed opposite me. It flapped its wings for a moment before it settled itself on the wire. It put its head through one of the gaps and began to drink from the dish. I was talking to it, when, suddenly, I heard a scuffle behind me.

Pavel Yuskov had banged into a box that someone had left on the landing, and now he was cursing.

In turning to see him, I pulled the dish away from the cage and startled the bird, which flew off, into the shaft.

'What are you doing, boy?' asked Yuskov, who was clearly drunk.

'I am giving the bird water,' I said.

'Water? Water!? What are you on about?' he growled. 'Where is this bird?'

'Gone,' I said. 'It has flown off.'

'Good!' he said. 'There's been enough talk about birds. *People* want to use that lift.'

He swung his arm towards it, in a way that sent him off balance. He stumbled towards me.

'*I* want to use it.'

He lunged, or tripped (I wasn't sure which).

I dodged him.

He clattered against the gate to the lift.

It sagged, heaved him back – as if repelled by his monstrous embrace.

Along the landing, the door of our flat opened. My mother stood on the mat, the light of our hall behind her.

'Arkady! Get here! Now!!' she said.

Yuskov dragged himself to his feet. He seized the lift's gate, as if it were the coat of a man who had offended him, in a bar, or on the street, and he shook it… while letting out a horrible yell.

In bed that night, I imagined Yuskov, not the pigeon, as the prisoner of the shaft.

I saw him shaking the gate – this time *inside* the trellis – sobbing for his release.

Suddenly, the thick, black cables that hung down the shaft came to life, coiling themselves around his legs and his waist.

His fingers, which were poking through the holes of the cage, unhooked – one by one – as he was dragged, screaming, into the depths of the shaft.

The huge slab-like weights that drove the lift sheared from their stays. They plummeted to the bottom of the shaft where, after a great crashing sound, Yuskov's ugly yells finally ceased.

Next day, when I came home from school, I found a number of the residents gathered at Elizaveta Entina's door.

When *would* the lift be working again? they wanted to know.

Marusya Klimova, who'd felt the pigeon's pellet on her hand, was no longer interested in omens of good fortune or anything like that. Our building's stairs were bad for her poor knees, she complained.

Old Golubkin said that, without the lift, it was a long way, for someone of his age, up to his flat.

Above all, Yuskov was there, waving a sheaf of papers. Nothing in his tenancy mentioned denial of access to the lift, he snarled, especially not for the sake of *a bird*.

Elizaveta Entina said she was still waiting for the engineer, but if the engineer did not come—

At which point, she saw me… and stopped.

The others noticed me also, and melted away to their flats.

The next day – coming back from school – I saw my father. He was taking a black bag to the bins outside our block.

Something told me it wasn't rubbish that he was carrying, and I asked him what he had.

He said it was a rat that he had killed for Elizaveta Entina (for whom he sometimes did jobs in and around our block).

He threw it in one of the bins and told me to keep away in case it was diseased.

I walked with him, back to the block.

As we entered our block, we passed Elizaveta Entina. She was hanging a dustpan and brush in her cupboard in the hall. Further down the corridor, the lift whirred (in its familiar way) then clanked to a stop. Out stepped Golubkin, who came towards us in the hall.

'Dobry den,' *('Good afternoon')* he said.

'Dobry den,' said my father… while I said nothing at all.

As Golubkin passed us, my father glowered at me in rebuke for my rudeness.

He walked to the lift.

I ran up the stairs.

That evening, I went out onto the landing. There was no sign of the bird. The residents were using the lift just as they always had.

I thought about the pigeon. I thought about Lev – the crazy ideas he might have had to bring freedom to the bird: sawing through the cage, blowing-up the car, even taking someone hostage: Marusya Klimova, perhaps.

Suddenly, the lift's door opened in front of me.

Pavel Yuskov staggered out.

He stank of drink. (I'd heard talk between my parents that things weren't well between him and his wife – who had left… and who had their sympathy.)

'What are you waiting for, kid?' he said to me. 'Not still on about that bird?'

He stepped towards me.

'There is no bird. There never was any bird. No one but you' – he leaned over me – 'ever saw that lousy bird. You!' he said, snorting and swaying, '… a boy who can barely see.'

At this, I looked up and I stared at him.

Defiance surged through me.

'What are you staring at?' he snarled.

'With *this* eye,' I said – pointing to my false one – 'I see nothing at all, Pavel Yuskov, it is true. And with *this* eye,' I said – pointing to my good one – 'I see perfectly, and I also see – Pavel Yuskov – *nothing* at all.'

For a moment, puzzlement clouded his awful face.

Then his confusion gave way to fury.

He raised his hand to bring it down on me.

Yet even as he held it above my head, I heard something which he did not: the keys turning inside our front door. And, after this, my mother's voice, calling me in, from the hall.

I turned.

Yuskov lowered his hand.

As I walked to our door, I glanced back, and I saw him... staring after me.

I will never forget the look on his face: consumed as it was with the utmost meanness, filled with bitterness, angry at the world and every boy who walked upon it – young, expectant – as even he, perhaps, had once been.

His look told me our business was not done, that it never would be *done*; that if he ever left our block and went away he would find another equally hateful man to take his place and that, wherever I went in life, there would always be a Pavel Yuskov – jealous, bitter, with an angry hand always ready to be raised – who, with my one eye, I would have to watch out for.

I pushed our door *to*, and turned the key, thinking of Lev... and locking out Yuskov... and all men like him – for that night, at least.

WILL IT HURT?

The images lined the walls of the small and otherwise gloomy room. The effect was to make them seem like icons in a chapel of the kind where those seeking solace light candles and cross themselves. They were photographs, either tacked directly to the walls or, in the case of the most esteemed examples, mounted in frames, like trophies: pelts, or even scalps, which was not unreasonable given that their 'common thread' was human skin. So that, in some way, as well as a place of worship, the tattooist's parlour – seen up close – had the feel of a tannery: a human tannery, if you will.

Fanged serpents, death's heads, grim reapers, roaring bears, fire-breathing dragons and fierce eagles all stared down from snapshots of bare shoulders and chests. Not only men's chests: women's chests, too.

Cuter illustrations like butterflies, dolphins and pet cats and dogs (with names such as Sasha and Ludmilla) had their places. And there were hammers and sickles and flags aplenty. Hearts and cupids, also. But the ones that caught the attention of Fedor Turov were those that, to him at least, seemed particularly odd. A black crucifix, drawn on a drooping penis, being one.

'A priest's… ordered by his bishop… to make him desist,' Fedor heard the tattooist say.

Fedor found these *stranger* illustrations bewildering, mesmerising. In one, an owl's wings fanned spectacularly from a woman's inner thighs, her genitalia forming the bird's beak.

'I could have won an award with that. The privates of a schoolteacher. She was worried her mother would find out,' said the man.

Fedor nodded and moved on. Apocalyptic inscriptions swirled in the valleys of ears. Zodiac signs revealed themselves inside cheeks and lips. Eyes on the tops of eyelids made it seem as if their owners must never sleep. Elsewhere, hands reached alarmingly from the crevasses of arses. Bizarre, inked busts of Lenin, Marx and others adorned proud pink nipples: the owners' chest hairs groomed into silvering whiskers and beards. The famous domes of St Basil's Cathedral hung on some guy's balls. *I Love Russia* a scroll above his shaved groin proclaimed.

'So, do you *want* a tattoo?' asked the man.

Fedor turned to look at him.

The man – the artist – had greying, cropped hair, was well-built and wore a white T-shirt. To Fedor's surprise, he had nothing – in terms of illustrations – on either his head, neck or arms, merely some dark tails and tips… uncoiling and pointing from under the short sleeves of his top, where his biceps bulged… as if the markings were reaching from some hidden thicket.

Fedor had seen the man's flyer on the board in the downstairs hall. More than once he'd passed 'characters', who weren't from the flats, waiting for the man's services, on the stairs.

At times, he'd heard the buzz and whine of tools when the man's door had been ajar.

'How long have you been doing this… here?' Fedor now asked.

'I *was* in the market, but rents got expensive,' the man said. 'I started here only recently.'

Fedor couldn't remember him in the market but said nothing.

'So, have you decided yet?' asked the man.

'Are you licensed… and everything?' Fedor asked.

'Oh Hell no,' said the man. 'That sort of thing's for doctors and lawyers, isn't it? And look what merchants they are. Don't worry, I'll take care of you. I've been doing this forever. You'll be in safe hands with me.'

The man pulled a pack of cigarettes from under the sleeve of his T-shirt. He offered one to Fedor, who declined. The man lit one and started to smoke.

'I'm not sure what to have,' said Fedor.

'Look around. Think about it. Come see me when you know what you want. It's not a problem.'

'Will it hurt?' asked Fedor.

'You'll be fine,' said the man.

'If I don't like it, can I get rid of it?' asked Fedor.

'Oh there are ways of going over them, or rubbing them out,' said the man. 'Just like Stalin.'

'How do you mean?' asked Fedor.

'Well, I once had a guy, a big Party guy… from the old days… and he had me tattoo all the big leaders and revolutionaries on his chest. I'm talking Lenin, Trotsky, Stalin, Kirov, Zinoviev, Khrushchev, you know. It was a big job and a nice-looking job, even if I say so myself… all over his chest. Anyway, one day he comes rushing in and starts unbuttoning his shirt on me and demanding his money back. When he opened his shirt up – you know what? – there was only one man still there. Stalin. He'd rubbed all those other bastards right out.'

The man drew on his cigarette and stared at Fedor.

Fedor looked back at him, not knowing what to say.

Then the man started laughing. 'I'm joking, my friend. I'm joking,' he said. He put a hand on Fedor's arm. 'Now, let me see if I can help. Where were you thinking of?'

'My shoulders?' Fedor said, uncertainly. 'My back… perhaps?'

'Oh, the back is good… good territory for a tattoo… especially the upper back. An excellent canvas.' The man suddenly stuck his cigarette in a dish – as if seized by an idea. 'Please… take your top off.'

Fedor pulled his sweatshirt over his head.

The man turned him around and put his hands on Fedor's shoulders.

'You know what?' he said. 'I think you were made for… a shark.'

'A shark?' said Fedor.

'Yes,' said the man. 'Right across your shoulders. I think that's really you. Nice skin by the way. Some of the young guys who come to me have boils and spots full of puss and all kinds of shit. Strong-looking boy. Work out?'

'A little,' said Fedor.

'It's good to work out. Healthy body, healthy mind. That's what they say. Oh yeah, I can certainly do something with you.'

He handed Fedor his top. Fedor put it on.

'Maybe a small one – to start,' Fedor said.

'Okay, but it'll grow on you. Trust me,' said the man.

Instead of making straight for his parents' flat, Fedor walked to the metro and hung around the kiosks and shops. He bought a Coke and chewed some gum. He saw Oxsana Antipin (whose kid, Arkady, had been half-blinded in a freak accident with a snowball). Once – going back – he'd considered her hot: jerk-off material, in actual fact. Now, though, he felt different about her... different about a lot of things. Whether it was because she'd gone to look old and had stopped taking care of herself (after what had happened to Arkady), or whether it was because something had changed or was changing inside him, he didn't fully know.

She passed him with her shopping and headed for the crossing to their block.

He put his bottle in a bin and walked the same way.

As he did so, he found himself thinking of Arkady's dad (who went to the gym that Fedor had also started to use). He thought about how Antipin was a guy to be respected. Not only for the way he kept himself fit, but for how he'd got himself a woman like Oxsana (who must have been really stunning once). Above all he thought of Antipin's tattoos. They ran the length of his powerful arms – sea serpents, flowers, mermaids, wild horses. They were, to Fedor, like illuminations in ancient Bibles... of the kind he'd seen priests use in the days when he still went to mass. At the gym, as Antipin lifted weights, skipped and hit the punchbag, his tattoos came to life, blooming and journeying, with a beauty that Fedor found hypnotic. He'd been similarly fascinated by the tattoos of some of the other men and looked at their bodies while pretending not to. One had a wonderful Pegasus whose wings spread over the pectorals of his chest. Another had a red rose that rambled down his thigh and leg. When he stepped from the shower, it was as if the rose – on its twisting stem – was spotted with freshly-fallen rain.

Fedor had come to feel awkward about this fascination of his. He wondered if the attraction the tattoos had for him was rooted in something more than skin-deep. He'd thought about going to see Father Pyotr… to talk, if not directly then in the semi-privacy of confession.

But he'd decided against it. A tattoo… a tattoo was what he wanted… what he *needed*, he told himself. Then he'd be like the other men and he'd get a girl – a beautiful girl, a gorgeous girl… and no mistake.

Getting a girl. That was what Fedor's parents went on to him about. Not all of the time, but a lot of it. A *nice* girl, to be exact. Nadine, whose mother worked at the pharmacy the Turovs used, was a 'nice girl'… as was Lesya Vitsina, whose mother was on the counter at the post office. Even Alyona Goreva, who Fedor remembered being banned from their youth club after a catfight at a disco, had, according to his parents (and to his intense disappointment), turned out to be 'nice'.

Fedor's mother worked at the library, his father for the civil service. Fedor looked at them and said nothing while thinking about the sort of girl *he* wanted. And that was a *bad* girl… in stockings and heels – the badder the better, in fact.

Then, later, he wasn't sure if he even *wanted* a girl at all… no matter how nice or bad she might be.

'Decided?' the man asked as he showed Fedor in.

'The shark – I think,' Fedor said.

'Good. That's wonderful,' said the man. 'I think that's going to work really well. I've been picturing it. The big thing now is this: how are you going pay? You're a college kid, right?'

'I have a part-time job. I stack shelves at the supermarket... by the metro,' Fedor said.

'Oh, that's right,' said the man. 'I've seen you there – in your overalls.'

'Can I pay by instalment?' Fedor asked

'You might be in my debt for quite a while,' said the man.

'You'll get it all – I promise,' said Fedor.

'Really?' said the man.

'Yes,' said Fedor.

'Okay, let's do it,' said the man.

'Do I need the consent of my parents?' asked Fedor.

'No. You're old enough, in my book. Take off your top.'

Before the man started, he showed Fedor the equipment he'd be using: the different needles for lining and shading, the phials that housed the ink.

'How long will it take?' asked Fedor.

'A while,' said the man. He put out his cigarette, pulled on some gloves that were tight around his fingers and wrists.

'A tiger shark has forty-eight teeth. Twenty-four upper, twenty-four lower. Jaw to jaw. Did you know that?'

'The pain,' said Fedor. 'Will it...'

'It varies from person to person. But don't worry. Since you're a virgin... in tattoo terms, I mean... I'll give you something.'

The man moved things around in the room – adjusted the angle of a lamp, changed the height of a stool, checked several switches and plugs.

'Oh,' he said, 'before I forget...'

He took a brown bottle from a cupboard, held it away from himself, unscrewed the cap and upturned it, for a second, onto a wad of cotton wool.

'Okay, get on the couch,' he said to Fedor. 'On your stomach. That's it. Now… you won't feel a thing once you've smelt…'

The man put the wad under Fedor's nose. A sweet, gluey wave engulfed him. For a moment, Fedor had the feeling of being an animal in a slaughterhouse – one that had been stunned or shot and was on its knees… halfway to falling, or dying.

'…*this*,' finished the man.

As his eyelids were closing on the couch, Fedor looked at the man – who was on the stool, holding his gun, working his foot pedal.

To Fedor, he seemed like some old witch at her spinning wheel.

The icons on the wall – the beasts, satyrs, superheroes, cherubs and mermaids – all swirled around him, as if on a carousel.

Fedor felt something slapping his face.

'Hey, boy! Boy! Wake up!'

Slowly, groggily, his head throbbing, Fedor realised where he was.

'Weren't *you* the lively one,' said the man. 'I had to give you a second dose.'

'How long have I been here?' asked Fedor, blinking at the light.

'Five hours… approximately,' said the man. 'Do you want to see it?'

'Is it finished?' asked Fedor.

'As far as I'm concerned,' said the man, lighting a cigarette.

'Yes… yes please,' said Fedor.

'Okay, get to your feet… *slowly*,' said the man. 'You've been out of it, remember.'

Fedor planted his shoes on the linoleum floor. He still felt woozy. His trousers sagged on his hips. He saw that his belt was undone, which confused him because he couldn't recall undoing it.

'Here,' said the man. 'Come and stand here.'

Fedor stood in front of a mirror as the man fetched another, which he held up behind Fedor's back.

'There. What do you think?' he asked.

Fedor saw – first of all – the shark's grey tail, flicking over his right shoulder blade. Then, when the man stepped to the other side of him (in the manner of a barber in a salon), Fedor saw the shark's snout pointing outwards, over his left shoulder blade, as if it were about to leave his body entirely… and was just passing through.

The man bade Fedor turn at an angle to the mirror in front of him. He then held his own mirror in such a way that it ran like a camera along the length of the shark: from the tail, past the small hillock of its rearmost dorsal, over the stripes that gave it its name, beyond the pelvic and principal dorsal, through the wing-like pectorals and gill slits, on to the dead, black eye (that Fedor thought was like the Sun eclipsed) and, finally, to its jaws… of forty-eight icicle teeth – which encircled Fedor's left scapula, as if about to bite.

'Well, what do you say?' said the man.

'It's… *bigger* than I thought it would be,' said Fedor.

'Of course, it is! Of course!' said the man. 'We're talking about one of the most beautiful, ancient creatures on this planet. Something like that can only *command* its canvas. It must have its realm. It is not some little goldfish to be hidden on a postage stamp.' He paused then began again, 'So… do you like it?'

'Yes… yes, I like it. I like it a lot. Thank you,' said Fedor.

'Oh, don't thank me. The pleasure has been all mine.'

'How long have I been here did you say?' asked Fedor.

'Five hours,' said the man. 'Thereabouts.'

'Five hours?!' said Fedor. 'My parents! I must go!'

'Wait a minute,' said the man. He wrapped some bandages around the tattoo, tied the ends in a knot.

'What do I do with it now?' asked Fedor.

'Be careful with it… for a couple of weeks. If you get scabs, or anything like that, don't worry… just let them dry and fall off.'

'Thanks,' said Fedor. 'I have to go, but I'll pay. I promise.'

'I know,' said the man, and he lit a cigarette to replace his other, which had burned itself to ash.

Fedor kept the tattoo to himself for nearly two weeks.

In lectures at college and while stacking shelves at the supermarket, he thought of almost nothing else. Knowing that he had it gave him a confidence he'd never had before. Finally – one early evening after his parents had gone to church – he took off his bandages and looked at the shark. He propped his mother and father's bedroom mirror behind him as he stood before the one in the bathroom above the sink.

If anything, the shark seemed bigger than he remembered it – as if it had somehow grown on his back. The snout seemed further over… nearer his armpit… the jaws broader… than before. He wondered about this for a moment. Then he told himself he was a growing boy and that, therefore, it made sense that the shark was growing, too.

He imagined himself places, saw himself taking off his top, the shark – he would name it something – *rippling* on his back. He sensed the awe he felt sure there would be among the bathers at Sokolniki ponds come summer. He also pictured himself above Oxsana Antipin, her legs around him, her nails in the skin – the sharkskin – of his back.

He went to the gym. Normally he worked out in a T-shirt or vest, but that night he went at the weights and the punchbag in only his shorts. He sensed the sweat beading and glistening on the shark. Not only that but that the eyes of the other guys were watching and following him as they went through their routines – bars and dumbbells clanking... skipping ropes whooshing and slapping... canvas bags and leather punchballs swinging and being whacked.

In the showers afterwards, there was the usual banter.

Fedor felt good. He stood with his face inclined to a nozzle, then dropped his head so the warm water jetted down his neck and spread around the shark, as if putting it to sea... somewhere tropical.

In virtually one movement, they were on him: pinning his arms against the tiles, pulling the towel around his mouth.

Fedor went to the man's flat. He did not want to show that he'd been crying, but his eyes were red and his cheeks were pink and puffed-up.

The man came to the door.

Fedor saw that – behind him – his hall was full of boxes and crates.

'Yes?' said the man, in the tone of someone who was busy and hadn't wanted to be disturbed.

'The shark,' said Fedor. 'I want you to take it off.'

'Take if off?' said the man. 'Take it off?! *Why* should I take it off? Do you have any idea of the cost and the time of doing that? *You* who've not paid me a kopek. Not a single kopek! I have more rights over that shark than anyone, mister. Including you! And if I say you'll wear it, you'll wear it!! Now, get out of my face! I'm busy!'

The man yanked the door to. Fedor smelt the wave of a sickly odour that was familiar to him.

Before the door shut, he caught sight of the room off the hall, the chapel-like chamber... where it seemed all the photographs had been removed from its interior.

The room was now no more than an empty cell.

And Fedor knew... he knew that, perhaps even by the next day, the framed images would shortly be hanging from the walls of another flat in another block – quite possibly in a different city entirely.

Nailed among them: his own hungry, searching shark – and his pale and taken skin.

GLASSHOUSE

Tokarev thought of the carp in the glasshouse and, as he lay on his pillow, he imagined them moving with great discipline in their pond in the dark. Glancing at his wife Lidiya, who was snoring softly beside him, he eased back the covers and stepped from their bed. In the hall, he quietly put on his hat and coat (over his pyjamas) then left their flat and walked to the metro, arriving just in time to catch the last train.

Earlier that day, he and his wife had toured the botanical gardens at the university, an excursion of the kind the couple had been making since Tokarev's retirement from the railways. For most of his career, he had driven engines at night, mainly freight on old trains and slow tracks from the Soviet days, but at certain intervals passenger trains also, such as the service that reached St Petersburg from Moscow near dawn. Since accepting his pension, he'd suffered from insomnia. Engines rumbled through his mind in the small hours of the mornings, brakes screeching (or so it seemed) as locomotives pulled into the stations of Moscow – Leningradsky, Paveletsky, Kazansky – grand and small. Tokarev fretted about fuel… scrutinised signals… pondered over points… clicked his tongue at timetables (his lips more often than not also moving with the names and numbers of tunnels, sidings and halts – even on those rare occasions when he seemed to sleep) no matter that none of these were any longer his formal concern. Acknowledging that his wife had throughout their long marriage invariably known what was for the best, he agreed with her that their trips out together, such as the one to the gardens, might, in time, divert his mind from his preoccupations and help him adjust to his new life without rails.

That day, at the gardens, the couple had separated according to their interests. She had wandered happily among the orchids in one of the great glasshouses, disappearing amid the fragrant blooms.

Tokarev, meanwhile, found himself studying a pond of ornamental carp. What began as casual observation on his part soon developed into careful examination. The cause of his captivation was the way that the fish – for much of their time utterly motionless – would, quite suddenly, move from one part of their pond to another. Although at times languidly achieved and, on the face of it, almost pointless, what impressed Tokarev was the precision of these journeys and the accuracy with which the fish would position themselves, before their condition of stillness resumed. Tokarev also noticed how certain of the carp swapped exact places with others in what was almost a military drill. He found this movement and symmetry both soothing and satisfying. He further discovered that using his wristwatch he was able to accurately predict the journeys and stops of a mounting number of the fish. The pond, as far as he was concerned, was a kind of aquatic railway hub, with branch lines, cross-country routes (between various kinds of weed) and platforms (on the pond's pebbled bottom). It even possessed the equivalent of engine sheds, amid the artificial rocks.

A timetable for arrivals and departures was, so it seemed, strictly observed by all of the fish in the pond. Responsibility for the longer journeys fell to the larger, older inhabitants; their smaller, swifter fellows undertaking the shorter, commuter-like, sprints. 'Come along now… time you were moving,' Tokarev whispered, tapping at his watch – and off the fish would dart, or heave.

When his wife returned and joined him, he thought about sharing his findings with her. But then he wondered what she – or anyone – would make of them (and him). So he kept his discoveries to himself. On leaving, he noticed that in one side of the glasshouse a low window was ajar.

Now, eight or more hours later and with the moon and stars at his shoulder, he climbed through that same aperture… and into the glasshouse.

Initially, its dark interior was a jungle to him. The trunks of giant plants blocked his path. Branches thick and thin batted his chest and face, and great hanging vines dragged at his shoulders and hat. With time though, his eyes adjusted to the dim light. Finally, aided by a moonbeam that penetrated the high panes of the glasshouse, he stepped out from a cluster of tropical palms and onto a path that took him to the pond.

When he came upon the fish, their orange and white forms were halted and quiet. Tokarev leaned to the water, and, in the faint silver light, their manoeuvres began: luminous shapes, submarining purposefully.

After observing them for some time, Tokarev laid himself on a wooden bench near the pond and went to sleep.

In the morning, Tokarev was woken by crows stalking and cawing on the roof of the glasshouse. At first, he didn't know where he was, and he gripped the bench with his hands – disorientated by the tall and exotic plants that enclosed him. In some ways, they were not unlike the birch forests and plantations of firs he'd passed through so many times on his night trains: trees that, in the mists of dawn, seemed to step up to the track.

After some moments, he came to his senses and let go of the bench.

What struck him next was the smell.

Yes, there had been times when, late at night or in the early morning, he'd stepped from his engines – in isolated sidings out of Moscow – to stretch his legs or relieve his bladder. And, while doing so, he had breathed-in what seemed to him the true air of Russia. But for the most part he had known the smog of the industrial areas, the stale atmosphere of the suburb (split, as it was, by a six-lane highway) where he and Lidiya lived. (They had never had children.)

What Tokarev, accustomed as he was to waking with a bronchial cough (and, after it, gasps for air that made him feel as if he were drowning), noticed now was the sweetness that seemed to surround him. This he took to be the perfume of the orchids.

After some while of lying there and looking at the roof, he rose and made his way through the vegetation to the window via which he had entered, which he now climbed through and pulled behind him... leaving it just a little ajar.

At the metro station, he caught an early train. The carriage was already crowded. A young woman, who looked to Tokarev like a student, rose and gave him her seat.

In the harsh light of the carriage, he was suddenly conscious of the flimsiness of his pyjama trousers below his overcoat, and he reached to smooth them against his sockless shins. No one else seemed to notice them, or his slippers for that matter. And, by the time of the next station, he had forgotten about them and was thinking about other things, particularly the pond and the fish.

At home, he re-joined Lidiya and he lay awake beside her, going over in his mind his night in the glasshouse, till she rose and came in from the kitchen with tea.

From that time onward, Tokarev went to the glasshouse at night – all spring and all summer: putting his coat over his pyjamas; taking the metro; climbing through the window; occupying 'his' bench; observing the carp.

And, in the waking hours between these nocturnal migrations, he felt himself relaxing at last, steadily losing the fears that had enveloped him in this new life he'd been allocated (with its unsettling lack of timetables and ordained destinations).

He and Lidiya attended concerts at Sokolniki park, picnicked at Strogino beach and even went on a day cruise on the Moscow River.

To Tokarev's frustration, Lidiya – as she had amongst the orchids of the glasshouse – kept disappearing.

Even when they had once been dancing at Sokolniki (to a folk song they both loved), she had somehow wandered off. The same happened at Strogino, causing Tokarev to roll up his trousers and enter the water and call out her name as people on the shore looked on. Somehow, she made her way home without him. When he returned, she was in her apron at the stove in the kitchen and (he seemed to remember) they hugged.

One midsummer night, a fierce storm struck Moscow. Lightning forked and flared. It made the glasshouse seem like some great haunted palace. Tokarev thought of Lidiya at home in their flat. Lying on his bench, he remembered a trip they had made to the cinema at that time when things in the city had started to change. 'Amerikanskiy,' the creased-faced woman in the booth had announced, as they bought tickets for the movie (through curiosity as much as anything).

It had been dubbed very badly and contained scenes of violence that Lidiya had not liked. He remembered her hand pressing his in the dark of the auditorium. The two of them had left quietly, before the end (despite Tokarev's interest in certain parts of the film that had shown trains, both over and underground).

Cursing himself now for leaving Lidiya alone in their flat, he hurried from the glasshouse and then waited more than two hours at the entrance to the station nearest the gardens, until an attendant arrived to open the station's streaming shutters.

At their flat, he took off his rain-soaked clothes and towelled himself dry, vowing to end the foolishness of his night journeys.

Yet he found himself drawn by the pond and its fish even so – an irresistible *something* that he would have had difficulty articulating to anyone else – and soon he returned as before.

Apart from the storm, Tokarev was only once seriously disturbed all that summer, waking one night to the sound of fleet-footed movement through the tops of the plants and the trees.

One moment the scurry and rustle would be on one side of the glasshouse, the next it was somewhere else.

Tokarev deduced it to be a squirrel.

He tried to track it but found the task hopeless due to the gloom of the glasshouse and the creature's eye-defying speed.

What disturbed him most was the way the animal's presence seemed to affect the carp, which, for all of that night, held fast their positions without undertaking any of their expected journeys.

It was as if, in their underwater world, they sensed the squirrel.

They know, Tokarev thought to himself. *They know.*

A picture came back to him of his father, who Tokarev realised he had almost entirely forgotten, holding a finger to his lips on a canal bank where the two of them had gone fishing when he was a child.

Come the autumn and its cooler nights, Tokarev was grateful for the warmth of the glasshouse, which he had found bothersome at times during the humid weather of the summer.

Students were now recommencing studies all over Moscow and Tokarev was conscious of greater activity in and around the glasshouse.

One night, he arrived to find his bench had been moved to a different side of the pond.

A new board stood where the bench had been.

It showed photographs of the carp and gave information about them.

This dismayed Tokarev, who – irrational as it may have been – was angry that he had not figured in any act of consultation.

'Lidiya!' he called out in alarm, hoping to summon her, thinking for a moment she might be somewhere amid the orchids.

'Lidiya!' he called again, needing to show her this… *violation.*

His mind imagined visitors making imbecilic remarks that, as with the squirrel, the carp would hear and be frightened by: halting their journeys, wreaking havoc with their timetables, scrambling the clocks that ticked in their brains, ripping-up the route maps they somehow held within.

To his utter dismay, he found the wrapper of a chocolate bar on the bench.

For a grievous moment, he felt that the fish were no longer his.

One morning, in what must have been late October, Tokarev awoke suddenly on the bench.

The voice of a woman – a young woman, it seemed – carried through the glasshouse. The altered position of his bench meant there was no time for him to exit as normal through the window, so he hurried into the nearest vegetation, in order to conceal himself.

Shrouded in greenery, and with the tendrils of something tickling an ear, Tokarev realised that he was without his hat.

He parted two large leaves with his fingers and peered through the gap.

The young woman, who seemed to be an employee of some kind, was talking and laughing into a mobile phone as she walked the footpath to the pond. She glanced around for a moment as if making some sort of check... and Tokarev saw her eyes fall on his hat. The astrakhan – originally his grandfather's: a man his parents had taken him to see only once in a village of wooden houses far outside Moscow – sat where Tokarev had left it: upright, on one end of the bench. The young woman walked to the bench and picked it up, telling the person on the other end of the phone what she had found. Then she walked off.

Tokarev had yet to cough that morning and, as the young woman moved away, he sensed the pressure rising in his throat. He fought to resist it, clamping both hands over his mouth. A small sound, like a strangulated sneeze, emerged, nonetheless. He parted the leaves a fraction and saw that the young woman had stopped and was looking back. After a moment she carried on, however, and within a minute or so she was gone. When Tokarev sensed the coast was clear, he made his way to the window and left.

Three days later – he felt it best not to make himself known *too* soon – Tokarev presented himself at an office at the gardens, where he enquired about lost property and, specifically, his hat.

He recognised the young woman he'd seen by the pond, who was now engaged on some other business in the office, and who said nothing to him, as a colleague located the hat.

Tokarev signed for it and left.

As winter set in, Tokarev's expeditions to the glasshouse continued, his checked slippers stepping across the lawns of the gardens with a crumping sound amid the early snows.

The way the flakes fell on the building in the moonlight made him think of remote cabins, and herdsmen and women driving elk in places of great wilderness… to the sporadic ringing of bells.

He seemed to see the animals' breath and hear their snorts as they moved over trails between trees, spurred by the calls of those who drove them.

Another matter that engaged and intrigued him was the way that, while the thermometer outside his kitchen window sometimes fell as low as minus twenty degrees, and Moscow's rivers were in places frozen from shore to shore, here, in the glasshouse, there was not so much as a splinter of ice on the surface of the pond. Sometimes, in the darkness, when the world outdoors was consumed by a near-Arctic cold, he heard a tail of one of the pond's bigger fish… flicking.

Then, one night, he was woken by voices.

Pulling himself up, he saw beams of white light flashing through the trunks and branches of the plants and trees in the glasshouse.

For several moments, he found it difficult to place where he was: his situation blurring with a time when a goods train he'd been driving had broken down in a forest a long distance from anywhere (a work party eventually reaching him and his engine, making their way, on foot, through the snow). Now, however. the lights were from the torches of watchmen, who were entering the glasshouse after finding, and following, a set of footprints in the snow.

Instead of fleeing through the window, Tokarev stepped into the pond and moved among its lily pads. Next, he stepped back out and clambered onto his bench. Then, without quite knowing why or fully realising what he was doing, he opened his overcoat, held his manhood and began to urinate wildly, as if wielding a hose against the leaping flames of a blaze.

The watchmen seized him – cursing as his member sprayed them as well as the surrounds of the pond.

Next, they frogmarched him to the office where he'd gone previously to reclaim his hat.

And there, again, he encountered the young woman.

When the watchmen told her what had happened, she reprimanded Tokarev severely.

He responded that she had sullied the pond with her 'horrible' sign and that 'clowns' were going there in the day and disturbing his fish.

How long had he been going there? she asked him.

That was not the point, he said. The point was the intolerable disturbance that was being caused to the carp. How could they be expected to go about their business after the 'circus' she had imposed on them? Was *this* what Russia had come to?

'You cannot come back here,' the woman said, raising her voice over his, at last. 'If you come back, there will be trouble. *You* will be in trouble. Do you have a home?' she asked.

'Yes,' he said.

'Well go home and sleep.'

'That's what I was doing,' he said.

'No more sleeping here… with the fish,' she said. 'That's final! Do you hear me? Do you have a wife?'

'Yes, of course I have a wife,' said Tokarev.

Yet, even as he spoke, he found himself uncertain… wondering how it could have been that he had slipped away, unnoticed, in the way that he had… so very many times.

'Only this summer, we danced at Sokolniki,' he continued, as if providing proof… giving information about a person who was – or might be – missing.

'Well, go to her,' said the young woman, 'and *don't* come back.'

Two police officers summoned by the watchmen questioned him in their car outside the gardens while running its engine to keep warm.

Tokarev looked at the hands of his wristwatch while sitting in the back seat.

'I must be getting back to my wife,' he said.

The patrol car's wipers pushed snowflakes from the screen as the officers drove Tokarev home. He stared at the road between their shoulders, as the car was strobed by the lights of advertising hoardings above and beside the highway. The road was new to him – he had never owned a car. The people and products on the billboards seemed to stare at him in a way that he found faintly monstrous.

Tokarev couldn't find his keys to the flat, and there was no answer at the door when both he and then the officers knocked it and pressed the buzzer.

The officers woke the caretaker for her spare set.

On finally letting him in, the officers asked if he'd be all right.

He responded that he would be fine, that his wife was in the bedroom sleeping… that she was a heavy sleeper.

One of the officers asked in a low voice if his wife knew where he went.

Tokarev said he'd judged it best not to tell her.

They looked down the hall to the door of the bedroom where he indicated Lidiya lay.

Tokarev continued to placate them, his voice hoarse now from all of the unaccustomed talking that he'd done. He was tired of his secret, he said, and in the morning he would tell his Lidiya… everything. .

'No more messing with the fishes, old man,' said the officer who appeared the senior of the two. 'Stay home now. You hear?'

Tokarev nodded meekly.

The officer looked again at the bedroom door (the thought seeming to cross his mind that he should wake and speak to the wife of this strange, wandering man).

'Promise?' the officer asked.

'Yes,' said Tokarev. 'I promise. There's no need for me to go back there. Really. You have my word.'

The second officer reminded the first of a call they had yet to make, and, with that, the patrolmen made for the front door and left.

Tokarev undressed and readied himself for bed. He entered the bathroom where he turned on the taps and ran the water gently, so as not to disturb his Lidiya in the bedroom next door. When he was satisfied that everything necessary had been done and all was as it should be, he re-joined her.

As he lay on the bedcovers with his head on a pillow he thought of the carp and hoped that, in spite of the night's turmoil, they might now be moving as normal… with assurance and discipline in their water in the dark.

Some hours later, Tokarev sensed sunlight on his face through the fine curtains of the bedroom.

He rose and went into the bathroom, where he put on the small strip light over the wash basin. Its glow rendered the gloom of the windowless room navigable without being over-bright.

Looking at the bathtub, he saw that certain of the carp – that he'd liberated first from the pond before the watchmen had reached him and then from the pockets of his overcoat after the policemen had gone – were moving in its water, with apparent contentment. Others calmly waited their turn, maintaining their positions in the white tub until it was time for them to move, just as they had in their pond at the glasshouse.

Remembering how he'd thought the better of mentioning the fish to Lidiya that very first day in the gardens, he now rebuked himself for the foolishness – indeed the selfishness (going off like some rogue engine) – that he'd shown. Hadn't the two of them always shared everything?

'Wake up, my darling!' he now called to her in a loud whisper that he hoped wouldn't worry the carp. 'There's something I'd like you to see.'

He turned from the tub for a moment and called her name through the doorway. 'Lidiya! Lidiya?'

Glancing once more at the fish, he began again: 'There's no need to worry, my love! Everything is working wonderfully. I shall be all right. *We* shall be all right. Everything is running to plan!'

Compass

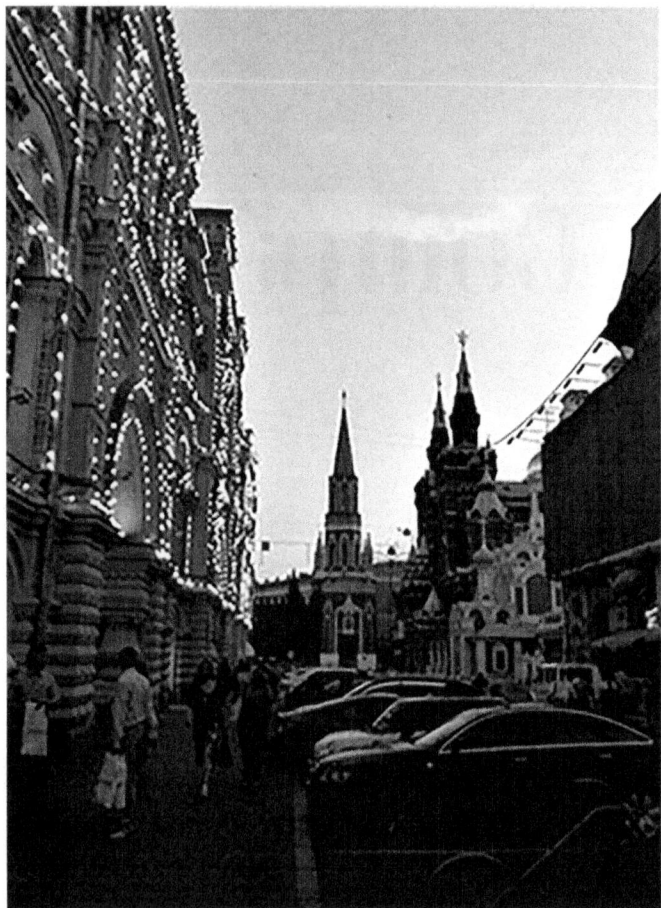

I don't think I can tell you… that I shall ever be able to tell you… *why* I took the horse. Even now, I don't properly know. What I *can* give you is my account of the events of that time and my confirmation that, yes, I was the one they called 'The Rider'.

When first I saw the mare, she was at the top of the steps that rise from and enter the metro station situated nearest my place of work: grimy, ordinary steps – of the kind found at a hundred or more Moscow metro stations – that I had climbed and descended many thousands of times previously.

A greasy rope tethered her by the neck to the end of a rail worn smooth by the hands of countless commuters.

I was, at that hour, on my way home with no intention or expectation of involvement in anything extraordinary.

I've a memory – a sense (it remains quite clear) – of my fingertips on the cracked leather of her bridle.

Before I knew it, I was on her back.

Soon, we were at a trot, then a canter… then a gallop, on the hard, slabbed pavement – the two of us running against the grain of the thickening tide of evening traffic.

There was shouting behind me but I – *we* – rode on, my bag strapped over my shoulder, bouncing against my hip, so that I felt myself to resemble a mailman in a tunic, from some history book.

The bag flew open and my dull work papers inside peeled from it self-importantly, as if they were the incendiary broadsides of anarchists, or the deathly decrees of Tsars. They blew against windscreens and shop fronts, and entangled themselves in rosebushes and the high branches of black-barked trees.

Ahead of us, an underpass disgorged commuters.

I drew the mare's reins to our left.

We wove through the traffic, as if fording a river, before zigzagging across a twin set of trolleybus tracks. A driver hit his klaxon, but the mare stayed calm and steady.

We headed down a side street that was mostly in shadow, and here, for the first time, I became aware of her shoed hooves, as the boxed-in nature of the street amplified their clatter.

An aproned woman came to the step of a grocery store, outside which were trays of fruit. A man in overalls eyed us from her shoulder.

At the end of the street lay a small park. I took the horse to a fountain and dismounted.

While she drank, I had my first proper look at her.

She was, as I have said, a mare: sorrel brown. I have no expertise in equine matters but to my eye she seemed neither wild (from the Steppes) nor a thoroughbred. While she had not been wholly neglected, she did not seem to have been treated particularly well.

In places, her coat was rough and matted. At her withers and reins, lay weals – possibly the result of an ill-fitting saddle or harness. These I made a point to avoid. There was, in any event, nothing in the way of saddlery upon her. She was bareback – that was how I – *we* – had ridden.

Her mane had a brittleness that made me think of the British in Crimea, whose ravenous horses – I knew from my past reading – had turned their teeth on their own hair and tails.

Her age was difficult to determine (for a mere layman, like me), but she was – I formed the impression – not young.

Why she had been brought to Moscow, I had no real idea. Strange now to remark, I had never seen an actual, live horse before – let alone ridden one. They were creatures I associated with Cossacks and the plains.

I saw that her neck and chest were wet with sweat. I felt guilty at the way we had galloped. Yet I could not help but think of the manner in which, together, we had swept past kiosks and malls, beneath bridges and across intersections, and how I had felt myself far more in *her* hands than she in mine.

It was as if she (and maybe all horses) possessed some inner compass that arrowed a safe passage, ancient and sainted, through the tar and the concrete and the metal of modern Moscow – a *way* that no man, woman or child might themselves divine.

My senses were gripped by a peculiar… exhilaration.

Around us, the city grew dark.

We walked on, through the warm night, past lit shop windows that flaunted handbags, televisions, cell phones and computers, all of which were of no interest to me, my mind intent only on finding somewhere we might rest… a place where the mare might safely graze.

We reached Sokolniki at dawn. The dry floor of the birch woods cracked beneath us as the first light fingered its way through the trees.

When we came to the ponds, mists were hanging over their still waters.

I left my clothes on a bank.

I led the mare through a shore of bulrushes till I was submerged to my shoulders, and she to her ribs beside me.

Then I let go of her.

She forged ahead, gently, through an island of lily pads, into the deeper, middle waters, until all I could see of her were her head, neck and back – the pond's surface also eventually closing over this plateau.

I swam to the bank, where, having risen from the pool, I dried and I dressed.

The mare lifted herself from the other side, the disturbance to the water making shallow ridges in the surface that sent a soft wake through its greenery.

She rounded the water's edge and came to me.

As I fell asleep, she moved quietly and pulled at the grass near where I lay.

Later, when the sun forced itself on us, we retreated further, to the shade of the woods.

For a while, that was how we lived: galloping through Moscow, in sun-tranced days and neon-lit nights, emerging then disappearing, in streaks and blurs and flashes.

To us, these crossings seemed not only natural but necessary.

A canter across the ground floor amid startled shoppers at the palatial mall at Kievskaya was an episode typical of the kind we undertook.

Another time, we circled the sides of the old Olympic pool at Luzhniki, between the oiled bodies of reclining bathers... before vaulting a wall and making good our escape.

One spectacular occasion saw us speed past the statue of Zhukov, in his stirrups, outside Resurrection Gate, and then on... into Red Square. We flew beyond Lenin's mausoleum and, while the police were still dozing, disappeared behind the domes of St Basil's and across the river bridge to Gorky Park.

Our rides took us past schools, libraries, markets and factory gates.

At night, we raced past high-end hotels whose staff wore livery, smiles and shining shoes; surging also past clubs, where the young and the fashionable turned from their queues to look at us... beer stalls and pharmacies, where those on duty poked their heads from small hatches to catch sight of our phenomenon.

As well as Sokolniki, we rested at Gorky (in the high ground amid the trees and streams) and the ferned and falcon-haunted woods of those gently tumbling slopes at Vorybyovy Gory.

We watered, after sunset, at quiet loops in the river and places like the ponds at Novodevichy; once also at the larger of the lakes at Chistye Prudy, where diners rose in restaurants on the shore to watch as we moved through the moonlit water, to the trees that lined the opposite bank.

At another time, we ran beside a metro train as it cut above ground to hammer through a strip of scrub seared by summer heat. Passengers pushed up against the windows, pointed at us and took our photograph.

More than once, I encountered our likeness, real or imagined, in graffiti. These depictions reminded me of photographs I had seen on the internet of men and horses carved into chalk hills in the countryside of southern England.

I learned later that some spoke of us as symbols, while others thought us angels, portents, or ghosts.

The Rider… that's what they called me – anchormen in TV studios who linked to women holding microphones who positioned themselves by fountains in parks, or at intersections, or at the feet of statues, or even at the top of cathedral steps.

The studio men would ask: 'So Olga / Irina / Katya / Olesya… just *where* is The Rider now?'

The women would pivot to a police officer, or city official, who'd sweat and stumble through some scripted lines while the reporter, more often than not lip-glossed and in furs, switched, as the moment suited, from the solemnity of a convent sister to the showy, look-at-me smiles of a courtesan.

I had never intended to make what people call 'a statement'. But when coincidence gave us the chance, we took it.

One afternoon, in Old Arbat, we charged from a side street and came upon one of these duos of diva-plus-cop. We leapt directly over them – mid-interview – and showed them our heels.

On a separate occasion, a news programme did something utterly unheard of: cutting off a Government

Minister in full flow, in order to broadcast some snatched footage of us turning a corner near Pushkin Square.

Another time, a crew quit covering a football match to – of their own volition – race with their gear through side streets till they glimpsed us: slipping into a monastery garden.

Such were our days and nights of fame and freedom.

I'd always hoped they would spare her, agree it somehow, amongst themselves. But when it happened – in one of those drab, nowhere places where bloodletting gets done – the bullets flew, from all directions.

Her front legs – perhaps unsurprisingly – went first. Thinking of it now, it was as if this wonder horse… this *danger* horse… was being brought to heel… taught to… kneel.

Next, her neck and head scorched the hard, dry earth.

Then she tipped over and just… lay there, on the yellow grass.

I was thrown. My head hit the ground.

I could see her side, rising and falling.

I heard a volley of shots, and then no further sound.

The pain from my thigh – a bullet hole, crimson with a black crust – brought me round.

I was on a bench in a part of the city I didn't know.

I made my way to a hospital where they treated my wound.

Two nights later, I limped out of there.

I returned to my home and, in time, my work. My profile at the office had never been high. No one seemed to realise I'd even been absent.

For a time, the television channels found other news: about children, sport, farms.

But there was only one subject on the minds of the people. They wanted to know about 'The Rider'… and 'The Horse'.

Graffiti – and questions – spread across the city. There were slogans on the walls of underpasses and the high sides of railway embankments. Flyers that had the look of having been printed secretly poured into the letterboxes of my and other blocks. Scrawled 'conversations' turned to arguments (and counterclaims) on the backs of doors in the bathrooms of bars and restaurants.

'They live… They are dead… They have never lived… I have seen them… You lie… I do not.'

It has been a year now. Last night, the TV said that 'The Rider' and his horse had been seen and that the authorities had confirmed this as a fact.

But I ride nowhere. Not even in my dreams. *That* is the truth.

To me, the city is a sick and steel-grey sea that I no longer have any wish to know, or cross.

Besides, I have no map, no charts, no sextant, no compass.

I am – like everyone else – lost… stranded.

Unhorsed.

Kamilavka

Alexei Lytkin was listening to his mother on his cell phone as he made for the downward escalator at the metro station at Park Pobedy on the western side of Moscow. The distance of its descent made it the longest stairway of its kind in Europe, and Lytkin's steps across the vestibule to the start of the conveyor habitually prompted a flutter of butterflies in his stomach.

At the other end of the phone, his mother, Nadia Agafiya Lytkina, was herself agitated. In her case, by a rather more real matter of mortality, namely the death of the priest in Alexei Lytkin's home village, some three hundred kilometres – and a world – away from the capital, the details of which event Nadia Agafiya was now relating to her son.

Father Fyodor had been killed by a tree. This catastrophe had happened as he was riding his motorcycle to early mass. Their district had seen nothing but rain for weeks and the ground everywhere was sodden – the whole countryside literally drowning in water. A wind had brought down the tree just as the father's motorcycle had come level with it – if such a curse could be believed. It had been a pine, Nadia Agafiya added breathlessly, as if knowledge of the genus would make some material difference to the circumstances of the father's death in the mind of her son.

With his exposed ear Alexei Lytkin could now hear the whir of the approaching escalator and its seven hundred and forty steps. His nostrils caught the warm, metallic smell of its machinery.

He re-focused on his mother's narrative on the phone.

Thanks Be to God in His Mercy, his mother continued, the priest – one of the best – had been killed outright. Old Polushin, the pig farmer, had discovered him while taking a sow in his truck. Polushin had rounded up various other men of the village and, together, they had sawed and rolled the tree from the trapped figure of the father. But by then it was too late: Father Fyodor's eyes – might he now rest in peace – being dead to this world and staring heavenward, as if their orbs were glass.

Alexei Lytkin envisioned the stricken form of the priest for a moment, and saw the back wheel of his pinioned motorbike, spinning on its side beneath the pine.

In front of Lytkin, a glow of light – heralding his near arrival at the mouth of the downward tunnel of the escalator – now distracted him: just a few more steps and he would be there… at the conveyor's cliff-like edge.

The funeral, his mother went on, would—

Like the priest, the signal on Lytkin's phone died suddenly.

Planting one hand on the black rail that ran downwards at his right, Lytkin breathed-in solemnly and began his descent to the platforms of the deepest-set metro station in Moscow.

Severed from his mother's chatter, he put away his phone, and – with a faint but distinct moistening of his mouth – he surrendered to the vertiginous steel waterfall that transported him, through lines of elegant white lights, deeper and deeper into the substrata of the Russian capital, as if he were permeating the city's crust on some primordial burrowing worm.

(Halfway down, he even opened his eyes.)

Several minutes later, and with his stomach now settled, Lytkin stood waiting for the train to his suburb. He found himself thinking of Father Fyodor. In particular, he wondered whether the priest had been wearing a helmet, or had instead put his trust in God, which would have meant that he had either been bare-headed or wearing his kamilavka or his skufia, his hats of clerical office. Of these, Lytkin thought it likely to have been the skufia since he remembered Father Fyodor wearing the stiff black cylinder of the kamilavka only at mass. What was more, he remembered he had seen the priest wearing the seemingly less solemn skufia while riding the lanes of the village on his various calls and visits in times past. The father did so, Lytkin remembered, in the traditional way, with the skufia pulled down over his ears: to keep them closed to gossip (so legend said). Not that there was anything in the village that escaped the attention of Father Fyodor, as Lytkin well knew.

Lytkin now pictured his mother: on the other end of the 'line' to his switched-off cell phone, calling out his name (as he knew that she would be), asking if he, Alexei, could hear her, while also complaining to her neighbour Irina Raspopova that Irina Raspopova's phone was no good.

His mother did not have, or want to have, a phone of her own. Instead, she went to the home of her neighbour and used hers whenever Alexei needed to be informed of something important in the affairs of their family or the life of the village.

These calls were made from an upturned zinc bath in Irina Raspopova's garden, from where the women had somehow found (or believed) messages to Moscow could best be relayed. The arrangement suited both women since it meant that Irina Raspopova, while being able to play the part of helpful neighbour, also got to know all of Nadia Agafiya's business.

In his mind's eye, Lytkin saw the two women quitting the upturned tub, amid the vegetable crops and heaps of compost, the pair of them annoyed at how the signal had deceived them, clucking and tutting and agreeing that everything in the world these days was either dying or already dead.

Quite suddenly, away from all this, Lytkin became aware of music on the platform… a melody, it seemed, from a violin: a solo that was somehow winding its way towards him over the heads of the waiting passengers…

skilled and confident sweeps of a bow, punctuated with brisk, determined dashes over the instrument's strings.

Lytkin looked for the player.

It was not the 'done' thing to behave showily on the echoey platforms of Moscow's metro stations, particularly at a subterranean cathedral of the line such as Park Pobedy. While, yes, there was a certain hustle-and-bustle nowadays (involving tourists, students and the younger element generally), a degree of decorum was expected from those who were a little older and had taken up 'positions' in the life of the city. To reinforce this, there was the presence of the police: albeit more often than not pale young cadets wrapped in grey greatcoats weightier than themselves, who patrolled the platforms in small and serious squads. On the whole, apart from peak periods (when a mood of abandon and a sense of 'every man and woman for themselves' could, on occasion, break out), people stood soberly, almost as if at mass.

Even so, Alexei now felt stirred to peer. He moved a few steps, leaning and glancing toward what seemed to him to the source of the music.

Beggars and performers of one kind or another were not unusual in the passageways, often boarding and pestering their way through the carriages of trains. Sometimes a saxophonist or harmonica-player would prove passably good. But to hear music like this – proper music by an accomplished hand – was out of the ordinary.

Alexei looked again, lifting himself on his feet.

Despite his discreet craning, he was unable to locate the player.

The arrival of his train drowned the music.

The people of the platform – the usual early evening commuters, peppered with the odd visitor from the country (obvious from their bewilderment and simpler dress) – swarmed to the carriages.

Lytkin – still interested in what he had heard – held back.

At the other end of the platform, a woman – a young woman, so it seemed – hurried over the concourse and into a carriage at the tail end of the train.

Could it be *her*? Lytkin wondered. Or was she someone who'd simply hastened from the halls?

As she disappeared, he stepped aboard.

Inside the train, he looked out at the platform, through the window of the carriage.

The train moved away with a jerk.

At the last moment, before entering the darkness of the oncoming tunnel, Lytkin saw it: the violin.

The instrument was in an archway, seemingly chained by its neck to the rail of a staircase, on perhaps the third or fourth step up.

Hanging.

That night, Lytkin struggled for sleep. The television set of the old woman who lived in the flat above his boomed laughter and applause from a game show that seemed to have no end. He suspected the old lady had fallen asleep in front of it.

He lit a cigarette from a pack beside his bed and went over his mother's phone call. Because of the way everything had to be choreographed in Irina Raspopova's garden (to catch the miracle signal to Moscow), there was seldom any point in dialling back, especially not after forty minutes underground on the metro.

At last, the noise from above him ceased. He put out his cigarette in an ashtray beside his bed and went to sleep.

Next day, at his place of work at the Department, Lytkin received the latest gallery of ghosts he'd been assigned to manage. Their files – for promotion on various platforms of social media – popped up one after the other on the screen in his pod.

First was Mick, a delivery driver who roamed the streets of London in his ageing white van. Mick's picture showed a broken-nosed but affable-looking man in a green body-warmer, with tattoos on his forearm. He gave a matey thumbs-up through the van's window. After him came Clare, a farmer and mother, who raised sheep on a farm in New Zealand. Next was Aadhya, a legal professional in New Dehli, whose relationship status was single. Finally, there was Magnus, a 'poet and free thinker', living 'off grid' on an island off Denmark, according to his fake particulars.

Lytkin set about processing his new charges and putting them to work.

At lunchtime, he left the office.

Instead of walking alone through the nearby park as he normally did, he made his way to the small cathedral he occasionally visited, in a back street not far from the Department's building.

He bought a candle from an old woman at a stall inside the door, which he lit in memory of Father Fyodor. He did this not because he was fond of the priest, but because it was a gesture he felt his mother would have appreciated, particularly as there was no prospect of him returning to the village to attend the funeral.

Studying the small flame in the cathedral's quiet interior, Lytkin found himself wondering at the thickness of the building's walls... how they managed to shut out the rest of Moscow – its crowds, its traffic, its noise – in a way that pleased him.

The aroma of incense – from some earlier mass or prayers – lingered in the aisles.

Lytkin stood for a moment in the nave, looking at the altar. He had lost his orthodoxy since leaving his village. If ever he spoke to anyone about a matter now, it was not to a priest but to a clinician he'd found in a neighbourhood near his own. He was not wholly sure of the man's credentials but addressed him, anyway, as *vrach* (doctor).

Alexei suddenly noticed a movement: a figure… a woman in a headscarf, leaning to an icon in a gallery to his right. The golden paint of the image of a saint issued a dull glow around her head and shoulders in the shadowy light.

Lytkin watched as she kissed the glazing, drew back and crossed herself.

He heard her steps behind him, a whisper of thanks to the old woman in the vestibule and then the cathedral's heavy door being closed.

After some moments, Alexei sensed himself growing cold, despite his coat and the presence in the cathedral of a potbelly stove.

He made for the exit, nodding to the old woman and thanking her quietly as he went.

Outside, the daylight – in the way it sometimes did on late-winter days – hit him with an abrupt, eye-bruising brilliance. The strong, white sun sparked and flared on dirty heaps of frozen snow.

As Alexei raised a hand to shade his eyes, his gaze fell on the railings that served as the curtilage to the cathedral's yard of old – and blackened – monuments.

In the middle of a section of fencing, a violin was hanging by its neck… in the same manner as the instrument he'd seen in the archway at the metro station. It was chained to the arrow-headed upright of a rusted iron rail, with its front facing him.

He walked towards it and studied the suspended instrument.

A ligature of dull, bracelet-like links looped the upper end of the fingerboard below the tuning pegs. Lytkin leaned to see if there was a lock but saw only a dense knot in the chaining. Moisture beaded the instrument's curved body: droplets glistening in the sunlight and streaking the dark wood with watery trails that ran to the chinrest and lower rim. A string on the left side curled loose near its peg at the top of the neck.

Alexei drew back and looked around him for the woman he'd seen in the cathedral. And, if not her, then… anyone. But, save for him, the concourse and yard were empty and still.

In the afternoon, at his desk, Alexei attempted to concentrate on the profiles he'd been given. He saw that Mick, the mythical London van driver, had acquired Followers and Friends.

A commendation appeared on Alexei's screen from Galkin.

Alexei sat up and looked over the wall of his pod, towards the pod occupied by his superior.

He thought for a moment about speaking to him about the violin. Not now, but afterwards, when their shift was done – except that Galkin's shift never seemed to be *done*. He was always there, at his screen. Besides, Alexei was worried about seeming 'green', still the 'country boy', even now.

Maybe the violin was a Moscow 'thing', he thought to himself, in the way that he knew that, in some cities in Europe, lovers left padlocks on bridges and riders hired bicycles which they left behind for others to use.

At the end of his shift, he hurried impatiently to the metro at Park Pobedy.

Setting aside his normal nerves, he hastened past others on the steps of the downward escalator, surprising himself with the determination of his dash and earning a rebuke over the speakers from the attendant in her cubicle at the bottom.

He took up the same position on the platform as the previous evening, and listened, glancing for any sign of the young woman and the violin.

The other passengers were, for the most part, as restrained as usual. Even so, there were small coughs, whispers, snuffles and shuffles, whose distractions annoyed him. As he concentrated with his mind and his ears, he felt the urge to shout and tell them to shut up.

But beyond their flotsam, there was… nothing, it seemed.

He listened again, this time closing his eyes, focussing his mind intently, shutting out the bodies that were around him.

And yes… there was… *something*.

Faint, higher pitched, delicately fine in its impression, but… *there*.

It was different somehow… *sweeter* perhaps, than the melancholy sound of the previous evening.

As with then, the passage of notes evaporated as his train pulled in.

He opened his eyes, hung back as the passengers boarded.

He scanned the platform left and right.

It was empty.

He jumped onto the train as the doors were closing.

In the carriage, he stood so that he might catch sight of the archway with the staircase and handrail where the violin had been hanging the night before.

In the seconds before the train drew into the darkness of the tunnel, he saw the rail. This time it was… bare.

It was dark, sleeting and the evening had grown cold, as Alexei walked to his flat from the metro station that served his neighbourhood. In his kitchen, he warmed cheese soup on a gas ring and looked up violins on the internet of his cell phone.

He scrolled through a website to a section about strings. Some were made of metal and others of catgut. The site explained the latter as an old term for animal intestines. Not those of cats, in fact, but usually from goats and sheep.

Scrolling on, he read that bows were strung with hair from the tails of grey stallions. Thinking about this, he realised that a bow was something he had yet to see. He mused that these had to be things the player, or players, carried with them: perhaps concealed in briefcases, or in the long inner pockets of coats. He realised also that, although he had studied the violin outside the cathedral very closely, he had not actually touched it, and for this failure he rebuked himself (wondering if such an opportunity would present itself again). He looked at a diagram and saw that the left-sided string, which, outside the cathedral, had been curled and broken, was a G – tonally, the instrument's lowest.

He ate his soup from the saucepan. He let the blue flame of the gas ring burn on, preoccupied with the desire to again hear – and see – the violin… and the violinist.

That night, there was no noise from the old lady's TV in the flat above Lytkin's, and the silence disturbed him. As he lay awake, he thought of the cathedral and the woman in the shadows, kissing the icon.

Later, as he slept, he dreamt that the woman's lips were closing on his. At what should have been their moment of contact, however, something kept her at bay, and she drew back. Later still, his 'personalities' from the department – his ghosts – paraded through his mind.

In a particularly troubling passage, he was with Mick in his van in London. They made endless revolutions of a roundabout near Buckingham Palace. Finally, they were on Tower Bridge, the highway ahead of them opening for the passage of a ship on the River Thames below. Mick, ignoring this fact, was all the while sounding off with opinions which he, Alexei, was taking down and Tweeting in the apparent belief that if he could only transmit them before he and his garrulous driver reached the end of the rising road, they would escape the increasingly probable prospect of plummeting to the waters below.

In his dream, Alexei's fingers flew madly at a keyboard on his lap.

Sending, sending, sending…

When he awoke, exhausted and sweating, it was to the sensation of his fingertips drumming his sides beneath his duvet.

He rose and made coffee. Remembering that it was a Saturday, he decided to breakfast in the market near his block.

In a small café, Lytkin ate a bowl of *kasha* grains and, after it, fried eggs on toast. He then wandered the market's stalls.

Grocers presided over stands whose citrus fruits, peppers. tomatoes and bananas were eye-catchingly bright amid the rusty frames and puddled walkways.

He passed an aromatic stand where a woman was busy bagging-up pastries. Near her another stallholder sold *borscht*, ladling the steaming, blood-like brew into containers.

Lytkin found himself entering a part of the market where the fish stalls clustered in a shanty village that was strung and stacked with all manner of fish: specimens that were fresh and oily; others that were frozen, so their sides were like tree bark; still more that hung, pungently smoked, or salted and crisp.

Eels, meanwhile, wriggled in glass tanks of green water, their eyes at times visible against the sides of the vats.

The cleavers of mongers thudded on various piscine heads and tails, while knives sliced open bellies that oozed blood and guts onto boards and slabs.

From time to time, stallholders plucked crayfish from butts and set them to scuttle on beds of ice, with the aim of capturing the attention of customers.

In places, the fish stalls shoaled together so densely that the coarse flanks and stiff fins of their ice-crusted merchandise snagged and stabbed at Alexei as he edged his way through.

Lytkin came to feel as if he were walking the bed of some submerged ravine. The hanging, staring salmon, sterlet, trout and other fish seeming to levitate and drift around him.

Eventually, he reached a stall curtained with catches, where the fish, as well as hanging thickly in bunches, stood across its front on their tails – their manner of doing so making it seem as if they were walking away from the shack, secretly, on tiptoe.

Amid their massed ranks, and to his great confusion, Alexei now, suddenly, saw the violin.

It stood upright between two lock-jawed trout that were coated with ice crystals. Each 'supported' the instrument in the style of creatures on a heraldic device.

Instinctively, Lytkin reached for it.

'You want help?' the monger whose stall it was called abruptly, from some hidden crevice.

The words caused Alexei to pull back.

He noticed a dark hatch, like a letter box, recessed within the stall, amid the carapace of scales and fins. Two eyes, that made him think of the flashing eels he had seen earlier, blinked within.

Alexei looked back at the violin.

He saw that on its fretboard a second string had snapped (his investigations of the previous night telling him that the string was the D, the second lowest and the third highest in the quartet that all violins possessed). It hung loose in ugly fashion, lifting in the draught that blew through the alley where Alexei stood.

For a moment, the sight made him think – more emphatically – of his brother Nikolai and, with him, a subject that the recent events, including the death of Father Fyodor, had brought to the surface of Lytkin's mind. Namely, the summer when, as boys, they had fished the lake near their village. One afternoon, in a fever of excitement, Lytkin had hooked some heavy piscine beast that swam in its deeps. Eventually, the fish ceased fooling with them, broke the line and reclaimed its liberty in the cloudy water beneath the lake's sun-sparkled surface.

It was still *there,* thought Lytkin. *It would never die.*

'How many?' the stall's monger now rasped from his hiding place, the seller unaware – so it seemed – of the instrument interloping so strangely amid the ranks of dead fish on his stall.

Puzzled… perplexed, Alexei stepped back, and away. He hurried on.

The alley before him now seemed to narrow and darken, the vendors and customers he passed becoming noticeably more ragged and poor. The stalls which they tended grew bleak, offering goods of a pathetic kind: worn shoes, cheap bric-a-brac, fake flowers that were shabby and stained.

Earlier, the day had been cold but clear. Now, though, snow began to fall through the gaps between the canopies, whose closeness permitted to the paths ahead of him only a faint and diminishing light.

In the gloom of one of these walkways, Lytkin saw a woman's face… looking back, over her shoulder.

Something told him immediately that it was the young woman from the cathedral *and* the metro… the player of the violin.

Fixing his gaze for a moment, she beckoned him with her bow, its horsehair beautifully luminous in the alleyway's dusky light.

As she moved away, something else showed itself amid the throng in the alley's murk: a cleric's kamilavka…

its black cylinder visible above the heads of the other people who were there. This kamilavka bore the veils of the klobuk, and the material lifted and blew back in the direction of Alexei on a gust of wind that sent the snow that was falling between the canopies of the stalls into a blizzardly swirl.

Alexei stepped after the young woman.

Presently, he came to an opening at what seemed the rear of some tenements, where only the crudest stalls remained.

Amid a small crowd, the woman he'd followed – she was dressed, he could see, in a dark cloak – was fiddling furiously, her hair a mass of fiery ringlets that shook as she played.

She acknowledged him with a flash of her eyes, and soon Alexei was locking arms with the other figures who were there, engaging in all manner of jigs and whirls.

The young woman's use of only two of her instrument's strings somehow caused the dancing to become ever wilder: the high pitch of her extravagant playing demanding *abandon* from those spinning before her, who, never mind the falling snow, grew increasingly frenzied in their claps, whoops, reels and calls.

Alexei felt himself sweating, burning.

He sensed himself streaming with those same rivulets he'd seen running down the woodwork of the violin on the iron railing at the cathedral, his perception growing that the woman was playing not merely the instrument, but *him* – dashing and sweeping her bow over his chest (which, in his mind, was naked)… plucking at his face with her flying, *flaying*, fingers… wounding him till he bled.

Flakes gathered on the young woman's cloak as her left hand flew at the neck of the violin, her right, meanwhile, sending the bow over its strings in quicksilver strokes of astonishing rapidity. The toe of a shoe-cum-boot protruded from under her cloak's hem, compelling her revellers with an ever-quickening beat.

Eventually, Lytkin – delirious – collapsed… the strains of the violin wreathing him, as he fell.

When he awoke, he was on his bed in his flat, fully clothed and shoed. He remembered the scenes at the market. At the same time, he was uncertain, wondering if they had really happened. After feeling his face, he plunged his hands into the pockets of his coat. His fingers encountered smooth orbs, harsh ridges and brittle filaments. Steadily, he drew from the depths of his pockets a strange array of produce: ebony plums, calloused oyster shells, odorous garlic and – to his shock – the moist and severed head of a fish. After these, came potatoes – still earthy – pears, carrots, and honey in a small, clear jar. All of these he lay about him on the bed, in the manner of comforts… offerings. And then he lapsed, once again, into sleep.

He dreamt of vast forests composed not of trees but of violins, all standing upright.

He wandered among them, lost in their endless plantation.

When he came-to properly, he rose and, with images from the events that seemed to have gone before still clouding his mind, he determined that he needed a distraction. Even though it was the weekend, he resolved to go to the Department. If no one else, Galkin would be there, as always – adjusting algorithms, studying graphs. Lytkin would take him some new profiles; nothing flashy or complicated, just good, sturdy ghosts for the Department's machine… ones he'd been thinking of for a while.

In the bottle-green gloom of his block's landing, Alexei now made for the lift. He slid shut the old, latticed gate and pressed the button to descend.

As usual, the lift passed shutters across the shaft at every landing, as it lowered. Except that now, inside each of them, silhouetted with the drab light of the various floors at its back, hung the form of the violin.

At first, he shrank from it, dreading its appearance at each arriving gate. Gradually, though, he stepped forwards and studied the instrument, as it appeared. Through the diamond-shaped metalwork of the lift-car, he looked at the neck… the fingerboard… the sound holes scrolled either side of the bridge.

It was unquestionably the same instrument he had seen at the cathedral and the market, albeit with something different. Only *one* of its strings – the topmost, the E – remained; the other three strings were snapped and in states of horrible disarray, either curling aggressively, or hanging broken and limp.

Finally, having reached the ground floor, he stepped into his block's foyer and out through the building's front door. Music… violin music – barely perceptible yet definitely *there* – emanated from the shaft behind him. The strains seemed to follow him into the night.

Instead of using Park Pobedy, he decided to exit the metro early. He walked the remaining streets to the Department, as snowflakes, like the downy feathers of owls, drifted around him in the evening dark.

He entered a courtyard set back from the street via an unmarked door in a high archway. Passing across its open space, where a small fountain stood frozen, he came to some smaller doors which took him to the staircase to the Department.

On the floor occupied by his unit, Galkin was – as Alexei had expected – the only person present. An aura of grey-blue light rose from his pod on the otherwise darkened floor.

Alexei went to his own pod, collected some printouts relating to his latest proposals and took them to Galkin for his approval.

Galkin didn't look up, instead continuing with his own work as Alexei placed the papers on his desk and withdrew.

Later, he sat watching the light over Galkin's pod in the darkness of the suite.

As Galkin shifted occasionally in front of his computer screen, the beacon of his little world flared and shuttered.

Alexei thought of the phrase Galkin liked to quote in English, about not being able to see the wood for the trees. 'To help people see,' Galkin would remark. 'Irony,' he would continue, by way of explanation. 'We must be the masters of it. We must be the masters of everything. For if *we* are not, somebody else shall be. You see that? You *understand*, Alexei, don't you? Woods, forests – we plant them for the good of the Motherland... for the good of ourselves.'

In time, Lytkin rose quietly and put on his coat.

'Going home?' asked Galkin from his pod. Galkin didn't look up but seemed to intuit that Alexei was by the door.

'I think so,' said Lytkin. 'If you don't mind.'

Lytkin arrived at the metro station at Park Pobedy almost unconsciously. The time of night meant that the station was quiet, and he passed over the vestibule and through the turnstile to the downward escalator without delay.

Somewhat to his surprise, he found himself the only person on the descending conveyor. To his greater surprise, the upwards conveyor – to his left side – was thronged.

A chain of figures rose solemnly, beyond the divide, their forms passing between the white lights of the waist-high wall that separated them from Lytkin. The figures were visible one moment, and then hidden by the dazzle of the individual lights the next: appearing, disappearing, and then appearing again.

First, he saw – coming towards him (though he wondered how it could be) – the young girl from the lake in his village, the one with whom he and his brother had gone into the woods on their way back from the fishing trip that summer. Her small form was scarcely tall enough to show above the barrier, but she was there: her pale features drawing ever closer between the torch-like lights.

Behind her was the much larger figure of Father Fyodor, who – as he climbed upwards – raised a hand and placed his palm on the girl's shoulder – as if to steady her – on the rising escalator.

After them, and on their heels, came a line of figures from his village who he knew could not possibly be there but who were climbing towards him, even so. Their chain included the elderly schoolteacher who surely had died years previously (hadn't his mother telephoned him about the fact?); the old station master with his antique pocket-watch – he rose there also.

Behind the station master stood various ancient villagers and elderly, creased-faced farmers – some Alexei seemed to remember, some that he did not… all processing towards him, as if on their way to a meeting, and looking out-of-place in the city world of Moscow – if that was where Lytkin still was.

The young girl was passing Alexei now, right beside him, in a gap between the white lights.

Her head turned towards him: her features empty of any conspicuous emotion yet, somehow, sorrowful, it seemed.

Behind her, and level with Lytkin now, came the large, spade-bearded countenance and black-robed form of Father Fyodor, in the dark pillar of his kamilavka.

Lytkin turned and looked upwards, after them, as their figures rose – high above him – towards the circle of light at the top of the slope.

And he saw now what the girl was holding in her left hand (hidden as it had been by the barrier between them): a dark case for an instrument that he knew could only be a violin.

At the last moment, before her form became diffuse (due to her altitude and the whiteness of the lights), she turned back... and stared.

Lytkin reached the platform in a trance-like state. He had the feeling that he was no longer at the station – or even in Moscow. The sense that he had was one of submergence – as if he were in the depths of the lake outside his village. He remembered – precisely – how, on that summer's day, he and his brother had fought with the fish – some monstrous carp of the deep; how it had snapped their line, so that – after all of their efforts and excitement – the line blew limp and useless on the water. He remembered also – how could he not? – their accidental meeting, by the woods, on their way home, of the girl... the girl from Moscow, who was staying in the village with her grandparents for the summer. And then – though he did not want to – he remembered and saw, again, what happened in the woods: the limbs... the light – vivid, stark; 'events' *not* lost to the birches and the pines.

A heat shimmer gave Park Pobedy's platform a molten, watery look.

Lytkin's ears seemed to hear a loud, sustained, high-pitched scream.

A train roared in... and onwards – a through train that was destined not to stop.

Lytkin stepped from the platform and met it, even so.

'The woods,' he said, in a whisper.

In their village, a red sunset spilled at the shoulders of Nadia Agafiya and Irina Raspopova, as the former, standing on the latter's upturned tub, heard nothing from her son's cell phone beyond the voice of a young woman stating – again and again – that it had not been possible to connect them.

Eventually, Nadia Agafiya and Irina Raspopova gave up – Nadia Agafiya stepping down from the tub.

Walking through her garden, back to Raspopova's wooden house, she told her neighbour that her son had never been the same since moving to Moscow... that he was, when all was said and done, no more than a ghost to her now. Perhaps that was what Moscow was: a whole, restless city of them, she wondered aloud. The young woman on the phone had been so cold (Nadia Agafiya thought to herself), telling her, over and over, that she was wasting her time. Had the girl no heart?

In the fields beyond Raspopova's house, a mass of rooks rose noisily from the trees and curled upwards in the sky in a great, black, cylindrical cloud.

This startled the women, who hurried indoors, fearing rain.

If only Father Fyodor had been alive, thought Nadia Agafiya: *he* would have known; *he* would have explained everything. Nothing in a village like theirs escaped the eyes and ears of its priest.

Flatlining

You could call it my own Cold War.

Day after day my thermometer taunts me… with a reading that's always the same.

Minus 22: the bad news temperature.

Fixed, locked, stuck there.

Bad – *evil*, some might say – for its cruel, hair's breadth proximity to Minus 23: the good news temperature.

At Minus 23, your brain – so I've read – starts to zing. Cross that threshold and you'll paint like Stravinsky, run the 100 metres like Dostoyevsky, bake cakes like Kandinsky, and write plays in the manner of Yuri Gargarin (when he wasn't doing his glass-helmeted thing out there in space).

Or so it's been said.

My treacherous tube (with its gruesome gradations) clings, like a parasite, to the concrete exterior of my flat… *needling* me through my kitchen window.

You know, I once sat there… in my kitchen… for 24 hours, with only the buzz of my refrigerator (irony of ironies) for company, eyeballing the mercury through the window (confident I'd catch sight of some crafty rise or fall).

But not a dart… not a flicker… not a pulse… nothing.

Minus 22.

All day long.

My neighbours have precisely the same thermometers as me.

They were screwed into our walls some date around 1970.

I suspect they were the product of one of those Planned Economy cities not famous for quality control. A Thermometer City where they made thermometers and precious little else.

Of course, I can sympathise with the workers there – how bored they must have been! Their tedium causing them, understandably, to turn out the odd bad batch

221

(of several hundred thousand) while their minds were focused elsewhere: some titbit overheard in the queue at the post office, or perhaps the new curtains put up by a neighbour – you know the kind of thing.

And let's be fair, who really – beyond taking home a wage – would want to work in a plant like that? (I'll avoid the obvious joke about it being enough to give anyone a temperature.)

At times, I've wondered if in our neighbourhood we aren't all stuck on some default factory setting – *Outlook Gloomy* – that we've failed – or don't know how – to adjust.

I can't disclose my sources but there've been occasions when I've known for an absolute fact that – out there – it's been Minus 30, if not colder. Days... weeks even... when the Moscow River has been frozen from shore to shore. One guy traipsed over it to our office in Kropotkinskaya, for example (having sensibly checked by cell phone with his wife, who'd gone on ahead).

So, you see why I'm suspicious.

More than once, I've abandoned my duties at my workplace, and raced home (chasing trains and flagging down cars), convinced my cheating gauge has been ebbing and flowing (and up to all sorts) like crazy, behind my back.

In the course of these dashes, I've bumped old ladies aside and sent cats flying from the stairs of my block.

Yet, when I've reached my kitchen window, the story has always been the same: Minus 22 (as if set not in liquid, but in stone).

Please don't think I'm mad, but I've begun to wonder if the thing has ears... if it hears my keys when I slide them in the locks.

I've taken to turning them softly... slipping off my boots, as silently as I can manage, on the mat in the hall.

Sometimes, I pass the kitchen door and make a feint for the bathroom... only to cut right back – fast as an arrow – to the kitchen and its window.

Yet that damned, demonic thermometer is always one step ahead: stuck... stock-still ... there... motionless: Minus 22... even though I absolutely *know* it's been dancing all over the place in my absence – *mercurially*, you might say.

I can tell you that I have, in all honesty, considered climbing the front of our building... drainpipe to drainpipe, balcony to balcony... like some sneaky thief of birds' eggs or jewels... *just* to get the better – for once – of the blasted, bloody thing.

How wonderful that would be!

You know, in winters like this present one, it can feel as if we're on the Moon here. Apart from car engines, pumping out fumes, the only sound sometimes is the cawing of the crows. To my eyes, the snow – at certain hours – can seem grey and not white at all.

One day, quite recently, some sunshine broke through. And, on the pavement, I met an old lady dressed all in black.

She had set down her shopping to raise her face to the sun (her creased countenance surely as old as the walls of the Kremlin).

Her eyelids were closed and she was smiling and whispering, as if in receipt of some joyous message.

Given her age, I would say that this private epistle could have been an epiphany of some kind, from those saints on their icons that old ladies like to pray to.

Had she been younger – much younger – it's conceivable it might have been a piece of *samizdat* – as some call it – to secretly pass on.

My thermometer, of course, was having none of it.

'It's Minus 22... you dumb bastard,' it sniggered, when – after seeing the old lady – I went in and looked.

'Don't go getting any ideas – idiot.'

One day I'll drink that bloody mercury, I tell you.

And then we'll see who's boss.

Nesting Season

Storks. Her father would talk of nothing else, said Natalya Nikonova. His head was full of them – and their nest. The one he was convinced they were building behind his back. He was in hospital – a serious matter to do with his heart – but he didn't give a damn about that. The storks were all he cared about. He'd been getting out of bed, calling her at night, talking endlessly on a cell phone as he paced up and down his ward, hooked to one of those drips on wheels that trundled with him as he spoke.

Recently, a nurse had seized the phone and snapped down the line that this behaviour of his would have to stop. There were others to consider, the nurse said, not least his fellow patients and staff.

Natalya Nikonova had heard cries in the background (aimed at her father): 'Shut up, you old fool!', and her father, responding, 'Shut up yourself! Fat arse!' After what sounded like a scuffle, he had come back on the line till, finally, it went dead as he was speaking (… about storks, of course).

Semyon Solnikov didn't really know Natalya Nikonova beyond that she was a neighbour who lived on the floor situated two above his and therefore shouldn't even have been there, at his door, badgering him about birds in the way that she was. It wasn't the first time she'd loitered there. As he turned his key in his topmost lock, Solnikov wondered what her *real* intent was. He sensed her peering over his shoulder into the hall of his flat – at his calendar of scenes of Rostov-on-Don, his barometer whose meteorological terms were in a curling French script, the corner – also – of his bed… visible through an internal door that stood ajar.

'It's their nesting season,' continued Natalya Nikonova. 'My father's convinced they're going to block his chimney, so that when he next lights his fire or stove the whole place will go up. That's what happened at a neighbour's when I was a young girl. I'm going to go there, to make sure the place is all right. Light the fires. Keep the pots warm. Once those storks feel my heat on their arses, they'll soon fly off.'

'Very sensible, I'm sure,' Solnikov said, stepping inside his flat. And then, not even realising that he was speaking (and intending nothing of any consequence at all): 'Let me know if there's anything I can do.'

He closed his door, turned all three keys in their locks and breathed out… heavily.

That night, Solnikov sat in bed – smoking.

He was restless over a move Gennady Golubkin had made at their chess club (prior to that business on the landing with Natalya Nikonova about storks).

Solnikov had found Golubkin's attack strangely irresistible. It had sent him to a rare and seemingly unavoidable defeat, his pieces falling as if cut off at the knees by some great, sweeping scythe.

Solnikov thought of Natalya Nikonova's father. He pictured him: gaunt in his hospital bed, consumed by the matter of the storks, the veritable bell tower of sticks and twigs the old man felt sure they were building on his chimney pot.

Three days later, against all his judgment but somehow powerless to prevent it, Solnikov found himself boarding a train to Natalya Nikonova's home district (having received a message via Elizaveta Entina, the caretaker of the block, in which Nikonova had called on him to honour his *pledge* of assistance in the matter of the storks).

When the taxi dropped Solnikov outside her father's house, which stood down a lane on the edge of a country village, Natalya Nikonova was waiting. Not in the coat and headscarf in which Solnikov normally saw her but in the costume of her province: a white, lace-trimmed blouse and an embroidered red dress, her hair woven in plaits.

Solnikov saw no sign of storks, but Natalya Nikonova immediately urged him onto the roof of the property.

'We must strike while they are gone,' she called, as Solnikov – well past the first flush of youth – hoisted himself upwards, with difficulty.

'Scoot to the stack and throw me their sticks,' Nikonova instructed him. 'Eggs, too, if any are there.'

Solnikov edged uneasily along the ridge of the roof, as if astride a yakutian horse in a plain of deep, winter snow.

'Their nest? Is it there? Can you see it?' Natalya Nikonova called out.

Solnikov continued carefully along the roof's apex, queasily remembering his distate for heights. He thought how strangely different Natalya Nikonova looked… below him… away from the drab landings of their block: as if she were about to dance the *kalinka*, or maybe milk a cow.

Poor cow, he thought (and he didn't mean Natalya Nikonova).

Through no more than half-open eyes, Solnikov saw the nest.

It was huge… resting on top of the chimney, like some great, big platter.

He took hold of and threw down its sticks and its straws: singly at first, then in bundles that fell around Natalya Nikonova, like showers of spears.

She gathered them hungrily and piled them outside the front of the house.

When there was nothing left to be thrown, Solnikov climbed down, and Natalya Nikonova filled him a bath of hot water inside the house.

He declined an offer by her to birch his back with certain of the twigs they had salvaged.

Having taken the precaution of wedging the bathroom door shut, by means of a chair against its handle,

Solnikov reclined in the steaming and pleasant waters of the bathtub, drinking black tea.

As he did so, his thoughts turned again to Golubkin and the chess match.

Solnikov had known Golubkin for twenty-five years. Golubkin was a tailor who'd been forced to hang up his needle and thread. His competence in terms of his ability to cut a fine suit or coat, and to effect adjustments and repairs, wasn't in doubt. The problem lay in his inability to direct the correct garments to their rightful owners. Across Moscow, men were wearing clothes that belonged to someone else. A plumber who had, for example, asked Golubkin to patch-up some overalls would find, on receiving or taking home his parcel, that he was actually in possession of a suit meant for some swank in Khamovniki or Rublyovka. Rumour had it that Golubkin's late wife, Galina, had finally persuaded him to retire when an army colonel, who'd received some new decoration to be attached to a tunic, received, by return post, half a dozen old socks. All darned beautifully, of course.

Solnikov rose from his tub.

The now cold water fell from him noisily in the quiet of Natalya Nikonova's father's house.

In the bedroom that Natalya Nikonova had shown him, Solnikov lit a cigarette and lay in a towel upon the bed.

Whilst he was still contemplating (in a distracted manner) Golubkin's strange route to check and checkmate, Natalya Nikonova entered the bedroom, hitched up her dress and straddled his loins.

Soon she was bouncing on him energetically.

Mentally, at least, Solnikov (who was – when at work – a civil servant in the Moscow ministry for road salt, and – at home – a bachelor in late middle-age with an interest in barometric pressures) remained detached from Nikonova's engagement of him.

All he could think of was Golubkin's hand… slapping the clock beside their board at the chess club, and, after that, his own hand slapping the clock back.

Never mind the vigour of his seductress, Solnikov imagined himself not beneath the buttocks of Natalya Nikonova (which were stretching and compressing like generous balls of dough) but on the chessboard in his match with Golubkin… *physically* on it, that is, dressed in the garb of a knight.

Solnikov saw himself wandering the board… crossing its chequered squares… a sword and a shield in his hands.

In this vision of Solnikov's, the fingers of his rival, Golubkin – which were pale and long – manoeuvred his queen first this way, then that. Golubkin did so as if he were engaged in some particularly intricate piece of embroidery or stitching, the art or skill of which came to him quite naturally, so it seemed to Solnikov. Golubkin's queen demolished Solnikov's defences utterly, taking his own hapless figures, one by one.

Wandering as he was, mentally and also, in a sense, *physically* on the board, Solnikov, who had never previously been beaten by Golubkin, came to see that his defeat had been due to one thing and one thing only – the total chaos of Golubkin's attack, which had been both senseless and… immaculate, like the tailoring of Golubkin's twilight years.

By contrast, his *own* moves, Solnikov now realised, while undeniably methodical and effective in their way, like, say, the distribution of salt on the highways of Moscow's Boulevard Ring, had also been entirely predictable, prosaic and machine-like.

Solnikov now lifted his hands to Natalya Nikonova's shoulders, causing him to think of her for a moment as if *she* were on the chess board that he had envisioned (albeit that her hips were now working on top of him like pistons in some Soviet-era metal-pressing plant).

'Queen takes…' Solnikov murmured beneath her, whilst looking upwards, quite vacantly, from the mattress of the bed.

'Yes!?' Nikonova gave out, with a shriek.

'Knight!' Solnikov, his voice now rather more energised, cried back (as, for him now, all the pieces of Golubkin's mysterious victory – at last – fell into place).

His eyes gleamed, under the rising and falling form of Natalya Nikonova.

'Yes!' responded Nikonova, who still surged and sank above him albeit that she did so now with a heavy, slow relish – her body like that of an express train that had arrived at a station of the line yet was not quite at a stop.

'Shakh!' Solnikov shouted, his voice much louder, and with a look on his face that seemed to marry both agony and ecstasy.

'Maty!' Natalya Nikonova screamed – to the rafters – in response; her body shuddering like a wind-caught larch in the forests that Solnikov had seen through the windows on his railway journey.

'Maty!' Solnikov almost chimed with her, a second late, so that their voices overlapped, as if in an echo.

'Eureka!' he then added, with a gasp (in reference to what he could now see had been Golubkin's chaotic route to glory).

And, with this epiphany, a beatific quietness overcame him on the bed, like the stillness of a boiling pot whose contents had overflowed.

Downstairs in the house, Natalya Nikonova's father, who, unbeknown to his daughter, had discharged himself from hospital (with his stork-induced torment unconquered), stepped back from the fire he'd laid *not* in the hearth of the kitchen but on the kitchen table – using the kindling he'd found helpfully piled outside the property.

'Let this burn your arses to Hell, you bastard birds!' he called out, shaking his fist at the ceiling (unaware of the coupling of those other lovebirds in their nest above his own throbbing and confused head).

Natalya Nikonova was first onto the sill of the bedroom window, her arms outstretched in the sleeves of her white blouse. As the smoke and flames rose around her, Solnikov gave her a push, and she plummeted to the vegetable patch in the garden below.

When Solnikov jumped after her, a gust blew back the robe he had put on, so that, momentarily, it both exposed his lower half and filled-out around him, in the manner of a parachute.

As the house blazed behind them, Natalya Nikonova wept angry tears, on all fours among the leaves of beetroots and radishes. Solnikov staggered beside her, dragging his feet in cucumber clogs.

From the furrows of the vegetable patch, they saw – through the windows of the house – the figure of Natalya Nikonova's father, who was running around in the kitchen, flapping his arms – as if in weird mimicry of a bird – his hair and head awfully aflame.

Grasping two bean canes (in a manner that made him look – in his cucumber 'footwear' – like some caricature of a cross-country skier), Solnikov wondered why he had ever forsaken the four walls of his flat: the safety of his 'castle defence'.

Amid the mad scene, he remembered an article (of a somewhat arcane kind) that he had read: a theory that the *lad'ya* (the chess piece called in English 'the rook') owed its origins to a giant bird of prey: the *rukh*… of Persian mythology.

For her part, Natalya Nikonova – mired as she was in the earth and crops of the vegetable patch – sobbed and cursed the costume she had asked Golubkin, the tailor, to make. Why could she not simply have continued her spinsterhood and her employment as a secretary at the sweet factory? How she now longed to smell again those boiling vats, with their odours she had so foolishly affected to despise. Never again would she thrust her bill into the life of any man.

Beyond the village, a pair of storks – that might have been mates – swallowed rabbits and mice in a marshy field by a wood.

Moonbeams fell on the great, scissor-like bills of the birds.

Between feasting, the storks 'clattered' these, so that the sound of their *clacking* carried through the darkness of the evening, to the bonfire that the old, wooden house of Natalya Nikonova's father had become.

It was an odd and eerie sound – almost a kind of laughter – that, as the floors and walls of the house burned and collapsed, seemed to get louder... and closer.

Memoir of a Moscow Dog-Killer

It began with the granny… one late afternoon in the early part of that summer… the day's last sunlight on her shoulders, like a shawl of amber and ruby flames.

My good friend Sergei and I had been making for the stairs of our block when she leant out from her door and, with a curl of her finger, called us in from the landing.

She seated herself at a table laid with a dark red cloth, in the lounge of her flat, which was fusty and dim, save for the sinking sunlight.

A little out of breath and with a voice dry as an old pine nut, she came to her point directly, and asked if we would 'take care' of her dog.

The dog was in a basket in the corner of the room, its head and mouth on the edge of the wicker.

The animal looked at Sergei and me as if it were listening to the granny and understood the words that the old lady was saying.

It was a good dog, a nice dog, she said, but it was old, like her, and not so good on its legs. What was more, said the granny, she didn't have the money for a doctor for the dog and there was no one she knew who could… 'take care' of it.

Would *we* take care of it? she asked.

Under her fingers, on the tablecloth – holding our attention as much as her words – were notes of money.

The granny's eyes, which were watery (not in a tearful way but in the way that old people's eyes can be), stared into mine.

She said to us that we were nice boys from good homes and she felt sure she could trust us to take care of her dog.

Her twig fingers began to push the rouble bills towards us across the tablecloth.

I sensed Sergei looking at me as the granny fixed me with her eyes.

I stepped forward and took the notes from under her right hand. Without a word, Sergei then did the same, regarding those which were under her left.

At my nod, he took hold of the dog, under its middle, and lifted it from its basket.

Other than raising its head to the granny for one moment, the dog offered no resistance and did not make a sound.

We didn't ask the granny its name, or how many years it had, or any other questions of a personal nature like that. We just took the dog, and the money – and left.

To be honest (and honesty – as they say – is the best policy) we really didn't know what to do with the dog. We took it to the basement of our block, which Sergei and I used as a meeting place – our 'secret place', if you like. None of the adults went there unless there'd been a failure of some kind with the boiler, or they wanted to dump an old mattress or a sofa, of which they no longer had need.

Sergei and I smoked a cigarette and talked about the dog, which lay on its side by the boiler, whose system – at that time of year – had been turned off.

Sergei got out the rouble bills he'd had from the granny and counted them… or tried to (he was never the cleverest of teenagers when it came to things like that).

From time to time, the dog lifted its head and looked at him, as Sergei bumbled through his sum.

After some while, we left to go back to our parents' flats. Turning out the light, we left the dog there in the dark (hoping, I suppose, that by morning it might have died or found its way out and been off with itself, maybe joining up with some strays and generally doing dog 'things' with other dogs).

The next day, however, it was still there.

So Sergei strangled it, as I held it down.

To be honest, it didn't put up much of a fight. Like the granny had said: it was a very old dog, a bag-of-bones dog.

Privately, I was amazed at the power that my friend Sergei had in his hands: the dog's eyes going all stary, as Sergei gripped it by the throat.

When Sergei let his fingers go, the dog seemed dead. But we weren't sure if it was *totally* dead. We were just boys and we didn't know how you took the pulse of a dog, or things of a scientific nature like that.

I didn't like to, because it had a smell that was unpleasant, but I put my ear to its side and listened.

There was no sound in the dog that I could hear, but it was hard to be sure. There were noises down in that basement: the rushing of water in pipes and the sounds (albeit low) of TVs, washing machines and goings-on in the flats of the floors above.

One thing we knew for sure was that we didn't want that old mutt in our place. So we rolled it in a rug that somebody had dumped down there and took it upstairs, to the roof.

Once there, we were uncertain what to do with our 'parcel': how to 'take care of it', so to speak. Certain of the residents grew things up there come summer: tomato plants, cucumbers, flowers and the like. But there was insufficient soil in which to bury the dog. So I told Sergei to throw it off the roof and be done with it. And that is what he did.

We watched from the edge as its body fell – all twenty-four floors.

An utterly senseless act, I know.

For one thing, the dog must have dropped right past the granny window.

Anyway, we stood there… looking.

The dog lay on the ground, near the front porch of our block. It didn't lift its tail, or bark, or do anything that showed life. There also appeared to be a mess in its middle... where its belly had broken and its insides had come out. So we felt pretty sure that it was *truly* dead.

Satisfied that no one had seen us, we went downstairs and out of the block's backdoor, to go and mooch by the metro station and see what – if any – new movie posters had been put up.

That wasn't the end of the episode though. A day or so later, we heard that the granny had discovered the dog – there outside the flats – as she carried her shopping home from the market.

Apparently, she had a heart attack and died, right there, next to the dog.

As crazy as it sounds, that's how it all started, that summer... our season of killing dogs (and – by special arrangement – other surplus and troublesome pets).

What happened next was that a few days later – with school now 'out' – Sergei and I were walking for no particular reason through our neighbourhood park. A woman I half-recognised from our block came towards us and made a big thing of nearly fainting and falling over, in front of us, forcing us to a stop.

She 'struggled' her way to a bench by the side of the path and waved her hand up and down in front of her face, as if gasping for breath.

The fact was that this woman did not have a good name in our block and only some weeks previously she had stepped from her door to shout and swear at Sergei, myself and certain other teenagers, for congregating on 'her' landing in a way she did not like.

Even so, good manners obliged me to enquire after her health.

'A turn,' she said. 'That is all. I shall survive.'

Sergei and I went to walk on... only for the woman to become agitated all over again.

'But maybe not,' she said. 'Who can tell? With this terrible exhaustion… of my nerves… that I have.'

We watched as she took a tissue from her bag and dabbed at her cheeks: a needless task, I thought, since they were as hard and dry as the concrete exterior of our block.

Again, I went to walk on with Sergei, only for the woman to quickly pull from her bag some cigarettes, whose pack was already open, with the ends of those inside extending towards us.

'Go on. Help yourselves. Please,' said the woman.

And we did.

She sprang from the bench and lit our cigarettes as we cupped our hands around hers, which were thin and bony, like the claw feet of a hen.

'Ah, you are *b-i-g* boys,' she said, smiling and showing her yellowy teeth.

We stood there and smoked.

'Yes, it is the exhaustion,' she began again. 'Oh, how I long for the quiet life.'

Once more, I was about to step away, only for the woman to re-begin her babble.

'The dog,' she said. 'The noisy dog. *Who* will save me… who will save *us*… from its terrible noisiness? What I would give,' she said, collapsing back on the bench, 'if there were someone who could *take care of* this terrible problem.'

Since this woman was a near-neighbour – albeit not of my storey – I happened to know the dog that she meant. It was a little, noisy thing that barked all day and all night. Many were the times I had lain in my bed on weekends, and before school, cursing it, or praying for my father's enormous snores to begin their volcanic rumble and drown-out its yaps and yelps.

'It is driving me crazy,' said the woman – now with her hands over her face. 'It is driving *everybody* crazy. Is there no one who will perform a service for the people these days? Where are our leaders? Is this what our fathers and mothers fought for?'

I looked at Sergei.

He waved away a wasp.

I looked back at the woman.

'For taking care of this dog,' I said, 'there would be a… reward?'

'A reward? Oh *yes*. Most definitely. A handsome one. Both here and in heaven. Thanks Be to God.'

I looked again at Sergei.

He spat on the path.

'We will…' I said (pausing for a moment to look at her) '… take care of this problem.'

'Can you *really* do that? Do you *mean* it?' said the woman, her green eyes lighting in a way that was bright and fierce, her claw-hands clasping tightly at the top of her bag.

Without further delay, the woman told us that the couple whose dog it was took it down to the front door at six o'clock every morning, so the dog could cock its leg. That was when we should *strike*, she said.

I had reservations about rising at such an early hour, but I thought about the easy money that had come our way from the granny. Besides, Sergei would be with me and do the 'necessaries', I knew.

'Come to me when it is done,' said the woman, her emerald eyes all a-gleam.

Next morning, Sergei and I waited behind the trash skips outside the front of our block. As amateurish as this may sound for 'assassins', he was armed with a heavy frying pan that belonged to his mother.

The man referred to by the woman appeared on the block's doorstep in his dressing gown and pyjamas, just as she had predicted.

He told the dog to go for its leak, while he stood there, farted and lit a cigarette.

Little by little, sniffing and pissing, the dog came around the corner of the skips to where Sergei and I silently lurked.

On seeing us, a confused look came over its face, as if it were thinking, *To Bark or Not To Bark?* That *is The Question.*

We heard the man coughing on his cigarette on the doorstep.

And that was when I signalled to Sergei to strike with the pan.

He whacked the little mutt right in the gob.

Before the dog knew what had hit it, Sergei – needing no encouragement from me – smashed it again: this time above the eyes.

And the dog went over, on its side, and lay still.

The man on the step – who we could see from around the edge of the skip – finished smoking and now started calling for the dog.

Sergei and I didn't move, or whisper a word, in case he should come over and find us. But he just stood there, on the step, calling 'Natalya…Natalya' and whistling a bit. Then he stopped and went inside, probably because he had to get to work.

A couple of minutes later the curtains on the flat where he and his woman lived flew open, and the woman was standing there in the window in her nightdress (which was not at all sexy) looking out.

Then she, too, came down to the front door and called out for the dog – 'Natalya… Natalya!' – and she looked up and down the street while calling, 'Baby… Baby!' (which made Sergei and me snigger somewhat, I must admit).

Then the woman went back inside also.

We didn't have much of an idea what to do with this noisy dog we'd silenced. So we threw it in one of the skips. Sergei's father was a dustman and Sergei said the bins would be emptied that morning and all of the trash would be taken to some big dump out of Moscow, where no one would find this dog that was now dead because it would be buried under a load of shit like old mattresses and broken vacuum cleaners and shit like that.

That night, we knocked the door of the woman we had seen in the park. We said her problem had been taken care of and could we please now have our reward. But it turned out that this woman was a sly thing and she kept the chain on her door and she said through the crack that she had seen what we had done with the granny's dog – how we had thrown it from the roof and everything and how the granny herself had died – and that if we didn't shut up and clear off she would tell our parents and the police, and our families would be thrown out of the block and we boys would be put in jail.

Then she shut her door on us.

The bitch.

This deceitfulness by the woman with the claw hands didn't seem fair at all. It was a total disgrace, Sergei and I agreed. Who knew where a witch like that might stop?

One thing I learned pretty early in my life is that if you want people to take you seriously you sometimes have to teach them a lesson.

So it was that, the following night, Sergei and I hid ourselves behind the door to the basement steps, where we looked out on the block's downstairs hall, and waited.

We watched as the women of the block did their thing of putting down food for their cats and talking nonsense to the lazy animals, which ignored these women completely and just crouched there filling their faces, with their bellies on the floor.

We waited till the sly woman (who we knew from past sight to be the keeper of one of these creatures) had set about this same nightly ritual, with a tin and a dish. Then we watched her go around the corner to see old Izolda Kuklova, our block's caretaker (no doubt with a complaint about something… sour cow that she was).

Anyway, as soon as she was gone, Sergei sprang out and cut off her cat's fluffy grey tail. This he did with his father's sharp cleaver: its thick blade going *chunk* as it went through that cat's tail and came down on the linoleum floor.

Together, we stuffed this 'scalp' in that evil bitch's post box in the hall, then hurried back and hid behind the basement door once more.

You won't be surprised to hear that a big commotion broke out among all of those cats (on account of Sergei's action).

Spying through the crack of the door, we watched as that cheating witch came back and shouted at the other cats. (I swear to God we saw her kick one up its arse and pull another by its tail.)

She snatched up her animal and put it in a carrier that had a gate on the front, as if it were its own little jail.

They then headed up to their place in the lift – that ghastly, green-eyed snake of a female cursing all of the other cats, in the most unholy language, as the lift's doors closed behind her.

In my bed that night, I pictured her – behaving in the way that I had no doubt a woman like her did: ears and claws to her walls, listening to her neighbours and writing letters of poison to our local police. And yet, I felt a great sense of superiority, as I lay there on my pillow, knowing what Sergei and I had done: 'the righteousness of our cause', it might be said.

Next morning, she went down to the hall to collect her mail from her box… and – Holy Moley! – how her screams *rang* through our block. They were bloodcurdling, indeed. All Moscow must have heard her. It was wonderful – a truly beautiful dawn, believe me.

Sergei and I never heard anything from the woman after that. In fact, if she ever saw us, she crossed the street, and hurried on.

Serve her right, for her shameful example to our nation's youth!

About this time, there was much turmoil in my home life. My father walked out on my mother and me.

He had a job dressing-up as Stalin and smiling for the cameras of tourists at our city's various places of cultural interest. My mother said it had gone to his head. When he left, she moaned and groaned around our flat all day and all night, smoking one cigarette after the other.

The cruel thing was that this job of my father's had been my mother's idea (after he was fired from his *real* position at the brick factory because of what his manager complained was his *complete inability* to make an acceptable brick). He came home drunk from the factory social club one night… and there was my mother, busy as a bee, sewing the hammer and sickle onto an old uniform that had been my great-grandfather's. My mother told my father he had always looked a little like Stalin. (She said he had his hair, or eyebrows, or something ridiculous like that.)

They danced around the kitchen and my father squeezed my mother's backside and winked at me in a way that I found disagreeable. They also giggled, which made things worse. To be honest, I found it hard to believe they were adults. As I was leaving the kitchen, my father was telling my mother how he would grow a bigger moustache – if she would polish his boots.

And so his great act began.

For a while, he was earning good money. He posed for photos with foreign tourists and country people from Siberia, who he said were impressed to meet a *personality* like him. When a new fish stall opened at our market, he cut a ribbon – and people even clapped. He wasn't the only Stalin in town. That much I knew. I myself had seen several of them on the excursions I took from time to time as a teenager approaching adulthood who was keen to find out what the world – or at least Moscow – had to offer to a young man-about-town. Many of these imitators were very impressive. Our society had, I knew, moved forward. Yet when I saw them I couldn't help but think that we were also somehow ruled by, or from, our country's past.

My father insisted that *he* was the best – the one customers looked out for. He said there were guys who did Brezhnev and certain of the other old leaders, but – in his opinion – no one wanted them anymore because they weren't sexy… and being sexy was what it was all about, in this new world in which we were now living.

One night, he was on Moscow TV – a half-minute (if that) at the end of the news. A woman with lots of hair and red lips – who 'did' the weather – interviewed him in a doorway where he sometimes hung about and drank black tea when it rained.

Closing the show, the head news reader made an unfunny joke about how it would be good if they could get Stalin to order some nice weather for us (which the weatherwoman, for some inexplicable reason, found completely hilarious, as if it were the funniest thing she had ever heard).

My father made a recording of this nonsense (that no one else was allowed to touch). One day, he stayed home and watched it over and over until the machine got really hot and the tape inside became tangled. He pulled at it in a temper, and it got completely stuck. Some short while after, he left home… and never really came back.

I saw him one time, in his uniform, feeding ducks on the big pond at Chistye Prudy.

He said certain of the other ex-leaders had grown jealous of his success and had joined in league against him. He'd had to leave his best places and find work in other areas. And now he was lucky if he got two pictures a day. It was a terrible comedown for someone in his position, he said.

I had my doubts about the truthfulness of what he was saying. But he was my father…

He didn't ask one word about my mother and me.

I suppose that was when, and why, it became important… the killing of the dogs, I mean.

There was a boy in our year at school by the name of Vasily, who was not at all liked. The cause of his unpopularity was his cleverness. He didn't live in our block and wasn't in any sense a friend of Sergei or of mine, but his cleverness and his isolation caused me to think he would be useful in our activities.

I invited him to attend what I described as 'a board meeting' for a small business that I said I was 'getting off the ground'. I told him to be discreet and, above all, to say nothing to his parents.

He showed up in his thick glasses at our basement one evening, as asked.

As I suspected, his friendless state – both at school and in his block – made him keen to join us in our fledgling concern. He needed no encouragement from me and quickly outlined what he felt to be 'the array of opportunities' in the new Russia that our leaders were building.

The key thing we needed to do, Vasily told us, was to advertise (but in a way that kept our own involvement 'at arm's length'). When I asked him to explain what he meant by this, he took a pad and a pen from his briefcase (he cut a mature figure for schoolboy, it has to be said) and he began to write on a sheet.

'There!' he said, handing me what he had written.

Pet Problems?
Permanent Solutions.
Enquire Within.

'Very good,' I said, impressed with the neatness of his writing and his spellings (which all seemed to be correct). 'But enquire *where* exactly?'

That, he said, was where we would have to use our brains. The location would need to be a prominent one but entirely *un*connected with ourselves. Enquiries could be left there in writing with a figure who could be trusted and who would receive a benefit for the use of his or her address. This was a strategy used by many companies that required confidentiality, Vasily assured me, both in our own country and elsewhere.

And – as the fates would have it – I knew the very person and place.

According to my mother, Alexei Pirogov was 'a pervert'. On no account – she told me, more than once – was I to go anywhere near his store. Naturally, I ignored her, as was to be expected of any self-respecting youth; besides, where else was a teenager like me to obtain his supply of 'everyday essentials': cigarettes, vodka (when the opportunity permitted) and imported magazines with educational photographs of women.

Pirogov's was truly a mean place: a shitty little shop of the kind left over from Soviet days, which had the sole advantage of being near our block, drawing its custom mainly from people who were too feeble or lazy to make their ways to the supermarkets situated on the parade near the metro station. He himself was a tall and skinny man with a grey pallor and a few isolated strands of brown hair stuck down with oil on the top of his head, like dead grass in swamp water. He wore a white coat, and his principal occupation, when not serving in the most sleazy manner, was the slicing of cooked sausages and other meat – as thinly as he could possibly manage – with a machine he had, behind a counter on one side of the shop.

Yet, to me, Pirogov had been… 'useful'. Disgusting as I considered him, he liked me, I knew. I understood this from the way that, when unable to steal what we wanted from his store, Sergei and I actually bought, with our pocket money, some small trifles that we fancied. At such times, Pirogov would always insist on me having the useless few kopeks of change, placing them in my palm with his horrible, womanly fingers (with their smooth, cold nails), which he would drag over my open hand… right to its very edge… as he stared into my eyes, with the sickest of smiles.

Although I had no girlfriend back then, I have always thought of myself as very firmly being 'a ladies' man' (and even saw myself as a 'bit of a catch'). Why Pirogov flirted with me in the way that he did, I don't entirely know. Perhaps it was the 'spice' of a certain sense of… danger.

Concluding our meeting in the basement, I suggested to my associates that we make our way to Pirogov's premises, in search of some refreshments that we might consume in the park.

Heading to his miserable store, it so happened that we trod a particularly turd-littered path, whose disgusting, dog-soiled slabs only served to increase my sense of the nobility of our new mission in life.

Sergei – never the most nimble of boys – planted a sole right on top of one of these stinking specimens.

He stopped to clean his shoe on a scruffy piece of grass.

And, at that moment, I was struck by my flash of inspiration – *genius*, you might even say.

'No! Leave it!' I commanded.

And I marched my comrades on… to the threshold of Pirogov's door.

Inside, Pirogov's was its usual ratty place. He was slicing away with his meat machine in his customary highly concentrated fashion, noticing nothing… as we boys crept in.

I whispered to Sergei to drag his shitty shoe over the old and grey tiles of the shop's aisles.

The foul turd – clearly the product of some obese and gluttonous mutt – fell away on the floor.

Satisfied with the fruits of Sergei's labours, I instructed him to stop.

The three of us then made a play of 'shopping' – in a conspicuous way that would attract the attention of Pirogov… our trio 'innocently' browsing his rack of magazines and so on.

At that precise moment, Kseniya Lapotnikova, whose job it was to drive the vehicle that cleaned the platform at our metro station, came in and said, 'Alexei Pirogov, there is a terrible smell in your shop. It smells like… a dog's unpleasantness. What on earth is it?'

And then she looked down on the floor and saw the Turd From Hell that Sergei's shoe had smeared everywhere – and I mean *everywhere*. Whereupon she put her hand to her mouth and ran out saying, 'Dear Lord, I think I am going to be sick.'

Pirogov came from behind his counter in his white coat – Vasily now pointing to a clump of shit that was still hanging around Sergei's heel.

'My God!' Vasily said. 'You must have trodden in it, Sergei, after that mutt finished its performance right outside the door. It's disgusting. What's more, it's probably illegal – shit like that, in a shop like this. A police matter, I should think.' (An unscripted and highly impressive intervention by Vasily, I have to admit: a boy who'd been singled out by our teachers at an early age as 'university material'.)

And that was how we came to talk terms with Alexei Pirogov. If *he* would put our notice in his window and make sure those wanting our services left their requests in writing in envelopes that were sealed, *we* would ensure that any dogs that went near his shop were *taken care of*, meaning there would be no further cases of turds on his tiles.

Things were coming along really quite nicely with our business, when we experienced our first hiccup. To my irritation, the couple who owned the noisy dog that Sergie and I had taken care of so successfully put up a notice on the board in the downstairs hall of our block. It had the word *Lost!* above a photograph of the dog, which had a pink ribbon tied in a bow around its neck. The dog's eyes followed me in a way I didn't like, as I went about my goings and comings.

At first, I tried to ignore the notice, but on the second or third day I took it down and burned it on the waste ground behind our block.

The dog's eyes stared at me as the paper curled in the flames.

I said to it that it was no good it looking at me like that, and that what had happened had been its own fault because of how it had annoyed people with its terrible noisiness. 'You brought in on yourself,' I said. Such was life… and death, noisy dog, I remarked.

A couple of days later, another notice went up, this time with the word *REWARD!* above a new and different picture of the noisy dog (now in a little check jacket, beside a red toy ball). I found myself thinking about the woman who was sly and her cat. I realised that, with this talk of rewards, we boys would have to watch a venomous type like her… very carefully.

Just as I was about to take the notice down, Izolda Kuklova, the caretaker, came out from her room and asked me why I was in the hall. I told her I was hoping to find information about a school or evening class where I might learn English or some other skill, so I might go to university and move to some other, more pleasant block.

'Off with you! Now!!' she snapped. 'Or I'll speak to your parents!'

That evening, I went downstairs again.

Kuklova's TV was booming from her room with the sound of a soap opera about doctors and nurses, that I knew that she watched.

I looked for the notice about the noisy dog but could not see it.

Just then, Veniamin Ilyushkin, an old boy whose wife had died and who now spent all his days trying to grow flowers at the front of our building, where the cats did their business, came in through the door (carrying his watering can).

Mindful that I should not be placed 'at the scene' – even by an old-timer like Ilyushkin – I stopped looking for the notice and went back upstairs.

When I went down next morning, the poster was nowhere to be seen – and, after a short while, I forgot all about it.

What had actually happened, it seems, was this: a driver from a pizza firm had pinned a menu on top of it. Then someone with a sideboard that was free to whoever would collect it had pinned their own notice on top of that. Then a woman who said she made nice dresses and also altered men's trousers put *her* notice on the top of that one. In turn, hers had a card put on it for a guy who fixed cars and said he was cheap. So it was, that the noisy dog fell from sight… and from my mind.

After a slow start, our business grew quickly – possibly on account of how word of our service got around. It is not necessary for me to go into details (I have no desire for personal glory), suffice to say that as well as dogs, our business embraced creatures of all kinds: caged birds, cats, rodents, insects, tropical fish, you name it. A good number were already deceased – their owners seeking merely a dignified burial for their much-loved pets. Frankly, we didn't have time to waste on such matters, so, typically, an expired budgerigar would be flushed down someone's toilet, whilst a dead dachshund would be given a smoky send-off on the waste ground behind our flats. Occasionally, we achieved a side-deal with Gleb Usoyev, who ran a snack stand near the metro station, thereby also lightening our load.

There were mishaps and close brushes along the way, of course. Sergei's shattering (with a stone from his catapult) of the window of a couple who had hired us to take care of a pestilent squirrel, being one such. (We didn't get paid for that job.)

But, as I say, despite a few 'difficulties', business took off and it was not uncommon for us to have three cases come in at once, at times necessitating our travel to a distance of three or even four metro stops.

On one such busy day, our cases concerned the stick insects of a student who'd gone camping with his friends and whose mother wanted the 'dreadful bugs' out of her place (this I delegated to Vasily); secondly, the seizure of a lizard that had scared its owner by eating its own tail (this I felt a job for Sergei); and, thirdly, the capture and removal of a mouse (which I myself took).

I read the client's letter on the train to the given address.

It is a pet mouse that has got loose. It is a large mouse. That is true. But it is not a rat. It is a mouse, as I have said. Please come quickly and take care of this <u>mouse</u>.

Yours faithfully,
Yelena Z.

In all of this I somehow smell a rat (and not a mouse). But my head was full of the stick insects and the lizard and the opportunity that had clearly been presented to introduce the student's bugs to the hungry reptile. Besides, in those days, such were the pressures on me, as leader of a successful and expanding small business, that I scarcely had time to catch a flea.

When I got to the woman's flat, she told me the mouse was in the lounge. We had to drag away from its door an absurd barricade of furniture which the woman, aided by certain neighbours, had put there. As I entered the lounge, she grabbed the door shut and ran into the kitchen, where she jumped onto a chair. 'Can you see it? Have you got it? Is it dead yet?' she shouted through the wall. 'What's keeping you? Hurry up with it!'

I saw the hairy devil in all his glory in a corner near the base of a lamp. And I have to say it looked *p-r-e-t-t-y* big for a mouse. But – like the true professional – I set to work. We'd smartened up our operations a lot by this time, and I took from my jacket a small net and a pickled onion that I had taken with me for the task. Originally, I'd had some cheese, but I'd eaten it – absent-mindedly – on the train. So, anyway, I chucked down the stinking onion and it rolled on the floor and came to a halt on a board… in sniffing distance of the snout of that rodent.

The creature looked at me, and I at it: eyeball-to-eyeball.

Our situation put me in mind of those duels faced by hunters in Africa and such places. Of course, I knew the low, snaky-tailed thing was no match for my brain… and never could be. And, as the woman kept on with her shouts from the kitchen, I wondered how long the big-eared beast would hold out before it gave into its desire for that onion, even though it must have known I was there: hunter… assassin… the one-and-only (as I sometimes thought of myself back then) Stiva K.

Well, my counting didn't even get to two before the dumb animal made its dash to damnation. Down went its teeth on that onion – and down went my net on top of it, followed by several heavy bashes from Sergei's father's torch. All – let it be said – in the natural order of things.

I shouted to the woman that the job was done, the monster (!) slain.

I heard her get down from the chair in the kitchen, after which she came nervously to the door of the lounge (where I was wrapping Mr Mouse in my net). The woman gave me a kiss on the lips, which in turn gave me a feeling (the particulars of which we can gloss over) in my 'downstairs' department.

She put two decent notes in my hand as payment, giving me a kind-of *look* as she did so (maybe on account of the bulge in my trousers).

I suspect that a psychiatrist may have diagnosed in all of this something that I gather is termed 'the thrill of the kill'. But I don't believe there was ever anything sadistic in what Sergei, Vasily and I did. We were public servants. It was as simple as that. (And we were in it for the money.)

That evening, when I got home, my mother was in the kitchen, smoking and staring into space. I put on the table in front of her one of the notes that the woman on the chair with the mouse had given me. This made me feel important, I admit (like I was the man of the house now). I thought my mother would be pleased, but – outwardly, at least – she was not.

'What is this? Where did you get it? What have you been doing? Don't think that because your father isn't here that you can do whatever you like. Because you *can't* and you won't!' she shouted. 'I won't stand for it! Understand?!'

She hit me with her hand on the side of my head.

I was, by that time of my life, comfortably as big as her, if not bigger, and could have hit her back… five times as hard. But I did not, because she was my mother. And, anyway, she did this because she loved me… I think.

I told her it was okay – that I had got myself a job for the summer.

She was still shouting when I left to go to my bedroom.

However, as I pulled the kitchen door behind me, I saw her snatch up the note and put it in her purse.

Over the coming weeks, our work continued with a steady stream of cases.

Our services were often booked by a jealous member of a family, such as a brother who hated his sister and, therefore, despised his sister's kitten or pet rabbit.

At other times, it was a wife who complained that her husband put his dog before her and that he was a cruel and heartless man. One man wanted a cat to be snatched back – alive – from a woman he had given it to (who was not his wife). He told us to *name our price*, but we decided that this was a messy contract that we could do without and, like Vasily said, 'a distraction from our core business', which was the taking care of animals in our own special way. Besides, none of us much liked cats.

By that time, we had only a couple of weeks left until we were due back at school, and it seemed our summer of dog-killing was done.

But then two things happened, which, in their different ways, conspired to change our lives… perhaps forever.

The first thing that happened was that my father got in trouble with the police. He was drunk and wandering around the park in Chistye Prudy, in the uniform my mother had made for him, when, for some crazy reason or other, he touched a foreign lady *inappropriately* and, in the scene that followed, caused her to fall into the pond, which, as you may know, can at times be a very snotty green. Why this lady didn't just climb out and slap my father's face and shout at him like any normal Slav woman and then push *him* in the water, God Himself only knows. But, anyway, she rushed off screaming in her wet dress to some policemen who were eating ice creams in their car and not wanting to be disturbed. Anyway, when they had finished these ice creams of theirs, they came back and arrested my father (after waking him up because he had, by that point, fallen asleep over the top of a bin). At the police station, my father gave our flat as his home address (even though he hadn't been there to see us for several weeks).

Later that day, an officer telephoned and told my mother what had happened. My mother shouted to the officer not to bring *the useless fool* here and slammed down our phone. A few minutes later, the phone rang again, but my mother wouldn't answer. So, I did. A female police officer said we needed to go down to the police station to pay a fine and once this had been *processed* they would bring my father home (when they were able). I wasn't totally sure what to do, but in the end I decided to go to the police station and do as the woman officer had said.

She got me to sign some forms and I gave her the money for my father's release.

'That's a big note for a young lad,' she said.

'I am seventeen years next birthday,' I said. 'And if you think that's big you should see what I have in my trousers.'

Okay, I didn't say that last part. But I felt like saying it because I sensed that this woman officer was making fun of me, even though it should have been plain to her that I was now the man of my house and that was why I was there: to deal with my father.

'Can I have the change, please?' That's what I *actually* said.

That night, the woman officer and a policeman who was a fat guy brought my father home.

My mother shouted at the officers for doing this and there was 'a scene' in our flat (which ended with my father falling asleep on the sofa in our lounge).

When the officers went downstairs, Izolda Kuklova, our caretaker, was there – all ears for gossip – pretending to be tidying.

She was taking down old notices from the hallway board and had got as far as the one that I've mentioned – concerning the reward for the noisy dog – just as the officers were walking past it to our block's front door.

The woman officer saw the picture of the noisy dog in its little check coat and said something stupid to her colleague like, 'Oh, so sad. What a cute puppy.'

The fat cop just gave a grunt and walked on.

But, as history shows, on such totally *tiny* things, great empires can sometimes crumble – and fall.

My mother kicked my father out the next morning. She hit his nose, as he lay snoring on the sofa, with the back of a wooden brush meant for sweeping the floor. He had blood on his chin as she pushed him out of our place. All of this sounds funny, I know. But he was my father and she was my mother. And none of that was nice to see.

The second important thing that happened was the arrival some while later of a letter – via Pirogov's shop. It was a letter like no other that we boys had received. This is what it said:

To those only whom it concerns,

I am writing to ask for your help. A woman that I know has an animal that needs to be taken care of. This animal is a pig <u>and</u> a dog, but he is different from other animals because he has two legs and not four. He has abused this woman of his and he has been a bad father to his son. He cannot hold down a proper job and he goes from one ridiculous thing to the next. He gives his wife no money and he is drunk all of the time. He is driving his brother-in-law's car as a taxi outside *(she gave here the name of a metro station several stops from our own)*. It is a brown car, and the number plate of the car is *(and here she gave the number plate of the car)*.

Please take care of this problem.

With these words were three notes, the biggest rouble notes that I knew of in all of Russia. But the matter of real relevance was this: each of them had been cut in half, through the middle, and only half of each of these notes was there.

At the end of the letter, the writer said:

When the job is done, and I know this dog is dead, I will send the other halves of the notes so that you can put them together and your payment will be complete.

Yours faithfully,
Your client.

P.S. You will recognise the car because it is very dirty and has a bad smell. He is too lazy to clean it.

Well, we sat in our basement and smoked (Sergei and I, that is… Vasily, with his scientific brain, did not 'partake') and we considered this letter very carefully. This man certainly sounded 'nasty goods', but, as Vasily said, this was *a very different proposition*. I mean, yes, we had taken care of many things, but our business had been in budgies (that, for the most part had already fallen off their perches), rodents that were 'fair game' by anyone's imagination, and toothless old dogs that could no longer stand.

This writer was asking us to take care of… a man.

We thought about what the writer of the letter had said about this individual… abusing his wife and being a bad father, also his drunkenness and the fact that he would not clean his car.

He did not seem a very… *good* man. He did not seem a very… *decent* man.

We looked again at the halves of notes and we thought about how much money they were, the most we had ever seen.

'We'll take a vote,' I said (in my capacity as chairman of our board) '… in our free and democratic way. Those in favour,' I continued, 'raise your hands.'

I placed mine in the air.

Sergei, my trusty lieutenant since our nursery days, promptly followed.

I now looked to Vasily.

He seemed nervous, shocked even… his mouth open in a state of disbelief.

'And you, comrade?' I said to him. 'Where do you stand on this matter? Can I count on your support?'

In those moments, I sensed many things churning in Vasily's mind. It would not be too great an exaggeration to say that I half thought his brain might explode out of that big forehead of his.

I felt my eyes narrow.

'I'm waiting… comrade,' I said. 'And – if I am honest – my arm is getting a little weary holding my hand in the air. And I suspect Sergei's arm is also getting a bit achy with being aloft. And you will have noticed, of course, from our previous operations, how Sergei's hand is rather… large.'

Slowly, hesitantly, looking down at our table rather than at me, Vasily raise his hand.

'Then it is agreed,' I said. 'We shall take care of this one, last dog.'

Next day, we hung around the metro station to which the client had directed us… to assess the lie of the land. We made sure we kept a low profile, spending most of our time in a café at a table from which we could see out of the window (while drinking tea, smoking and generally blending-in with the other customers).

We saw the brown car.

It was an old and lousy Russian thing. Not a proper taxi with a sign that said *TAXI* and suchlike.

We couldn't see the driver clearly because his seat was pushed right over, and he appeared to be asleep.

But everything pointed to him being *our* dog – a driver of the maggoty type who did jobs the official drivers would not, such as taking men to prostitutes who had nasty breath; delivering stinky meals (that he himself, no doubt, half-wolfed) to seedy clients in miserable flats; a low fellow of the sort who (for a tip) carried a granny's shopping but made sure he helped himself to something nice and tasty from her bags on the way into her place. Yes, *he* was such a man. The evidence was there, before our very eyes.

As we sat at our table, we considered – quietly – how we might best take care of this dog.

Sergei was for using some kind of poison and spraying it into the man's mouth and possibly his ears and, if needs be, up his nose.

Vasily suggested a wire of the variety used for cutting cheese, which he felt could be pulled by the three of us – 'most effectively' – through this mutt-man's throat.

Sergei and I were a little surprised at this seeming bloodthirstiness on the part of young Vasily but agreed that the idea was not without its merits. I wondered, though, how and where we might get hold of such a wire. The cheese at Pirogov's shop, for example, came pre-wrapped from a factory. For a moment, I remembered my father once exclaiming to my mother – on a rare occasion when she had shopped there – that Pirogov's cheese was both uncuttable and uneatable: being, so he said, 'tougher rubber than a priest's condom'.

Asserting my authority, I said we would hire this low man to drive us somewhere dark and quiet and we would sit on the back seat of his lousy car and, when we got to that dark and quiet place, we would… strangle him… from behind… with… my dressing gown cord.

And that would be the end of it – and him.

As these last words came from my mouth, I thought how much like my mother I had come to sound (which pleased me, somewhat).

We returned to the café in the afternoon of the next day. From our window table, we watched the man's car come and go on a couple of taxi trips.

We hung about till it was turning dark, and then, as one, we moved.

We slunk from there, crossed the wide, trash-covered pavement outside the metro station, and crept alongside his vehicle.

He had his seat right back and, through his window (which was rolled half-down) we could hear his snores.

We opened – gently – the door behind him and slid in, across the back seat, one by one.

Vasily, who was last, *slammed* the door hard and the man came-to, with a jump.

He pulled his seat up quickly and moved his hands up and down his face, so as to wake himself more fully.

I had decided that what talking we would do would be done only by Vasily, on account of his abilities with long words and his way of sounding a man-of-this-world, never mind that he was still a small schoolboy who nobody liked.

He told the man the district we wanted and said there would be a tip in it if the man could hurry.

At first, the car wouldn't start and, several times over, it made dry and horrible sounds, which the man cursed, quietly, to himself.

Finally, it fired, shuddered and then steadied itself, like a drunk regaining consciousness somewhere squalid – a litter-strewn step or gutter.

Before we knew it, we were out on the highway.

Vasily gave directions to a neighbourhood two metro stops distant, situated on the way back towards the one in which we ourselves lived.

We knew of a quiet place there where old and rusty trains were parked and left to rot, and where there were piles of rubbish and weeds that in summer grew high as a man.

Apart from those words by Vasily, we said nothing and just sat there.

The car was filthy, and the driver stank.

His mirror was cracked, which meant that we couldn't really see his face, and he couldn't see ours.

He put on the radio and some old music began.

Then he lit a cigarette, whose tip glowed orange in the car's warm dark. The lid of his lighter made a *thunk* as it shut.

He wound down his window (to let out the smoke) and leaned his elbow where the window's glass had been.

The air that rushed in swept his full, farmyard stench all over us in the back.

Yet we boys had a calm about us, like that of priests taking the mass.

Above all, we had the certainty that this was a dog who deserved to die.

After a while, Vasily told the man to turn off the main road, and we followed some smaller roads to that place in our plan.

Soon there were no lights from other cars, just the occasional streetlamp and, eventually, not even one of those.

Vasily told the man to drive to the other side of some sheds that could just be seen in the dark.

The man asked if we knew where we were going. There was temper in his voice but also – I sensed – fear.

Vasily said *of course* we knew where we were heading and would he just be kind enough to drive to the other side of those buildings because there was a walkway there that was a shortcut to our blocks. We all would 'disembark' there and pay him for his services, added Vasily.

The man pulled round to the other side of the buildings.

The headlights of the car lit up the side of an old brick shed that had broken windows and a tree that had risen through its roof.

Vasily said it would be perfect for the driver to halt right there.

There was a crunching sound of stones as the car came to a stop. Small clouds of dust rose in the beams of its headlights in front of us.

The man seemed to look for the walkway we had told him of, and he appeared to be about to speak.

But before he could say even one word, we had the dressing gown cord around his throat – in a loop – and were pulling it, as tight as we could: Sergei at one end, me and Vasily at the other.

The man jerked from side to side in his seat.

His left arm bashed against his door.

His feet kicked down near the pedals (as if he were trying to run from our hold).

Reaching past him, Sergei snatched the key from the ignition with one hand, then quickly went back to pulling with both.

For a lazy man with a seedy life, the fight in this dog surprised me. He was like some wild thing – a bison perhaps – that, never mind that it had been cornered and lassoed, was determined not to yield.

He reached to the cord around his throat.

We boys had it so tight it was practically *sawing* his head off.

And *still* we kept pulling.

The man now made horrible sounds of gasping and choking.

Suddenly, moonlight lit up the car.

It was as if we were caught in a kind of camera-flash.

I saw the man's eyes – which looked as if they were about to burst – in his shabby, broken mirror.

The cord in our hands was so tight I feared it would snap.

The man's face was dark and monstrous in the moonbeam.

I seriously wondered if his head would explode.

He was no longer kicking with his feet or bashing with his arm now – just trying, for all his worth, to breathe.

His eyes met mine again in the mirror.

I looked away, and, with Vasily and me at one end, Sergei at the other, we pulled – ferociously – on that cord, as if in a tug of war.

'S-t-i-v… u-h,' the man seemed to say, as – finally – his head flopped on his fat neck, and his chin fell to his chest, and the cord in our hands – that had been tight as a piano wire… a tent rope… a fat lady's trousers… or anything you care to name – slackened, at last.

The man slumped forward onto the steering wheel, like a bum of a boxer who'd been beaten, or even a bear who'd been shot.

I feared his heavy thud would set off the horn or something, but, like I say, it was a lousy old Russian car, and nothing happened. It was as if the car itself could not give a shit about this man, who lay there, over its own steering wheel... dead.

Sergei, who knew about these things on account of his father being a binman, reached forward and switched off the car's headlights.

Above us, clouds concealed the moon, and the car fell dark once more.

In our stillness, we now became aware of the fact that the radio was playing – something that our ears had become strangely separated from during those events that I have described.

A woman was singing in English. Some song from years ago... about the summertime.

Hearing her voice was a funny thing.

It was as if she had been there, through all that we had done; that she had been listening, as well as singing, and that she... *knew.*

Sergei turned off the radio. The light of its tiny white bulb died to nothing.

In the darkness, silence fell over us.

I pushed Vasily to leave.

A weak yellow glow lit the car's interior as we opened the back doors to get out.

An icon of St John was swinging from the man's cracked mirror as we left him... in his lousy car (which wasn't even *his* lousy car), there, in the blackness, amid the trash and the weeds.

Taken care of.

After that, the three of us didn't meet up again for several days. Eventually, I had word from Sergei to say there was an item of mail for us at Pirogov's. Vasily brought it to the basement one evening.

The back of the envelope was taped down.

Inside were the other halves of the notes our client had promised.

We each took the half that was ours.

We parted without saying much. Sergei said he was going to buy a cell phone and possibly some training shoes, Vasily that he would be putting his share towards his future university fees.

And that was it.

The mood was... muted. We all knew in our minds and our hearts that something inside us had changed. That we had made, in more ways than one, a journey on that night in the taxi. That – from that point on – no matter whatever else happened to the three of us in our lives, there would now be no going back to our youth... let alone our childhoods.

I returned to my parents' flat and sat on my bed in my room. I taped the two halves of my banknote together with a roll I took from the drawer in our sideboard (where my mother kept her needles for sewing and her rubber bands and coupons for her shopping and similar small things).

Later, I went into the kitchen, where she was smoking, and I laid the note down on the table in front of her.

She didn't say or do anything... which disappointed me, to be honest.

She just sat there looking at the note which I had placed on the tablecloth in front of her.

At the end of the week, we boys got ready to go back to school.

We went to Alexei Pirogov's and took down our notice from his window. We stole some cigarettes, which we felt was 'fair play', on account of the fact that we were no longer in league with him.

To be honest, I was glad our association with him was at its end.

On the third morning of our return to school, we were called out of class… one by one.

Izmaylov, the deputy headmaster, marched each of us down the corridor to the study of Krupin, our headmaster.

Izmaylov knocked the door and sent us in while he himself stood guard outside.

Krupin was sitting behind his desk.

The woman police officer who had that time before brought my father home was also there.

When Izmaylov pulled the door shut I became aware of her fat colleague, who was standing in the corner.

Krupin had on a green and white tie (and I remember thinking what a horrible thing it was to wear).

When I went to sit in the chair facing his desk, he went crazy – ordering me to stand still and take my hands out of my pockets.

I learned later that Sergei had been first to tell about the things we had done that summer. Sergei's father had been there, in Krupin's study, when the woman officer started asking all of her questions. Sergei started sniffing and crying and nodding his head and saying things to her like, 'Yes, that is right'. He was then taken out and made to sit in an office with Oprinchuk, the sports master, who was in his red tracksuit.

Vasily held out longer. More than once, I learned later, he asked the woman officer to explain herself (in a sort-of game of cat-and-mouse). He said to her things like, 'And your point is?' and also 'I'm not sure where you are going with that'. But then his mother was called in by Krupin, who himself said to Vasily something like, 'We are talking about very serious matters here,

Vasily; matters that could have consequences for your education, your career and your entire life. Make no mistake about the gravity of all of this.'

On hearing this and on seeing the look on his mother's face, Vasily, too, began his confession. As the woman officer read through a list of certain of the pets we had taken care of, he lowered his previously proud head, nodded and also began to cry. His mother went to give him a handkerchief, but Krupin shouted that she was to sit back down *immediately* and keep her hands to herself.

Vasily was then escorted by Izmaylov into the office where Oprinchuk was still wearing his red tracksuit – and made to sit at the opposite end from Sergei (with no permission to speak).

When Krupin, finally, spoke to me, he said there was no point in me denying anything as full confessions had been made by Sergei and Vasily, who had, he said, not only *implicated* me in everything but had also identified me as the leader. He was in 'full possession' of the facts, he said.

Although I had not said one word to him, Krupin said our conversation was at its end. My activities would be a matter for the appropriate authorities. That would be all.

Sergei and Vasily were taken away in a minibus by a woman with a clipboard.

I had expected to go with them, but the woman police officer and her fat colleague put me in the back of their police car instead (where I found myself in a kind of cage).

I suppose it's fair to say that, at that time of my life, I would have preferred if all of that business could have been done – if it *had* to be done – a little more… spectacularly: a gunfight, a car chase, maybe a grappling match on the top of a fast-moving train. The involvement of a glamorous female agent (who was secretly in love with me) would also not have gone amiss.

But life is not like that, as I have learned. The painful truth is that you get tripped up by the hum and the drum and find yourself being marched from your flat, with a blanket on your head, in front of all of your neighbours who say to the TV and the papers that they *always* suspected you were nasty goods, but had, in fact, never stopped knocking your door for spare cubes of sugar or leaves of black tea.

Through the wire of the cage in the police car, I asked the woman officer how she had found out… about us boys and what we had done.

As we crossed over lights and swung around corners, she said she'd seen the poster about the noisy dog in our hallway and then, by chance, some while later, had called in at Pirogov's for a *Coca Cola*. Our sign about taking care of pets had been right there in his window. While she hadn't been able to act on it immediately because of more pressing matters, she had made a 'mental note'. She hadn't needed to be Sherlock Holmes, she said. Besides, Pirogov had been 'most helpful': he was 'known' to them.

So that was what this was all about? *Just* the animals? I asked.

And wasn't that enough? she responded. 'The Dog Killers of Moscow.'

She began to read out her horoscope from the newspaper. 'Don't go buying a cat in a sack. Success for you means taking a difficult dog by its tail.'

She closed the paper, and snorted, with a horsey kind of laugh.

When we appeared in court, it was the first time I had seen Sergei and Vasily for weeks and it would, I thought, have been a time for hugs and slaps, or, at least, civil handshakes between us.

But those boys barely looked at me and said even less.

We had places in a boxed-off part of the room, separate from everyone else.

A woman with red hair read out a list of the pets we had taken care of (which was quite long). She lost her way at one point and there was some coming and going between certain of the officials. This occurred where the details of one particular case ran over several pages. As the red-haired woman read through the list, there were gasps and groans from some of those present in the room – and even little shrieks.

As the woman droned on, I looked around.

Sergei's father was sitting, with a tie on, and looking mad as hell. (I made a point to avoid his eyes.) Vasily's mother was crying into a tissue as his father held one of her hands.

My mother was there, too, sitting apart from the others.

I waved to her, but she just stared back.

In one corner, a woman with pink-painted nails was writing everything down. (I learned later that this was a reporter on our local newspaper.)

Anyway, the woman who was reading the list about those pets we had taken care of seemed to be doing this mainly for the benefit of three people – two men and a woman – who had on black gowns and were sitting behind a long bench on the other side of the room: the magistrates, as I, in due course, discovered them to be. The man who was in the middle started talking, but I didn't pay a great deal of attention because I was concentrating on the young woman reporter who was writing very quickly in a notebook and turning over the pages so that they made a slapping sound. I guessed there and then that she must have been preparing an article for the newspaper about what had occurred. I thought to myself that this would at least be more interesting than the usual material they printed… about young people doing well at university and grannies enjoying a coach trip somewhere miserable and dull.

However, it irritated me greatly that she was hearing only of our 'cruelty' – as it was described – to the toothless old mutts and half-dead (or even *fully*-dead) birds we had taken care of, rather than the true history of our service to society, as I have explained it, here.

After a sort-of interval, the head judge (as I learned him to be) started talking again (as if he hadn't said enough already).

I'm sorry, but I had lost all interest in him by that stage. Meanwhile, the reporter was writing so fast I thought her notebook might catch fire.

The next thing I knew was that Sergei and Vasily were being led out of our box.

They were snivelling and crying and making complete fools of themselves in a way that I found very disappointing.

There was quite a scene as Vasily's mother started to wail in a way that was embarrassing to everyone present. Her husband, Thanks Be to God, finally took her in hand and dragged her out.

I was following Sergei and Vasily when a man swung shut the gate of our pen and ordered me back (as if I were a naughty little boy, or dog).

The head judge, who was a tall, thin man whose features set me thinking about the stick insects we had dealt with so efficiently, now started off again – this time at me, in a high and mighty way, of which Krupin, our headmaster, would have been proud.

For a while, I was angry and thought to myself 'Who does this fellow think he is?', but after a time I simply 'tuned out', as the expression goes.

Eventually, he stopped, nodded and the one who had pushed me back in my pen – not before time – let me out.

I was glad that the whole pantomime seemed at its end.

I looked to where my mother had been sitting, but there was no sign of her. I presumed she was waiting to meet me outside (where there'd be an almighty telling-off from her, I felt sure, and maybe a strong clout (or three) in front of passers-by), after which we would go home.

But then two men in uniforms led me a different way from Sergei and Vasily, and we three went down the many steps of a staircase that sank beneath the room in which we had been… so that the noises from above us became ever quieter, till the only sound was that of our feet… going down.

❦

I have received a letter from Vasily. He has told me that he and Sergei are at a special school where they will have to stay for the next five years. It is apparently like an ordinary school, except there are bars on the windows and the young males there are not allowed to go home at night. His letter informed me that I also am detained but, in my case, only *indefinitely*. Vasily explained that our 'differing fortunes' have been due to the fact that I am a year older than he and Sergei. I should perhaps explain that my being in the same year as them at school was on account of the fact that in the time before we went into business I never really went to school that much. Krupin, our headmaster, put the authorities onto my parents and he told my mother that he would be 'holding me back' a year to begin with and, if necessary, for longer. Therefore, in a strange way, my lack of schooling has, in this particular case, made me more mature than my fellows and, to boot, *a responsible person* in the eyes of 'The Law'.

Still, all of that is by the by, as they say. The main thing is that I am being held here *indefinitely* – a term of which I was previously unaware. And that is good news, of course. Far preferable than to be here *definitely*. If *that* were the case, who knows when I would get to see my friends, my home and the world again?

So, one day, Reader, I shall be 'out', on the streets… off my leash.

There will be some small debts to repay, of course… a ledger to balance – it might be said (… with Pirogov, for one. You know, at night, I hear his meat-cutter… slicing, almost *musically*, in my ears).

Beyond him, once I am free from this 'kennel', there will be far bigger fish to fry, of course.

Our capital, I hear, is these days stalked by a big and very bad wolf… one who might need a pup – so to speak – to run with (for a while), and perhaps even to 'take care of' him, in the fullness of time.

Who better for that job than a son of Stalin?

Priest

The track seemed different: darker and more secret than I remembered.

When I reached the bottom, Lena and Viktor's kids – Little Viktor and Alona – were shrieking and running around a paddling pool of the blow-up kind… whose bright blue-and-yellow plastic unsettled me for a moment after the cool conformity of the pine forest.

The children were naked.

When they saw my car, they stopped running. They stood by the pool with their arms by their sides and they stared as I drove out of the trees.

Their father appeared from around the back of the house. He was carrying some logs, which he set down in a shelter by the side of it. As I stepped from my car, he came over and we shook hands. Lena then came out from the house.

'Mikey,' she said, and hugged me.

She told me that I had lost weight… then her eyes looked away for a second, as if she felt she had said the wrong thing.

She spoke to the children and told them to dry themselves and to put on some clothes. The kids turned their heads after us as we grown-ups climbed the steps to the house.

In the kitchen, Lena poured iced tea and we stood around their table, which had flowers on it in a blue jug.

Lena and Viktor asked me questions about Moscow, where they hadn't been for some time. And when I answered, they said things like 'No!' and 'Really?' and 'You're kidding!', as if my replies were interesting or important, when really we all knew that they were not.

I said I'd forgotten how far off the road their place was and how I'd wondered if maybe I'd gone the wrong way at a fork.

We talked about the kids, who came in after a while and clung to Lena as they looked at me… Lena doing up certain of the buttons and buckles that Little Viktor and Alona had left undone.

Later, she showed me my room and I left my bag on the small bed.

Then we went outside, and she had me look at her vegetable patch.

She slipped off her sandals and stepped neatly through the plot, while I looked on from the edge.

Her pale feet pressed over the soil, which was grey and dry.

She pointed and said, 'Radish… lettuce… cucumbers… *small* cucumbers (my speciality)… beans…'

She smiled and moved her hair from her face and knotted it at the back of her neck (in the way that I remembered).

She saw me looking, and she began to talk of something else. 'And over here… raspberries… currants… gooseberries…'

Viktor joined us and the three of us sat on the porch for a while, talking about people we knew in Moscow (Elizaveta Entina being one).

I said she was still caretaking my block even though she had to be a hundred years old – at least – by now. I recounted how she'd told me off – her finger jabbing in the air – when I lost my keys at Christmas: once without her teeth and then all over again when she'd put her teeth in.

Lena slapped my knee… but laughed, all the same.

Viktor then said he wanted to go fishing before supper, and he fetched rods and tackle from under the stairs of the house for the two of us to use.

Viktor and I pushed his small boat from the shingle beach where his ground gave way to the lake. He rowed us out, towards the darker, deeper water. The oars rubbed the locks as the blades scooped at the lake. He rowed well –

steadily, smoothly – smiling at me from time to time as he worked the oars: the two of us enjoying the lovely calm of the early evening and the sweetness of his rhythm.

Eventually, he pulled in the oars and we set up our rods.

Viktor opened a box and took out a rainbow-coloured lure. At its end hung a trinity of hooks, like a miniature grappling iron. He began to tie it to my line. As he did so, a barb snagged his thumb. It drew a tiny teardrop of blood, as he unpicked it.

'Damn!' he said, and he put his thumb in his mouth.

Having fixed a lure for his own rod, we then cast our lines and let the boat drift.

Behind us, on the shore, Viktor and Lena's house had grown small… to the size of a matchbox… if that. No other could be seen amid the trees that came down to the lake.

'I love it here,' I said, when some time had passed.

'I know,' said Viktor.

'Especially after Moscow,' I said.

'Especially after Moscow,' he repeated, and he nodded and smiled.

'How long has it been?' I asked. 'You had Alona,' I said, trying to remember, 'and Lena was carrying Little Viktor. There was a thunderstorm,' I said. 'Do you remember?' I half-smiled. 'I seem to be a bit of a rain-maker.' And then I added: 'I'm sorry it's been so long.'

'But you're here now, Mikey,' Viktor said. 'You've made it. That's all that matters.' Viktor took some beers from a box beneath his seat, and we snapped them open.

I lit a cigarette.

Frowning, he took one from me, which I lit for him.

'How are you all anyway?' I asked.

'Good, Mikey… we're good,' Viktor said.

'That's good,' I said, and we drank our beers and smiled and let our lines drift.

A breeze created a swell under the boat's red hull.

It was refreshing, pleasurable even (after the stuffy heat of my car journey), but I zippered my jacket, all the same.

Suddenly, there was a pull – a big one – on my line.

My rod dipped and – as I gripped – it bent into an arch.

'You've got one!' said Viktor, excitedly. 'Careful now. Let him run. Let him run, Mikey. And then we'll reel him back. Run and reel, Mikey. Run and reel!'

The fish ran strong and deep. I struggled to keep hold of the rod.

'Jeez, Viktor!' I said. 'It seems… big!'

All of a sudden, there was a pause. My line slackened, but still bore a weight.

It was as if whatever it was that I'd hooked was resting, re-grouping, considering its next move… out there, in the depths of the lake. And not only that, but that it was *daring* me, somehow.

'How deep *is* this lake?' I asked Viktor.

'God knows! I've never been down there… thankfully,' he answered.

We sat there, not talking for a moment: me holding the rod, Viktor staring at the water, an intermittent bob to the boat.

'Now!' said Viktor, suddenly, and I struck at the reel.

The fish fought back.

My rod arched anew; its line like piano-wire in the water.

'Let him run now!' Viktor commanded, looking out onto the lake.

And I, again, let the line unreel.

'Okay, *now* bring him back!'

And, once more, I attacked with the rod and the reel.

I felt the power of the fish: in my shoulders, all the way down my back, in my hips, my thighs and even my groin. It was pulling *me* – it seemed – as surely as if the hooks on that lure were embedded in my own mouth.

Viktor was rapt. I wondered if he even remembered that I'd been ill.

'Oh, he's big!' Viktor said. 'Don't let him go!'

'*How* big?' I gasped.

The boat was rocking now as Viktor moved around in it.

'It's time. Bring him in, Mikey,' he said. 'Bring him in!'

'I'm not certain I can,' I said.

'Sure you can!' he said. 'Sure you can!'

He kept looking at the water – his eyes had grown huge.

Suddenly, the fish broke the surface. Not in a leap, or anything majestic like that, but with a grey heaviness, like some rising submarine.

'Hell! He looks big!' I said.

'*Now* Mikey! Take him! Take him!!' Viktor shouted. 'Reel him in!'

And I did as ordered and went at it again with the reel.

The fish flapped and ploshed and came our way, awkwardly, another metre or so, in the water.

'I think you've got him. Stay strong now, Mikey. You can do it,' Viktor said.

My lungs felt empty; my hands as if they'd been burned raw: casualties of some skin-scorching passage through my palms of the tarred rope of a tugboat.

I sensed the strength fading from the fish. Yet, because of this, its weight was now gaining tonnage in the water. It was as if I hadn't hooked a fish at all but that I was reeling-in – through the fathoms below us – the very bed of the lake… dredging-up its silt, slime, mud, and weed. Even, for that matter, its secrets – the dark treasure that might lie buried in the primordial strata lurking below the cold, black water.

In those last, lumbering moments – as we saw the fish breaking the surface, near the boat – it seemed no longer piscine.

I half expected it to show a human face.

'Reel him in, Mikey,' Viktor said. 'Reel him in now. Steady. *E-a-s-y*. Okay, you're going to have to move over so I can try to get him in here.'

'Is that wise?' I asked. 'Maybe we should let him go… if he's *that* big. Just take a photograph or something. Right?' I gasped.

The fish twisted heavily, showing us its silver belly in the water.

It bucked the side of the boat, shifting us on the lake.

For a moment, Viktor seemed to lose some of his swagger.

He threw a net over the side of the boat, which landed on the tail end of the fish. Then he took a step back.

The fish now seemed to rest there, on its side, in the water… its dark eye looking up.

'Come on!' Viktor said. 'It's ready for us. Let's get it!'

I dropped my rod, and he and I leaned over the side of the boat and took hold of the net.

'Watch your fingers, Mikey!' Viktor barked. 'This bad boy may have some teeth.'

Together – in a series of jerks and pulls, amid curses and gasps – we heaved the fish in.

Although the *real* fight had gone from it, the fish humped and flapped in the bottom of the boat… as if pride made such a show necessary.

Viktor and I looked on and panted.

'That's a fifteen-kilo fish… at least. What *is* it?' I asked.

'A taimen,' said Viktor, '… if I'm not mistaken. I didn't know they were even in this lake.'

'Taimen?' I answered.

'Gods to some. Wolves to others. Look at its jaws. Not a fish to be messed with.'

'We did,' I said.

Viktor raised his eyes from the fish and met mine.

'And we won, Mikey,' he said. 'No more big bad wolf in *my* lake.'

'How do you think it got here?'

'I don't know. Perhaps he's always been here,' said Viktor. 'Come on. It's getting late. We should get back.'

'Do we let him go now?' I asked. 'Put him back – in the lake, I mean?'

'Hell no! Not this one. Not after all that. He's going with us. We're taking him in.'

I rowed us towards the shore, with none of the oarsmanship Viktor had shown going out, the taimen all the while seeming to stare up from the bottom of the boat – contemptuous, or so it appeared, of my skills.

The blueness steadily drained from the sky, surrendering to a more leaden look.

Near the beach, we got out into the water and dragged the boat over the shingle to the grass.

Together, we lifted out the taimen and laid it on the ground.

Its grey and black-flecked flanks made me think of the armour of ancient warlords.

I knelt in front of it… and experienced a kind of awe.

I thought of the thousands of years that had submitted themselves to creating this fish, to sculpting the proud spines of its fins… the centuries of evolution, stacked longer than any felled forest pine, that had shaped and smoothed each and every scale in its sides.

As I did this, the fish came to life before me.

It beat its tail and banged its head on the grass, in the way you'd imagine of some shackled escapologist, or that a dead man walking might protest in his last metres and minutes.

Viktor sucked his thumb.

He handed me a club.

'Lena's uncle's,' he said.

The weapon was carved from wood that was old and dark. The shaft rose to a bulbous fist.

'Can *you* do it?' he asked, peering at his wounded thumb (with, what seemed to me, deliberate distraction).

'The priest,' I said, taking the club from him. 'That's what they call this thing in some countries. Did you know that? England, for one.'

He raised his eyebrows, as if impressed by my scrap of knowledge, while standing there, boyishly, his thumb in his mouth.

Removing it, he said: 'Well, it's a funeral, I suppose.'

I hit the fish hard, twice… to its head… above the eyes.

It seemed to watch – and even bait me – as I landed each blow.

I gave it a third.

Big as it was, it now lay still.

I wedged open its jaws with the shaft of the priest.

Mindful of the taimen's teeth, Viktor brought me a glove from the boat – and I put my right hand inside the cavern of its vast, white mouth.

My gloved fingers located the grapple hook, buried in its cheek.

I slipped it backwards and drew it out.

Looking down on it, I wondered how old the fish was.

Forty or fifty years. Maybe more, said Viktor. Fifty was about the typical life of a taimen… in the wild.

That was older than us, I said. Was it right? I asked him. What we had done: killing a creature that was older than us?

'Maybe it wasn't such a nice fish, Mikey… and, besides, it's done,' Viktor replied, with an air of finality.

He picked it up and took it, over his shoulder, to the house.

The kids ran to us and tilted their heads to look into its eyes, as Viktor carried it.

They touched its tail – nervously – and skittered away, calling for their mother.

Viktor put the taimen in a freezer in a shed next to the house, where he kept a snow-shifter and various ropes, tyres and tools. The taimen's rust-red tail stuck from under the freezer's lid. Viktor said that, ordinarily, he would have cut it into steaks, but it was getting late. Standing in the shed's doorway, the kids stared at the tail, with saucer eyes. Lena, eventually, called them away.

For supper, Lena served beef goulash with bread she'd baked. Listening to Viktor's account of our fishing trip, she said she couldn't believe he'd allowed me to row all the way back.

It was okay, I said. I'd managed. It had been a relief, though, I admitted, to finally reach the shore.

Lena gave me 'a look' across the dinner table.

Viktor reached over and squeezed the biceps of my arms.

He pulled an awed face, as Little Viktor and Alona laughed.

'Mikey the hunter!' he said.

That night, the stockpiled heavy heat of day and of the preceding days, which had filled the forest and the lake with a pregnant stillness, leaving the timbers of the house warm to our touch, broke to a storm.

Thunder rolled over the water and the tops of the trees.

At first, the rain was squally and light and did no more than spit against the window of my room.

But then it changed until it was sheeting, then drumming, on the roof, in a way that made me get up and, in spite of the torrent, slide open the sash window.

I looked out onto the lake.

In the grey, mid-summer light, the water seemed higher. It appeared to have extended at its edges so that the shingle beach could no longer be seen.

Rain sluiced the sill in front of me.

The air was thick and had that particular odour given off by timber that has been treated and coated with preserver.

I pulled the window part of the way down and lit a cigarette.

I lay on my bed and smoked and – as the rain continued – I thought of the barb in Viktor's thumb, the droplet of blood it had provoked.

Whether the drumming of the rain drove me to sleep or kept me from it, I don't know. But I grew to have the sense that I was diving through the dark waters of the lake, twisting and turning, like the taimen we'd taken from it. I lost count of the times I went to the dripping window to look at the lake, which seemed always to be rising. In my fragments of sleep, I saw myself luminescent in the lake's black water. At my sides were the angry eyes and cavernous mouths of a shoal of taimen whose muscular flanks enfolded me so that I could only dive with them, deeper and deeper, into the underworld of the lake.

In time, I came-to and felt myself warm and dry-throated on the bed.

I went to the window.

The lake had risen so high I was convinced it had to be climbing the steps at the front of the house. Unnerved by this sight, I drew down the pane, closed the curtains and lay back down on the bed.

Before long, I was roused by sounds from the window.

I flopped from the bed, went to it and opened the curtains.

In the way that happens if you're at the cinema and too close to the screen, I struggled to make sense of what it was that was before me, the 'thing' that had seemingly been thudding against the frame and scraping the glass.

Slowly, it became clear.

It was the red-painted prow of Viktor's boat: the waters of the lake had, it seemed, climbed as high as the house.

I wanted to call out to Viktor, to summon Lena, through the dry darkness, in the rooms and halls of their home. But my energy had been wrung from me… by the length of my journey, the heat of the day, the illness I'd had, and, capping it all, the exertion of my duel with the taimen, and then, afterwards, the long (and slow) row back to the shore.

I was exhausted and lay on my bed *beaten* – like the taimen.

I thought of it: awaiting its execution on the parched and alien grass, the blows of the priest… raining from me… in the early evening sun.

When morning came, I was the last to rise. I drew back the curtains and looked out of the window. The lake lay in its bed, just as it had for thousands of years.

Alona was sitting in Viktor's boat on the grass.

At breakfast, Lena asked if the storm had kept me awake. She said Little Viktor had crept into her and Viktor's bed in the night, wriggling between them – like an eel – to sleep in her arms.

I went to ruffle his hair, but he moved from me and hid behind Lena.

She gave an embarrassed laugh.

When I put my things in the car, the children were at the door of the shed, looking at the freezer and the taimen's protruding tail.

Lena hugged me, then Viktor pulled me to him and said, 'Mikey'.

The children turned to watch our goodbyes but didn't speak.

The pine forest was sweetly fragrant after the rainstorm… shafts of sunlight crossing my windscreen as I drove.

Near Moscow, the sky became grey. Lightning forked over the sprawl of the city. Occasionally, it plunged as if with particular intent.

A woman carrying shopping flagged me down in a somewhat panicky way outside a mall at Sokolniki.

As I drove, I found myself wishing I'd made a better job of cleaning out my car.

When we got near her neighbourhood, I said it wouldn't be a problem for me to take her to her door and that I'd give her a hand with her bags. But she said it would be fine for me to drop her at her corner… when we came to it.

She produced a blue purse that I waved away.

After that, she smiled and said something about having to prepare supper for her husband.

Rain spotted the windscreen as I watched her walk away.

About a week later, I phoned Lena. For several nights, I'd been struggling for sleep. The thump of the priest on the taimen's head haunted me. Likewise the image of the prow of Viktor's boat. I imagined it against my flat's bedroom window – never mind the height of my block and the floor on which I lived.

When I called her, it was late and I'd been drinking.

'I'm sorry about the time,' I said. 'Is everything okay,' I asked her, '… with you… the kids?'

'Yes, Mikey,' she said.

I seemed to see her thinking… pulling back her hair, in the way that I knew she did.

'The fish…' I began. 'It didn't…'

My line to her was poor. And her responses to me grew distorted and petering.

'… the taimen,' I continued (wanting to talk about other things but somehow fixated with the fish).

'We're fine, Mikey. Trust me,' her voice came back. Her words were somewhat clearer now yet seemed small and (I seemed to notice) *youthful*. It was as if she were speaking from somewhere not only distant but enclosed: a vortex, or a cave.

She began again: 'We love you, Mikey. We *all* love you. Go to sleep now. It's okay. The monster's gone. The monster's gone. You beat it, Mikey. You won.'

When she went, I left my phone off the cradle, hoping my line to her might somehow stay open, so that, later, in the stillness of my flat, I might perhaps catch the sound of the children… shrieking and laughing by their pool, likewise the grind and beat of Viktor's oars in his boat on the lake, and, above all, Lena's account of everything that was good and growing in her garden.

Thanks

Matthew G. Rees expresses special thanks to Rhys Hughes for so generously reading these stories and finding them worthy of comment.

Smoke House & Other Stories
(Periodde Press)
Tales of the liminal and the uncanny with photographs
by the author

"His writing is truly imaginative, dark, but also at times darkly amusing.'

Frost Zone

'Matthew G. Rees oxygenates language and playfully conjures up the oddest things and happenings while making them seem casual, almost everyday events as he mesmerises the reader, holding our attention in a velveteen vice … a writer at the top of his game and then some.'

Jon Gower

'Rees has crafed a superb "smorgasboard" of weird, unusual and often terrifying characters and events which make up this unique collection of short stories. "Unputdownable" is often an overused adjective, but never has it been so appropriate.'

Sally Spedding

'We have no hesitation in recommending this collection to anyone with a taste for the macabre and bizarre or indeed anyone who appreciates exquisite story telling.'

AmeriCymru

'By turns bawdy, hilarious, thrilling, breathtakingly inventive – effortlessly exploding imaginative horizons… such beautifully-crafted work. With Rees, you never know what's lurking around the next page.'

Keith Davies

'I laughed out loud and was unsettled in equal measure. I highly recommend this anthology to anyone who enjoys intelligent, original horror'

Reader's 5-star review on Amazon

For more about Matthew G. Rees and his books please visit www.matthewgrees.com

Printed in Great Britain
by Amazon

78064371R00174